Selfish Love

A Reverse Age Gap Musician + Single Mom Romance

Cheryl Terra

bang it out
WR TINC

Bang It Out Writing

Content Warnings

While not a dark romance, this book covers some heavier topics. I have tried to reflect those here as best I can without providing spoilers, but if you have concerns about any of the items listed and wish to know more, please reach out to me via email at **info@cherylterra.com**.

As a steamy romance, this book is intended for adults and contains multiple sexually explicit scenes with an older woman/younger man relationship.

A past abusive relationship featuring physical, sexual, and emotional abuse is pivotal to the story, as are mentions of a traumatic and abusive childhood and parental abandonment.

While not overly graphic, explicit discussions regarding and reliving this past abuse—both physical and emotional—occur within the text.

There are also scenes featuring characters who obtain or discuss abortion, religion, and divorce within this book.

Author's Note

While this book can be read as a standalone, it is part of the collaborative Afterglow Studios series. You don't need to read the other books in the series to enjoy Selfish Love, but if you would like to, the series order is:

If you have previously read the other stories but it's been a while or you would like a summary of the other stories prior to reading Selfish Love, please read on. **While this summary may contain minor spoilers for the previous books, major plot points that don't affect Selfish Love will not be shared.**

No Strings Attached: A Rock Star Single Mom Romance

Em Reilly is a single mom who takes in her brother, Jimmy, who is eight years younger, after he runs away from home. Finally having a stable home lets Jimmy go after his grand aspirations of being the next big rock star, leading him to be an overnight sensation. Unfortunately, Jimmy's rise to the top comes at a cost, and he begins overindulging in the rock star lifestyle as he becomes convinced of his invincibility.

Former rock legend Alex Franzetti lives a quiet life. After walking away from the rock star lifestyle, he opens a recording studio in Pueblo with his sponsor and mentor, Mike Acton. When the out-of-control Jimmy Reilly comes in for a photoshoot at the studio one day, Alex sees a reflection of himself in the young man and can't help himself from getting a bit of revenge after Jimmy loses it on him. Writing a scathing article under a pseudonym, Alex sets in motion a series of events that culminate with Jimmy being dropped from his label.

Unfortunately, Jimmy's fall from grace has a negative effect on one of the people he loves more than anyone in the world; his niece and Em's daughter, Leia. Devastated that her uncle isn't giving her the guitar lessons he promised, Em approaches Alex and asks if he'll teach her. Neither of them expect the chemistry that occurs between them, but nothing happens until after hitting rock bottom, a sheepish Jimmy approaches Alex for help. Alex, feeling guilty for being the one who wrote the article, agrees, but only a short while later, ends up giving into his feelings with Em and spends the night with her, despite the age difference of twenty-some years. Eventually, Alex reveals that he's the one who wrote the article about Jimmy. But Jimmy's turned his life around so much that he forgives the older man... even after finding out about Alex's relationship with his sister.

Santa Mike: A Later In Life Romance

Mike Acton is a legendary music manager who owns Afterglow Studios with his business partner and former client, Alex. As the kind of man who can get anything for anyone, Mike isn't the kind of person anyone should mess with, but beneath his curmudgeonly exterior, Mike is fiercely loyal to those he cares about... including Leia, the little girl who is like a surrogate for his own estranged daughter.

When Leia asks to put on a Christmas concert to raise money for charity, Mike goes above and beyond to make it happen, right down to agreeing to play Santa Claus at the event. The timeline of this book crosses over with the timeline of Selfish Love.

One

"I'm not going."

Sighing, I wordlessly held my hand out for the skimpy black bikini and fire-engine-red one-piece swimsuit Em had just yanked out of her suitcase.

"No," she said. "This is a terrible idea, Kelsie. I don't even know if these fit. I'm not going. I'm calling Alex right now to tell him I'm not going."

It would have been a lot more convincing had she not just stood there, her knuckles turning white as she clutched the swimsuits, instead of calling her boyfriend to tell him she wasn't going on the trip to Mexico he'd been planning to surprise her with for *ages*.

Not that she knew she was going to Mexico. *I* knew she was going to Mexico because Alex had zero concept of everything that would have to happen for him to pull his whole plan off without a hitch. I guess that's what happens when you're a former legendary rock star turned recording studio owner who made it to fifty-something without having to do anything for yourself, only to fall madly in love with a woman half your age that deserved the best of everything.

1

Despite my frustration with his inability to do something as simple as plan an all-inclusive vacation for his single-mom girlfriend without her knowing about it, I did like Alex. The age gap was a *thing*, sure, but it made sense for the two of them. Neither Alex nor Em had a particularly easy life; Em wasn't even thirty yet, but when you start raising your kid brother at the age of eight because your parents are pieces of shit who should've never been allowed to have kids, you tend to mature a little faster than most. And Alex... well. He'd lost everything young. Not his money or his career—just the stuff that had mattered.

Like I said, neither of them had easy lives. But Alex loved Em with everything he had, and Em returned that love with all she had and more. They were happy, and what were a few decades between people when they had that happiness?

Well, except for me blaming Alex's age on the fact that he had no idea how to plan a fucking vacation. This entire trip wouldn't be happening without me, and I wasn't even going.

"Put it on," I ordered, nodding at the bathing suit Em had in her hands.

"What?"

"Put it on," I repeated. "You're so concerned about them not fitting, give it a try."

It took another few minutes, but she finally conceded and stripped down. I would've looked away to give her some privacy, but the way things were with me and Em, that would have been weird. She'd seen—and photographed—me mostly naked a bunch of times. As for her, well. She used to do some "modelling" of the explicit variety, which made sense. Em was born gorgeous and she'd die gorgeous. Long, lithe, and tall, she was covered in tattoos and had thick black hair, sparkling bright eyes, and unfairly perky tits considering how big they were.

I, on the other hand, had a dump-truck ass that would give the Pixar moms a run for their money. I also had dump-truck hips that had never quite gone back to normal after I'd given birth, a poochy stomach, and slightly below-average tits. If mom-bod was a thing, that was what I had. Only my mom-bod was contrasted by the vibrant colored hair and multiple piercings I'd gotten after my divorce.

I mean, I figured if I was gonna be a divorced single mom escaping from a quiet life under the thumb of a mature church-going counsellor who wanted little more than a trophy he could sometimes scream at, I might as well go all out.

Anyway, the point was that despite her being a literal model and me looking more like I'd been sculpted out of modelling clay, neither Em nor I were modest around each other. So I stood there with my arms folded as she stripped down and squirmed her way into the bright red one-piece.

"Hmm." I toyed with the piercing in my lip as I studied her. "You're right. That's going to be a problem."

She groaned. "See, I told you I—"

"Alex won't be able to keep his hands off you. I mean, you'll never even make it to the beach when he sees you in that. It's just going to be pound town, twenty-four-seven, and then why did he even bother with all the fancy vacation stuff? He could've booked a room at the Motel Six."

She rolled her eyes and snorted, but her face lightened a bit. "You're so full of shit."

I watched as she turned to look in the full-length mirror, twisting and evaluating the way the stretchy fabric sat on her chest. After a moment, she frowned.

"Wait," she said. "The beach?"

"Or the pool, or the hot tub, or whatever," I said smoothly. "And if there isn't one of those, you can just wear it in the hotel bathroom so Alex knows that if he wants to see all of *this* next time, you expect a beach."

"You have a lot of confidence there'll be a next time," she muttered. "I'm still not even sold on this time."

I passed her the black bikini to try on. "What's this really about?"

Even though she hesitated, she didn't do me the discourtesy of pretending she didn't know what I meant. "I don't know if I'm ready to be away from Leia."

Fucking finally. I sighed and sat on the edge of her bed.

Of course it was about Leia—Em's daughter, and my daughter Baylee's best friend. Spitfires, the both of them, but Leia had a habit of wrapping people around her sticky little fingers. She was charming and seemed to melt hearts simply by blinking her big doe-eyes. Baylee, on the other hand, was more likely to get in trouble for being one of those girls who was "too much." She was going to be too loud, too outspoken, too dramatic, too unabashedly herself.

I might never win Mom-Of-The-Year, but if my daughter turned out to be "too much," I'd consider my parenting to be a resounding success.

But of course, that would be when she was older. Right now, Baylee couldn't seem to tell the difference between standing up for herself and talking back to me, and I couldn't seem to go through a single day without claiming I was going to sell her to the zoo.

Not that I'd ever say that to Baylee, of course. Just to Em. That's what best friends are for: making fun of your parenting skills and commiserating when you were wondering how in the hell your DNA came up with that squalling turd of a child.

Personally, I blamed Baylee's dad, but that was mostly because he was a squalling turd of a man.

In any case, I'd told Em time and time again that she could make fun of me all she wanted, but that I was going to do the same damn thing to her once Leia realized how easily she could get people to bend to her every whim and start using it to her advantage. And honestly, if Em kept pulling this "Call it off, I'm not going" bullshit, I was going to spill the beans to Leia and get *her* to convince her mom to go to Mexico for her week-long fuckfest with Alex.

"Okay, look at it this way," I said. "The next time Leia starts learning a new song on her guitar and Baylee demands to sing along and Pepper's in the background whimpering because the girls are singing in tones only dogs can hear and you think to yourself, 'Man, I wish I could get away from it all for five minutes of peace,' ask yourself again if you're ready to be away from Leia."

That made her laugh. "Okay, fair."

"I've watched her a million times before. I know what I'm doing." I folded my arms. "Are you questioning my mad parenting skills, Em? Because if so, I'm not sharing my flask of whiskey with you next time we have to shiver through a soccer game."

"You also work," she pointed out.

"Jimmy already agreed to watch Leia when I can't. I'm still trying to convince him he should take Baylee."

"I'm sure he'll watch both girls if you want him to."

"No, I mean permanently. I even offered a friends-and-family discount. Way better price than I'd give to the zoo. But for some reason, he keeps saying he'll give her back after."

Em snorted back another laugh.

"You can call Leia every day if you want to. Just keep in mind, that means you're going to be subjecting yourself to an impromptu over-the-phone concert. But Em, she's going to be *fine*." I nodded towards the bikini she was still holding. "Try that one on. See if it's a little less likely to give Alex a four-hour erection before he even takes his Viagra."

"He doesn't need Viagra," she huffed, but peeled the red bathing suit off.

She managed to pull the black bikini on. I declared it even worse than the red one piece, telling her we were going to have to go to Target and find her one of those old-lady swim dresses so she wouldn't give Alex a heart attack.

"You're such a bitch," she scolded, laughing as she untied the straps of her bikini.

"It's not my fault you look like that," I replied. "Nor is it my fault that Alex is going to lose his mind and fuck you until he—"

And of course, that was the moment *someone* flung Em's bedroom door open.

"Is Pepper's ball in here? The girls want to—oh, *Jesus*, Em!"

"Ever heard of knocking?" Em asked wryly, not managing to cover her tits before Jimmy's face turned red.

"How the fuck was I supposed to know you were naked?" he muttered.

"Oh, I don't know." Em pulled her t-shirt on. "I mean, you could assume that I'm naked at all times when the door is closed and then you'd never have this problem."

"Kelsie was in here with you," he replied. "Why would I think 'oh, my sister and her best friend are in her room, better double check that neither of them are naked before I go in'?"

"Prior experience?" I suggested helpfully.

Well, helpful in that it made me cackle with laughter as he glanced up, a haughty look of annoyance unable to mask the embarrassment on his face. His scowl had been his trademark, once upon a time. With dark eyes and high cheekbones, that glare had a dual purpose of intimidation and dampening the panties of any girl attracted to the rebellious type of rock-star-esque guy who would piss off her dad.

Only in Jimmy's case, he sort of *was* a rock star. Or at least, he had been, back when that scowl had been his trademark. It felt weird to say "back when" about a guy who was just old enough to buy alcohol for himself, but his star had burned bright and fast. Before turning twenty-one, he'd had a record deal and more money than he knew what to do with. A total overnight sensation. Which meant, of course, that he drank, smoked, and snorted a lot of that money away while the people clinging to his star power blew so much smoke up his ass that his head started to swell.

He was barely twenty when it all came crashing down. That combination of money and drugs and the inherent sense of invincible immortality that boys that age seem to have pissed off the wrong person: Alex.

Yes, that Alex.

But it all ended up working out, in the end. Alex wanted to bang Em, Em wanted to bang Alex, Jimmy ended up with a decent job at Alex's studio with him as a mentor... what's a little career destruction by a pseudo-father-figure who wants to bang your mother-figure a.k.a your sister who practically raised you?

Em was eight years older than Jimmy. She'd left home when he was only ten, but when their parents kicked him out just a few years later, she took him in, even though she was a single mom with a toddler who was trying to get her shit together. As a photographer, she made decent money, but around the time Leia started kindergarten and with an eighteen-year-old brother-slash-pseudo-son-wannabe-rock-star who was on the verge of a big break, things had started to get tight.

Luckily, that was around the time my ex-husband began paying his child support, so Baylee and I were able to move into a small townhouse across the street from another single mom and her daughter who *happened* to be in Baylee's new kindergarten class. The girls declared themselves best friends the moment they met, Em and I declared ourselves best friends as soon as we realized both of us were sneaking Baileys into our coffee cups during morning drop-off, and the rest, as they say, was history.

"Will you help me build up my portfolio?" she asked me while we were watching the girls at the park a couple of weeks after we'd met.

"Sure," I said. "If you really think my face is going to sell people on your portrait skills."

"Gorgeous as it is, it's not your face that I want to take pictures of."

I snorted and took a swig of wine out of my travel mug as the girls played on the monkey bars. "What, you want pictures of my ass or something?"

"Yep."

I laughed, but she was serious.

"I want to start doing boudoir photos. I know what it's like in front of the camera and how to pose people to make them look their best. There's good money in it. But I need some photos of someone other than me."

"And you think my dump truck ass is going to sell people on your boudoir photos when you've got photos of *you* posted right next to it?" I asked in disbelief.

"You have a nice ass. So yes."

I scoffed. "Sure, Em. Why not? I guess it'll be a testament to your skill if you can make me look sexy."

And I mean, to her credit, I did look damn good in them.

We took them in her bedroom the following weekend while the girls were at a classmate's birthday party getting hopped up on cake and goody bags. Em drew the sheer curtains across the windows to filter the natural light and give her room a soft, sensual feel. I was kneeling on her bed, holding an oversized men's shirt taut against my breasts so the hypothetical person who would eventually look at these photos could see the hint of my nipple piercings poking through the fabric.

And I mean, I wasn't uncomfortable or anything; I might have had a dump truck ass and a poochy stomach, but that didn't mean I felt the need to hide those things from the world. It was entirely possible to recognize that I didn't have a supermodel body and not hate it at the same time. But what was life if I couldn't poke a little fun at myself now and then?

So there I was, mostly naked, legs spread, doing my best to pretend I was some pretty young thing and not a mom in her early thirties with stretch marks and pink hair and one or two more wrinkles than I was willing to acknowledge in the corners of my eyes. And there Em was, contorted around the edge of her bed with her camera pressed to her eye, trying to pretend like we weren't in a small, cramped bedroom as she took my photo.

And then a skinny, dark-haired eighteen-year-old threw the bedroom door open and barreled in.

"Hey Em, guess what I—" The man looked at me and his eyes nearly popped out of his skull before he looked at Em with a wild expression on his face. "What the *fuck*?!"

"Jimmy!" Em exclaimed, which answered my unasked question of who the fuck he was. "What are you doing here? I thought you were touring the rest of the month."

"I am, but I—" He couldn't seem to help himself from looking back at me, red splotches dusting his high cheekbones. "What the fuck?"

I pressed my lips together, amused. "As much as I love having someone look at me half-naked and repeatedly wonder 'what the fuck,' perhaps you and Em could go have this conversation somewhere where I'm not distracting you?"

His face went even redder. "No, that's not—I mean, you're not... *You're* not what-the-fuck, the situation is what-the-fuck. You... you're..." His eyes flicked helplessly down to my tits and I was pretty sure almost every drop of blood in his body was concentrated in his face. "You're naked."

"That's very observant. Thank you."

He cleared his throat. "And hot, I mean. You're naked and hot. Or wait, no. Pretty. You're... uh—"

"Jimmy," Em said flatly.

"—like you're pretty but I mean that in a respectful way and—"

"Jimmy," she said again.

"What?" he asked.

"Shut up." She pointed to the door. "Go to the kitchen."

I managed to wait until he'd hightailed out of the room before I burst out laughing and flopped back on Em's bed as she sighed.

"So anyway, that's my brother." She rolled her eyes. "Let me go find out what he's even doing here."

So, all of that was to say, it wasn't the first time he had burst through Em's bedroom door and discovered there was a naked woman behind it, though maybe since this time it was his sister, he'd learn a lesson or two about knocking. Especially since this time it was just to find the dog's ball; at least when he'd barged in on me naked, it was because he'd signed with his record label and was so excited to tell his sister that he'd driven up to Pueblo to share the news in person.

It was part of the reason his intimidating scowl didn't quite work on me. I mean, my first experience with the moody wannabe rock god was him stuttering as he tried to find the line between offending me for commenting on my body and offending me for not commenting on my body. Every time he put that scowl on his face, I remembered the particularly sweet shade of red his cheeks turned and the slight waver in his voice as he spoke.

For reasons related to the fact that he was my best friend's brother and also much, much younger than me, I tried not to remember the absolute thrill I felt when he couldn't seem to take his eyes off me. I mean, yeah, maybe it was because he was in shock, but I liked to pretend it's because he wasn't just trying to be nice when he said he thought I was hot.

But I digress.

"Ha, ha," Jimmy said flatly as I laughed at his scowl. "So can I take that to mean Pepper's ball isn't in here?"

"Actually, it is." Em pointed at the dog bed in the corner, the bright red ball tucked into the raised cushion as if the owner of said ball was hiding it from prying eyes, which he probably was. "But before you go, I need to ask you something."

He pointedly looked away as he went to fetch the ball. "Can it wait until you have pants on?"

"It's a bathing suit. I wear this to the beach."

"No way Alex is going to let you go to the beach in that."

"Alex doesn't get to 'let' me do anything," she snapped. "If I want to go to the beach naked, I will."

He straightened up after grabbing the ball, raising his hands defensively. "Right, okay. I just meant that—"

"—that you think because Alex is a man and we're in a relationship that he gets to dictate what I wear?"

"That neither of you is gonna see much of Mexico if you wear that since Alex is probably gonna be popping as much Viagra as he can handle so he can keep you in the hotel the whole time," he finished. "Trust me, as much as I have zero desire to know how hot he thinks you are, he never fucking shuts up about it."

"See, Em?" I said. "That's the exact same thing I said, save for the part where *someone* clearly wasn't threatened with the wrath of his boss if he spilled the beans on the location."

He grimaced. "Shit."

Em whirled towards me. "He's taking me to Mexico?"

"I refuse to confirm or deny these allegations," I said.

A bright sort of energy seemed to vibrate off her as she struggled to maintain the cool, collected composure she was known for. "I've never been to Mexico."

"And you might never get to go," Jimmy said. "I mean, who knows where Alex is taking you? Show him the bathing suit and he might just rent a room down at the Motel Six."

I hooted and nudged him with my elbow. "That's *also* what I said."

A hint of a smile broke through his haughty expression as I touched him.

"What was the question?" he asked, looking at Em.

11

"You're going to be okay watching Leia when Kelsie can't?" she asked.

"Of *course* I am."

She didn't look convinced. "You can't just be cool Uncle Jimmy while I'm gone, you know."

He rolled his eyes. "I know."

"This is different from taking her out for ice cream or having a movie night," Em said. "You're going to have to balance work *and* going out *and* taking care of my kid, and if that last one isn't your highest priority, then—"

"Leia is always my highest priority," he said fiercely. "I show up to *everything*. When I do drink, it's usually with you. I've been working for Alex for ages and you can even ask him and Mike, I've been—"

"—doing a damn good job of being a responsible, slightly disrespectable adult, since being respectable is completely overrated," I interrupted, looking at Em as I attempted to put an arm around Jimmy's shoulder. He was too tall, though, so I settled for resting my hand on said shoulder instead. "And Em's doing the 'typical mom' thing with worrying about leaving her baby for an extended period, but she's going to remember that it takes a village to raise a child, and me and Jimbo here are part of her village."

"*Jimbo*?" he repeated, his voice twisted with a strange mix of repulsion, shock, and laughter.

Em snorted back a laugh. "It suits you."

"It does not!"

"Sure it does." She picked up a shirt she'd discarded on the bed and began folding it. "You're part of my village, remember? You can be the village idiot."

"Oh, fuck off," Jimmy groaned as I dissolved into laughter. "If I'm the village idiot, what does that make her?"

"Town bicycle," I said before Em could reply.

Jimmy couldn't stop himself from laughing that time and Em rolled her eyes.

"Leaving my kid with the village idiot and town bicycle seems questionable," she muttered.

"You've left her with us before," he said. "Kelsie and I have this down, Em."

"We make a great team," I added.

He nodded. "You need this vacation. Let Alex spoil you a little and stop worrying."

Em took a long look at her brother, then at me, then sighed.

"Okay," she said. "You're right. Just... you know I'm gonna want to talk to her like, three times a day."

"How?" I asked. "I have a feeling Alex is going to make sure you spend a lot of time with your mouth full."

She tried calling the whole thing off again, but Jimmy and I were laughing too hard to pay any attention to it.

Two

TRUE TO HER WORD, Em called an average of three times a day.

True to my word and Jimmy's word, Leia was completely fine.

While Em may not have been away on a tropical vacation before, there were times that Jimmy and I had taken care of the girls before. She was a photographer, which meant she occasionally had photo shoots or events scheduled at weird times.

And, like me, she sometimes got sick of being around her kid. It happens.

Either way, it meant that Jimmy and I had a system in place, though it *was* the first time we were testing it out for such a long stretch.

I was lucky enough to have a job working for an amazing boss who let me make my schedule. It was the stupidest job: I worked in the warehouse of a specialty candle company, which meant my job was literally packaging up these stupid bougie candles and sending them to stupid bougie stores or stupid bougie customers. Day after day, I put glass-encased pillars of scented wax into cardboard boxes and lovingly tucked bubble wrap and packing peanuts around them so that somewhere, some rich lady who would be aghast at my colorful hair and multitude of piercings could unwrap it and display it in her bougie living room or bougie bedroom or bougie shitter.

At least my boss was nice and super easy going.

"I don't care if you're here at one in the morning or if you want to work split shifts every day," she'd told me. "So long as the orders are processed in forty-eight hours, you do what you need to do."

On top of that, if I needed to make a little extra cash here or there, she was cool with me taking shifts on the production line so I could get some overtime. It was a great job, stupid bougie products aside.

Normally, I started around seven. I'd package up Baylee's lunch and schoolbag, bring my sleepy headed daughter across the street to Em's, and she'd take care of morning drop off. Then when school let out, I'd pick up the girls, since Em's clients usually wanted photos done in the evening. Easy peasy.

With Jimmy, though, that didn't work. He worked at Afterglow Records, Alex's studio, and he usually worked in the evening. So while Em was gone, I took care of the morning drop off before going to work, and he picked the girls up after school and brought them to the studio to hang out until I picked them up. It worked out in my favor: Alex being gone meant Leia wasn't getting her usually scheduled guitar lessons, and since she had Mike, the crudgey old bastard who co-owned the studio, wrapped around her little finger, she could get some of her musical inclinations out of her system with Jimmy while she was there.

Some. Not all. She and Baylee made sure that there was a brand-new concert for me to begrudgingly listen to each and every day I was watching them.

It was the fourth day of Em and Alex's trip when everything changed.

I'd had to work a bit late, so I had just parked at the studio when Em's second call of the day came through. Rolling my eyes, I answered it as I got out of the car.

"She's fine," I said.

"I know she's fine," Em replied, staticky sounds of relaxed beachgoers in the background.

I used my hip to slam the car door shut. "Then why are you calling instead of sucking Alex's dick?"

"I need to talk to you."

The lack of snarky response to my comment paired with the serious tone of her voice gave me pause, and I frowned as I leaned against my car. "What's wrong?"

"Nothing's... wrong," she said. "I just... Alex asked me something and—"

My heart jumped into my throat. "That *fucker*! He proposed?"

"Oh, God no," she said hurriedly. "And I would've said no if he had."

I let out a heavy sigh. "Oh, thank God."

She laughed. "On Alex's behalf, ouch."

"Em. Out with it. Why are you calling?"

Another long moment of silence passed before she cleared her throat. "He... he wants me and Leia to move in with him."

The parking lot of the studio wasn't an especially loud place, but the world around me went quiet all the same.

"Move?" I repeated. "But you... I mean, he pretty much lives with you already, doesn't he?"

She sighed. "Yeah. But it's... I mean, it might be nice to have the extra space, you know? And like, it would be nice to live in a place a little more updated."

Updated. As in, not the shitty old houses we lived in.

"With more room for Leia to play in the yard. And a... you know, a safer neighborhood."

Safer. As in, not in the shitty low-income neighborhood we lived in.

"I mean, Leia wouldn't switch schools, of course. But she'd be able to have a bigger room and Alex said we could convert the basement into a photo studio so I could expand my business."

"Right."

"Kels?" she asked after a moment. "What do you think?"

What did I think?

My heart had dropped out of my throat, leaving a trail of nausea behind as it fell further and further down into my stomach. Here was my best friend, calling me from miles and miles away to ask my opinion on her moving in with her boyfriend. Which, like... fair. It made sense. I mean, we were best friends, and best friends are supposed to give advice in situations like this.

But we were best friends who also relied on each other. *Heavily.* And Alex had to know that. I mean, he *had* to know that Em and I had built our lives and schedules around each other because for a long time, it was just the two of us.

We didn't have other friends. We didn't have partners. We had each other. He knew damn well what he would be doing to me if Em moved away. And that was probably why he'd decided to ask her while they were on the other side of the continent.

So what did I think?

I thought Alex was a complete shitbag for using me to plot this whole thing, knowing damn well he was about to fuck me over.

I wanted to tell all of that to Em. I wanted to tell her I was standing in the parking lot of *her* boyfriend's studio, covered in dust and sweat with the scent of a thousand essential oil candles permeating my freshly-dyed pink hair, about to pick up *her* daughter that I was babysitting so she could have a luxury vacation. That I'd made tons of changes to take care of Leia. That I absolutely, positively, one-hundred percent did not want her to move in with Alex because that meant *my* life was going to get harder.

But I couldn't make it about me.

"I'm so happy for you," I managed to say. "Y-You should do it."

"Wha... seriously?" she said.

"Of course." My throat felt tight. Blinking rapidly, I stared up at the greyish fluff that made up the sky above me. "You love Alex and he loves you. And it makes sense, you know? You're hot enough to be a trophy wife, so you might as well get used to the finer things. Starting with a nicer house."

"Oh, shut up," she scoffed. "I'm not a trophy wife."

"Not yet." I laughed, but it sounded more like a cough. "But you can start practicing now."

"Okay, no. But seriously." She sighed. "Like, we do everything together. This is gonna affect you just as much as it affects me."

"Not really. I mean, one of us is going to end up sucking a lot more dick and it's probably not going to be me, so—"

"You're awful."

"You love it," I said. "So when do you think you'll move? Like, soon, or...?"

"I'm not sure," she said. "I wanted to talk to you. I haven't decided yet."

"I think you have," I said. "Which is great, Em. Like, *so* great. You'll have to give me a head's up once you decide when you're going so I can take advantage of my across-the-street babysitter and bring home a couple of booty calls before you go."

She laughed. "Oh, sure. Because you bring home *so* many booty calls."

"You're right. I usually end up at their place. I mean, it's harder for them to sneak out in the morning when they keep stepping on Baylee's Barbie shoes. That shit is worse than Lego."

We talked for another few minutes and I repeated my stance on her moving in with Alex, which was that I thought she should absolutely do it even though I secretly thought she absolutely shouldn't do it.

"Even though it's going to... like, what about school drop off and stuff?"

"I'll make it work," I said. "Girl, I don't want you to stop yourself from moving forward just because of what I need." Even though that was exactly what I wanted. "This is the next logical step for you and Alex. We'll make things work."

There was a long pause, then she sighed. "All right. You promise you're okay with this?"

"Yep," I lied.

"Okay. Do me a favor and don't tell Jimmy yet, please?"

Once we hung up, I took a deep breath and let it out, then wiped my hands beneath my eyes. When I was certain I could hide my heartbreak, I walked through the still-too-quiet parking lot to the studio and pulled the door open.

Noise poured out the moment I opened the door. The bustling sounds of chattering and singing and laughter burst forward and tugged me in, as welcoming as they were alienating. I paused just inside the door, glancing around the lobby. Normally, Jimmy was waiting up front with the girls, but I was now later than I'd anticipated and he'd obviously taken them elsewhere to wait. Across the lobby, the office manager—a churchy woman named Lini who was surprisingly cool with the rock n' roll types that frequented the studio—poked her head out.

"Hi, Ms. Bauer," she called. "Here for the girls?"

"You can call me Kelsie, Lini," I said for the thousandth time, though I forced my tone to be bright and cheery. "And yep, it's my turn to be on Baylee and Leia duty."

She smiled and motioned for me to follow her. "I've been informed I'm not supposed to tell you they're working on a little surprise for you."

Oh, good. Just what I needed. More surprises.

I kept my smile on and followed Lini towards the office area, where I could hear the muffled sound of music and the shrill laughter of my girl giggling with her best friend.

"So how was your day, Kelsie?" Lini enunciated loudly, and the music and giggling was swapped for the obvious rustle of two girls hushing each other.

"Oh, not so bad," I replied just as loudly. "How about yours?"

She pressed her lips together, though I wasn't sure if she was holding in a laugh or resigning herself to her next line. "Well, it happened to be one of those days where things were a little difficult. But you know, sometimes that happens, and—" She stopped and placed her hand on the knob of a closed office door, tilting her head to indicate I should stand in front of it. "—you need to, um, *shake it off.*"

And with that, she pushed the door open, I had a half-second glimpse of Mike sitting awkwardly behind his desk, and then two bursting balls of energy jumped into my line of sight.

"Hit it, Uncle Jimmy!" shouted Leia.

From the corner of my eye, I saw Jimmy sigh as he pressed a button, causing the dulcet tones of one Miss Taylor Swift to start playing as Baylee and Leia broke out into a shakily rehearsed dance routine.

My fake smile broke just slightly; a real one crept out, something that was touched at the joyous way my daughter was jumping around the room and giddy for the day she realized what a cringey kid she was.

I leaned against the doorframe as I watched, Baylee's blonde hair bouncing as she belted out lyrics, round cheeks flushed pink as she did her best to shake, shake, shake, shake, shake it off. There was a harrowing moment where she bumped into Mike's desk and the hula girl that sat there teetered precariously, but Jimmy lurched forward before the look of indignation even crossed Mike's grumpy face.

"Wow," I said as they finished and struck a pose, little lungs gasping for breath after they danced their hearts out. "Great job, ladies. That must have taken a long time to put together. I didn't think I was that late picking you up!"

"You were late?" Leia said.

"They've been working on that all afternoon for you," Jimmy said.

Their sweetness made my heart swell for all of a second before I caught the pleading look on Baylee's face.

"Aw, out of the goodness of your hearts? That's so considerate and thoughtful!" I said.

If I didn't know any better, I would have thought Mike had chuckled, but he was a grumpy old fuck so I figured I must have been hallucinating.

"Um, well, sort of," Leia said. "But also, we wanted to tell you that—"

"Mom, Ms. Lini told us that *Taylor Swift* is gonna do a concert here and Mr. Mike said that he thought he might be able to get tickets for us!" Baylee shrieked.

There it was.

"Oh, wow," I said, cringing at the fake brightness of my tone. "Well, that's pretty exciting!"

"I said maybe," Mike grumped grumpily in a grumpy growl. "I need to make some calls. Swift tickets ain't the easiest to come by."

"You don't say," I said flatly.

Mike raised an eyebrow at me, but I didn't say anything else. I mean, sure, it's not like he knew that I already knew about the Taylor Swift concert and had tried to get tickets for Baylee's Christmas present, only to realize I could barely afford the seats up in the nosebleeds even if they *hadn't* already been sold out when I tried to get them. And it wasn't Lini's fault she didn't know that Em and I had agreed to hide the knowledge of the concert from our girls so we wouldn't have to go to the concert, though Em's reasoning was more that she didn't like Taylor Swift.

I mean, she was fucking Alex, so it wasn't like she couldn't afford the tickets.

So it might not have been malicious on anyone's part, but that didn't mean I was particularly pleased about it.

"Not sure how many tickets I'll be able to find even if I do," Mike said carefully, and I heard the words he actually meant: Leia was the priority.

"You can find four though, right?" Leia said, looking up at Mike with her big, hypno-entrancing gaze. "For me and Baylee and Mom and Kelsie?"

"Or maybe Santa can help," Baylee said helpfully.

"Yeah!" Leia said, flapping her hand excitedly. "Mr. Mike, you can ask Santa, right?"

"I'll put it on my Christmas list, too!" Baylee added.

"I, uh, well—" Mike stuttered, then sighed. "Yeah, kid, of course. I can talk to Santa."

"Well, girls," I said before they could start screeching their excitement or break into another Taylor Swift song. "We should head home for dinner so Jimmy can get back to work. Where are your backpacks?"

They said goodbye to Mike and Lini, then raced out of the room to grab their things from the breakroom. I nodded politely at Mike.

"Thanks for checking into this," I said.

He looked at me grouchily. "I might not be able to get floor seats or anything. Maybe a box or something near the stage. You got a price point you don't want to go past?"

Fuck.

The answer to that was yes, I didn't want to go past the price of the cheapest available seats because even those had been almost out of reach for me. I didn't want to even consider seats that were near the stage or in a fucking box or something. I could pick up a couple of extra shifts to cover the cost of the cheaper tickets, but box seats? That would require calling Daniel.

And was it worth calling Daniel for something like this? He'd pay without question, I knew that, but he wouldn't pay without demand.

I thought of how excited Baylee had looked. I hated to say no, but... well. She'd be disappointed, but she'd survive; she'd understand, one day.

I swallowed hard, decided on the cost I was willing to pay, then turned to Mike. One bushy eyebrow flicked up as he sat behind his desk with a judgmental grimace on his grouchy old face.

"Nope," I said. "Just let me know how much."

Mike looked surprised, which I would have normally relished. But the price of that look of surprise wasn't worth it, not when I had blurted something out of pride that would likely cost not only a call to the person I hated more than anyone else in the world, but also whatever that person deemed reasonable to ask for in return.

But it did help me feel a little better.

"Thanks again," I said.

"Don't mention it," he grumbled.

I bit back a snarky response, nodded once, and went after the girls.

"Kels," Jimmy said, following me out of the office.

"Hmm?" I asked, not looking at him.

"You okay?"

"Yep."

The feel of a hand closing on my arm surprised me and I turned, almost shocked to see the concern on Jimmy's face.

"You're not," he said.

"Everything's fine."

"You look like you've been crying. Your eyes are all red."

A sharp laugh escaped my lips. "Yeesh. Someone needs to give you some lessons on talking to women, Jimbo. Does this uniform make my ass look fat, too?"

His mouth twitched, though I wasn't sure if it was with laughter or annoyance. "That uniform makes your fat ass look fantastic, but even though women with fat asses are hot as fuck, that's not important right now. What's going on?"

My mouth dropped open. The dark, pouty look on Jimmy's face faltered, the skin on his cheeks turning a muted shade of red as he tried to gauge my reaction to his... I didn't even know what to call that. Compliment? *Backhanded* compliment? No, it wasn't... was it? He said my ass was fat but that fat asses were hot, so was it more of a pickup line? Or just an admission that he liked fat asses?

A potential admission that he liked *my* fat ass?

Whatever it was, I froze, and he let go of my arm.

"Kels, I'm sor—"

"Everything's fine," I interrupted. "I'm fine. I just need to... I... work was hard today. I was thinking I... I might have to do some extra shifts, but you know what, that all works out because I have a little extra for Christmas." I laughed, hating the sound. "Thank you for asking. And for keeping the girls a bit later than you thought. I appreciate it."

"No problem," he said. "When, uh... when do you have to do the extra shifts? 'Cause if you want me to watch the girls, I just need to know—"

"I'm not sure," I said. "It can probably, um, wait. Until Em's back. That should still be fine."

"I can watch them this weekend if you need me to," he said. "I'm not working Saturday. I could even come watch them at your place. Maybe take Pepper out for a walk or something."

I tried to smile. "I work in the mornings, Jimbo. Pretty sure you don't want to be at my place at like, eight a.m."

He smirked. "You know I'm not up all night partying or anything, right? Sometimes I even work here at like, eight a.m."

I stared at him, then swallowed and nodded quickly.

"That would be helpful, yeah. If you don't mind."

He touched me again, a soft pat on the shoulder before guiding me down the hallway. "Anytime. I'm happy to help."

Three

I WOULD NEVER ADMIT it to anyone—not even to Em, and Em knew *everything* about me—but I was insanely thankful that I had a daughter and not a son.

Don't get me wrong. If I'd given birth to a boy, I would have loved him as much as I loved Baylee. He would never have felt neglected or sad or like his mom didn't care about him. And it wasn't that I'd spent my pregnancy praying for a girl or anything.

It's just that, when my marriage imploded, I couldn't stop thinking about how hard it would have been to have a little man in my life who was a reminder of Daniel.

Daniel had wanted a boy. He hadn't been at that appointment—he attended barely any of the appointments because childbirth was a "woman" thing and he had "man" things to do—after the doctor congratulated me on my daughter-to-be, I was certain I'd misheard. I couldn't be having a girl. I *couldn't*. Daniel wanted a boy and what Daniel wanted, Daniel got.

Otherwise, there would be consequences.

When he got home from work that night, I'd been the very model of The Perfect Wife. It was a role I played often while Daniel and I were married, which would have surprised anyone who knew me post-divorce. I couldn't blame them; it was hard to reconcile the multi-colored hair and plethora of piercings I sported now with the Stepford Wife I'd once been.

That was the woman Daniel had walked into see that day: his quiet wife, wearing a modest-but-flattering dress over her growing belly. Blonde hair neatly pinned back. A pristine apron over her outfit to protect it from all the splashes and splatters she hadn't dared let touch the fabric as she cooked. On the table was The Perfect Dinner: meat, potatoes, vegetables that could have used a bit more salt, but since salt was almost An Actual Flavor, I didn't dare use too much of it. After all, then it wouldn't be close enough to his mother's cooking, and that might make Daniel Very Mad.

He wasn't mad, though. He saw his Perfect Dinner on the table and his Perfect Wife in the kitchen, shaking palms hidden by the apron's skirt as she wiped them off before greeting him, and he smiled. He put his briefcase by the door and his keys on the counter and crossed the kitchen, sliding an arm around my waist as he leaned down to kiss me.

"Look at you. How could I be any more blessed?" he murmured, and I'd drunk so much of his goddamn Kool-Aid by that point that I straight-up *melted* in his arms. "How was your day, my dear?"

"G-Good," I responded.

One eyebrow flicked up. He knew I was lying, and I knew he was calling me out on it, and I trembled as I met his eyes.

"I had that doctor's appointment today."

Daniel nodded, intense eyes studying me. "And?"

"We... we're having a, um... a girl."

I'd imagined any number of reactions he might have. In my mind, I'd heard him yell. I'd heard him berate me. I'd watched him sneer and blame me for not being able to give him a son. I'd felt his breath as he huffed his derision, felt my heart crack as he wondered aloud what in the hell he was

26

supposed to do with a *daughter* instead of a son. I'd spent the whole day playing scenario after scenario in my head, trying to plan what I'd do if he got Very Mad.

I hadn't imagined a scenario where he stared at me before a small smile began to play on his lips. I watched it grow, hesitant to mimic the expression until it reached his eyes.

"A girl," he repeated.

"Yes," I said.

A gentle hand touched my stomach. "That's my daughter in there."

I nodded, and he embraced me in one of those ways that made me forget all the horrible things about him, thanking God for blessing our little family with The Perfect Daughter.

And really, even with all his faults—and there was an absolute *fuckton* of faults—I couldn't claim that Daniel didn't care about Baylee. I assumed it was more about his image as a Perfect Father rather than actual love for our child, but he cared. He cared so much that he'd tried to get custody back time and time again, but luckily for me, his anger issues had manifested in ways that left mountains of evidence and a paper trail that meant no judge could justify letting him buy his way into being Baylee's primary caregiver.

He was still entitled to some days with her and I was constantly battling with him about which holidays he got to "have" her for—Easter was always his, a battle he'd won but a war he'd lost in court because by permanently claiming Easter, the judge had given me Christmas—but for the most part, Daniel's role in Baylee's life was mainly monetary. Each month, he dutifully sent his child support payment to my bank account. It still never seemed to be enough, not after school fees and field trips and birthday parties and Girl Scouts, but asking for more money wasn't worth the cost of giving that much power back to Daniel.

I'd tried explaining that to Em once, but she didn't understand how horrid he was and I didn't like dredging up all those memories. All that meant was that she didn't know just how tight money was for me sometimes. To be fair, until Alex had fucked his way into her life, it hadn't mattered all that much. There were days I was insanely jealous of her: she didn't know who Leia's father was, so she didn't have to deal with a psycho ex every month.

I, on the other hand, had to talk to Daniel at least twice a month. Once on the first day of each month, when I confirmed I received his payment and informed him which day he was allowed to see Baylee, which was the second time I had to talk to him. He would agree and ask how much it would take for him to get an extra day or weekend with her, and I'd mentally tell him to go fuck himself before politely informing him he would need to speak to the courts about that. He would sigh, ask me if we *really* had to go through all of that again.

"It was one mistake, Kelsie," he would say.

"You put me in the hospital, Daniel," I would reply.

"I would never do anything to hurt her."

"You said you would never do anything to hurt me."

"I've changed. I'm not the kind of person who would do that anymore."

"So have I. I'm not the kind of person who would let you."

"She's my daughter, too. You can't keep her from me."

"I'm not keeping her from you. I'm giving you the court-mandated amount of time you're supposed to spend with her."

I did have to relent occasionally, especially since Baylee was still too young to truly understand what all the presents and toys and adventures to amusement parks meant. As much of a piece of shit as Daniel was, I didn't badmouth him to her.

And he was. He was a *huge* piece of shit.

"You're late," he said when he answered my call on the first of the month.

I stared at the front of my house from my spot in the car, hoping that Baylee and Leia wouldn't look out the window and realize I was home almost as much as I was hoping Daniel wouldn't be able to tell I had completely forgotten it was the first of the month until I was driving home after my shift.

Or at least, that's what I was telling myself. I mean, I must have completely forgotten. It couldn't possibly have anything to do with the crushing coil of dread in the pit of my stomach that had been growing and twisting for the past few days, ever since I realized I'd have to ask Daniel for money to pay for the stupid fucking Taylor Swift tickets.

"I had to work," I said flatly.

"It's Saturday."

"Yeah? Sometimes I work Saturdays, Daniel."

"You could have called on your break," he replied. "Or texted to let me know. Or, I don't know, let me have an extra day with my daughter since you were busy anyway."

"It was last minute. I have a babysitter for her."

"So you'd rather waste money on some unknown tween instead of letting me see her."

"She's with Em," I lied. "And you wouldn't have made it in time. And your day with her this month is the fifteenth."

"God forbid I get an extra day with her once in a damn while."

The coil of dread in my stomach pulsed and I almost puked all over my steering wheel. "Well, I was, ah... thinking about that, actually."

There wasn't so much as a gasp or a muted noise of surprise; Daniel simply went silent.

"Were you?" he finally asked.

I kept my eyes glued to the front door of my house, willing my lunch to stay where it was as I tried to remember the words I'd rehearsed over and over in my mind. The rehearsals had been useless; the only thing my mind seemed capable of doing was watching in horror as I stooped to his level.

"Yes," I said. "I... I thought maybe this month you should have an extra day with her. The fifteenth and the sixteenth. She c-could stay with you."

"Why?" he demanded.

My palms began to sweat as I tried to collect my thoughts, which apparently took too long.

"*Why*, Kelsie?" he repeated. "You have never offered an extra day with her. What's changed?"

"I—"

"Are you seeing someone?"

My mouth fell open. "Excuse me?"

"You're seeing someone."

"I'm not—"

"No? Because I can think of no other reason you'd offer an overnight visit when you've never so much as let me have an extra minute with my daughter before. Has she met whoever it is you're slutting around with?"

"Fuck you."

The words fell out of my mouth; I didn't think them so much as spew them, and it was only once they were out that I kind of wished I'd spewed puke instead.

"Excuse me?" Daniel said after a moment.

The dryness in my mouth was almost painful; I swallowed, hoping it would help, but it was like sandpaper coated my tongue and throat. It was disgusting, really, the way it had taken me years—fucking *years*—to muster up the strength to leave him, and then even longer to find the strength to stand up to him, and in one conversation, all that fragile strength began to crack.

I was not the kind of person who would let him hurt me anymore, I told myself. It was a bit of a lie, but I managed a shallow breath so I could speak again.

"First of all, it's none of your business," I said, my voice shaking. "Second of all, *no*. I'm not seeing anyone. Baylee wants to go to the Taylor Swift concert and I…"

I didn't need to finish the sentence.

"You need money," he said, sweet delight masked beneath the words.

"I thought it would be a good Christmas present," I muttered. "She wants to go with Leia."

"Hmm," he said, then fell silent until I couldn't stand it anymore.

"Will you help me or not, Daniel?" I asked.

"I will," he said.

I closed my eyes. "Thank—"

"But not for one extra day."

The absolute shitstain.

"What do you want?" I asked.

"Two weeks."

"Fuck you."

He laughed. "Language, Kelsie."

"You're not taking her for two weeks. She has school."

He made a tsk-ing sound. "Taylor Swift tickets aren't cheap, you know. And I'm not asking for a lot here."

"It's not happening," I said.

"Really? You're going to stop your daughter from getting to see her idol because you're too selfish to let me have her for a couple of weeks?"

"Not even," I spat back. "I'll get the tickets another way."

He chuckled. "Sure you will."

I *seethed*. "Goodbye, Daniel."

"Talk to you soon, my dear."

Four

I TRIED TO SHUT the front door quietly as I walked in so I could take a few minutes to collect myself after talking to Daniel, and I succeeded.

Then I tripped on a pair of stylishly beat-up Converse sneakers and stepped on Pepper's chew toy, which let out a shrill squeak that pierced through the sound of rock music coming from my living room.

"Sounds like your mom's home," I heard Jimmy say.

"Oh, *no*!" Baylee cried.

Any other day, I would have laughed. That day, a lump clogged the area behind the base of my throat. I kicked my shoes off and hung up my purse.

"What a welcome," I said, my voice dry as I peeked into the living room.

The girls were standing in front of the TV, Leia holding a plastic guitar and Baylee clutching a wireless microphone to her chest. Jimmy sat on the couch, sock-clad feet resting on the coffee table. A video game console was resting on the TV stand, the associated video game paused on the screen as all three of them looked at me.

"We just wanted to keep playing," Leia explained earnestly. "And if you're back, that means Uncle Jimmy is gonna take his games and go home."

"We were just having fun," Baylee said.

Jimmy caught my gaze for all of a second before he took his feet off the coffee table and stood up.

"Keep playing," he said. "Your mom and I are gonna hang out for a bit."

I raised my eyebrows at him, but the girls squealed in excitement and Baylee unpaused the game. It only took him a few long strides to cross the room, leaving me no choice but to step back and let him guide me down the hall to the kitchen.

"What's wrong?" he asked in a low voice.

"Nothing," I said, shaking his hand off my arm. "I'm fine."

"Right. That's why you've got that look on your face like nothing is fine."

I snorted as I walked to the fridge to grab a bottle of water. "Since when are you such an expert on what looks I have on my face?"

"Since I kind of like your face."

I glanced at him over my shoulder, showing him what my face looked like when I was unimpressed. "Bullshit isn't going to win you any points."

"It's not bullshit."

I turned back to the fridge and reached for two water bottles. "Flattery, then."

"It's not that, either."

"Whatever you want to call it, then."

"What, it can't just be that I'm flirting with you?"

I snorted and closed the fridge door. "Jesus, Jimmy, I'm not old enough that you have to pity-flirt with me like I'm an elderly lady in line at the CVS or something."

"I... what?"

I rolled my eyes at him and held out one of the water bottles. "Never mind. Drink this. Knowing you, you haven't had a sip of liquid since you finished your coffee this morning."

He rolled his eyes but chuckled, taking the water from me. "You know me."

"Hydration is important, young man."

"Not that young, you know."

There was some kind of snarky response on the tip of my tongue, but the soft rumble of his voice stopped me. He met my eye again, but before I could say anything, he cracked the water bottle open and took a sip.

"Whatever," I mumbled, and mirrored his action.

He put his water bottle down on the counter. "Talk to me, Kels. What's going on?"

I sighed, then procrastinated responding by taking another slug of water.

"Another rough day at work?" he guessed.

And see, I should have said yes. I should have made up some story about how there was an essential oil spill on the production line that caused a huge backup and that the whole warehouse now smelled like lavender which meant it was almost impossible for quality control to make sure the *other* candle scents didn't all smell like lavender, not that I knew what that was like from experience or anything.

But Em was still on vacation, and Jimmy was right there, dark eyes studying me as I struggled to keep my thoughts on the inside, and Leia and Baylee were in the other room screeching at the TV in an attempt to sing a song written years before either of them were born.

I mean, I couldn't tell him *everything*. Maybe it was pride or maybe it was shame, but I didn't want him to know how tight things were for me and Baylee. And I didn't want him to know *why* I'd wanted extra money from Daniel since that would require admitting I'd gotten myself into this mess because I was too stubborn to tell Mike how much I'd be willing to spend on the stupid concert tickets.

Above all, I didn't want to tell him all the things Daniel had done to me, all the reasons why I couldn't just demand money from him, all the ways my ex-husband could punish me if I slipped up even a little.

But I could tell him some things.

"I just got off the phone with my ex," I said quietly, though there was no chance in hell the girls could hear me over their yowling. "It's child support day. And I... well. Let's just say I needed something from him and his response was to tell me he wanted to take Baylee for two weeks in exchange."

Jimmy looked confused. "Two weeks?"

"He's supposed to get one day a month," I said. "He picks her up at eight and she needs to be home before bed. So he isn't..., it's not happening. He can't have her that long."

"Right," he said, his voice guarded in a way that I hated.

My annoyance surged and I looked up, glaring at him. "Let me guess. You think I'm a horrible, evil ex-wife who's trying to keep some guy's kid from him."

He scowled right back at me, though his smoldering glare was far more masterful than mine. "Give me some credit, Kels. I know your ex is an asshole."

"Sure you do."

"I do." He put his water bottle down and folded his arms. "And besides, why would I take his side over yours? I *know* you."

"You know what I want you to know," I muttered, but I couldn't bring myself to look at him.

"I know enough. You might not say much, but that doesn't mean Baylee doesn't talk about him."

I physically *felt* the blood drain from my face as I snapped my head up. "She... what?"

The scowl faded off his face. "Well, I mean... yeah."

"She talks to you about her dad?"

He glanced towards the living room. "Sort of. Like, not... Kind of in passing, I guess. Leia does, too."

The whole idea of eyes popping out of someone's head had to be exaggerated because if it was possible, mine would have shot across the room. "Does Em know?"

He shifted again. "Not... no. I haven't—"

I put my water bottle on the counter a bit more firmly than I needed to. Just enough that the plastic made a crinkling sound and water sloshed out of the top and pooled on the counter top.

"Jimmy, what the fuck?"

"It's not what you think. They're old enough to have questions about shit, you know?" He folded his arms and tilted his head as he looked at me. "But it was mostly today."

"What do you mean?"

He sighed. "I brought video games over because I thought they'd like them. Baylee got all excited and started telling Leia about this arcade her dad took her to. Before I know it, Leia starts wondering why she doesn't have a dad, and I mean, I know she's asked Em before but it's not..."

"She doesn't know if Em's telling her everything, so she asks you," I finished.

"Pretty much."

"What did you tell her?"

"The truth," he said. "That I didn't know who her dad was. But that her dad didn't know about her, either, 'cause if he did, he'd for sure want to know her. I thought that'd make her, you know... feel less like he didn't want her."

"Did it?"

He shrugged. "She still seemed pretty sad, so Baylee tried to tell her that all the things her dad takes her to and gives her and stuff aren't that good, but I think that just made Leia jealous." He cleared his throat. "So she, uh, shared probably a little more than she should have."

My body didn't know how to react. My stomach was dropping and tightening; my throat was dry at the same time that my mouth watered like I was going to throw up. "She... she never asks me about it. What does... what did she tell you?"

"I don't think she knows what happened to make you and him split," he said carefully. "She doesn't remember a lot."

"She was only four."

He nodded. "She said she remembers you went away on a trip and it was just her and her dad, and then one night you came back while she was sleeping. Then you went to the car together and all her toys were there."

Oh, God. I pressed my lips together, certain I was about to puke all over the kitchen.

"She said after that she didn't see her dad for a long time, and that she doesn't see him much now," he continued. "Look, she might not have said anything specific about why you split up, but from the sounds of it—"

"It's none of your business," I said.

"It's a bit of my business," he shot back.

"Excuse me? It is not."

"I give a shit about you, Kels," he said. "So, yeah, it's my business because I want you to be safe and, like, happy and shit."

I opened my mouth to respond, but I didn't know what to say. Instead, I picked up my water bottle and took another sip.

"I don't mean like you have to tell me whatever happened," he continued. "Just that whatever it was, I'm on your side. And that I understand why him asking for two weeks with her is upsetting."

I tried to smile. "Thanks. I... sorry."

"Don't be. Sorry that you're dealing with it."

"Did... did she say anything that made it sound like he..." I couldn't finish the sentence, but he knew what I was asking.

"She said she usually has fun, but sometimes they have to take breaks from the fun stuff since he gets tired because he's old."

My laugh that time was a bit more genuine. "He's not old. I'm old. He's fucking ancient at this point."

He rolled his eyes. "You're not old."

"I'm practically grandmotherly. Which makes Daniel a dinosaur." I smirked and drank more water, shaking my head. "I'm the same age now as he was when we got married."

He frowned. "How old were you?"

"Nineteen. My dad had to sign a waiver so I could have a glass of champagne to toast with."

"Nine—*seriously*?!"

His expression was hilarious. I mean, yes, the tension had built up so much that anything remotely funny would set me off in hysterics, but I couldn't stop laughing at Jimmy's face.

"Seriously," I finally said.

He shook his head again. "How did you even meet?"

"Through the church," I said. "I was a rebellious teen brought to him for counselling after my parents discovered I pierced my belly button."

"At nineteen?"

"Sixteen."

"Six—" He gaped at me. "What?"

"Sixteen," I repeated. "Don't worry, he patiently waited for me to turn eighteen and worked on getting into my head in the meantime. I was a very well-behaved, soft-spoken young lady by the time my parents handed me off to him after I graduated high school."

I didn't quite know what to call the expression on his face. Horrified, maybe. Disgusted. Sympathetic, borderlining on pity. Whatever it was, I didn't like it.

"It's in the past now, Jimbo," I said boldly. "It took some struggling, but now I have a wonderful daughter and I get to make my hair whatever color I want it. And you can damn well bet I put my belly button piercing back in literally the day after I left him."

"Good," he said. "Belly button rings are hot."

"Careful now. You're going to give this old lady a big head."

"You're not old," he said again.

"Older than you."

He smiled, but it didn't quite reach his eyes. "Can I, like, hug you?"

The request surprised me, but in that delighted, exhilarated sort of way. "You know I love hugs, Jimbo."

"Jimbo," he muttered disdainfully, shaking his head as he crossed the kitchen. I didn't have a chance to respond before he tugged me in close, enveloping me as though he was using his arms to tell me that it was all right, that it would all be okay, that I was going to be okay.

And honestly? They were pretty convincing.

Five

"I SAID YES."

Em wasn't looking at me. I don't think she could bring herself to. And I understood that, obviously. I mean, she knew her decision was going to change my life as much as hers.

She probably thought I was going to be upset about it.

And I was. I told myself not to be. I stared across the cafe, doing everything I could to push down the selfish little monster inside me that wanted to scream and cry and beg Em not to move in with Alex. They'd been back from vacation for a few days and even though she hadn't said anything up until now, I'd known, and I thought that would make it easier to pretend I was happy for her.

But hearing her say it was harder than I'd thought.

I took a shallow breath, summoning up that other monster, the Stepford monster, the one that knew how to put on a fake smile and nod and be agreeable. The one I'd been controlled by for years and that I wasn't sure I'd ever be free of, even after all this time away from Daniel.

"I'm so happy for you," the Stepford monster said.

"Liar," Em replied.

There was a mother with her son on the other side of the cafe. I didn't know what the occasion was, but the little boy had a cupcake and was eating it with such a pure sense of delight that I almost smiled for real. I focused on them for a moment longer; then, when I was certain I could keep my feelings all wrapped up inside where they belonged, I turned to Em.

"I am," I repeated. "I mean, girl, come on. Of *course* I'm a little bummed that you're moving across town. But it's going to take a lot more than physical distance for you to get rid of me."

She rolled her eyes. "I'm not trying to get rid of you."

"Good, because I'm not going anywhere." I grinned and used my toe to nudge her shin under the table. "You're moving in with the love of your life. I'm happy for you. You *deserve* happiness."

My Stepford monster must have been particularly convincing that day. Either that or Em knew I was faking it and chose to believe me anyway. She stopped fidgeting with her napkin and smiled at me, one of those radiant smiles that almost made losing my best friend worth it.

Alex was good for her. I couldn't deny that. I could question it a little, and I had, more than once. I mean, the entire reason we were at that cafe having coffee was because Leia and Baylee were at the studio helping Mike and Alex with some fundraiser thing. Somehow, Em had gone from the kind of person who was hesitant to even let her daughter *learn* how to play guitar and who was openly resistant to letting her *perform* to happily agreeing to let Leia plan some charity concert. I mean, Leia had a fucking YouTube channel these days. She was just a kid, and she already had awards and... I had no idea when Em became okay with that kind of shit.

Like, she was a good person. As a kid, she raised her little brother, and as an adult, she took him in. She was blunt and snarky and hilarious, but she was also kind and thoughtful. But I'd never known her to be the kind of person to do charity work. She didn't have the time for that stuff as a single mom, and it wasn't really her thing. There were more ways to be a good person than to do big, showy events or dedicate all her time to raising money.

Somehow, though, Alex had turned her and Leia into the kind of people that like... planned fundraiser concerts for fun. And that was a change, of course, and it was my job as her best friend to question when she changed her life and personality and heart for a man.

But how in the fuck was I supposed to question a change that had her doing charity work?

Even the monsters inside me couldn't justify it. Even if it meant I was feeling like I didn't know who she was. Even if it meant I was expected to help out with chauffeuring Leia and Baylee around a little more like I was that day so Em could do some photo sessions that night for some of the promotional stuff.

"You deserve happiness too, you know," Em said, pulling me out of my thoughts.

"Of course I do," I replied, taking another sip of coffee. "After putting up with Daniel's all those years, I absolutely deserve a penis. A big one, even."

It came out louder than I intended. The mother across the cafe looked up, alarmed, but her son was still chowing down on the cupcake and hadn't heard my hilariously clever play on words.

Em snorted with laughter. "I said 'happiness.'"

"And what is happiness if not a big, throbbing, hard—"

"You're awful."

I grinned. "You love it."

"I do." She sipped her coffee. "And so will the right guy. Once I'm done moving and things settle down a bit, you and I are going to go out on the town and find you a big throbbing hunk of happiness together. Then we can double date and shit."

I lifted my almost-empty mug to her in agreement. "And shit."

My inner monsters managed to maintain the slightly saucy cheerful humor as Em and I finished our coffees. Once she realized I was at least pretending to be happy for her, she chattered endlessly about the move in a way that made it very clear she'd been planning to say yes to him for a while.

"I want us to be there for Christmas," she said. "After the fundraiser, though. I can't plan a move and deal with that all at the same time. Probably at the beginning of December since it'll be that nice lull between people going 'oh shit, I need to order photos for Christmas cards' and 'oh shit, we didn't take a nice family portrait this year.' But that'll still give us enough time to settle in and for it to, you know, feel like home for Leia. And then Christmas will *really* make it feel like home, I think."

"Mm-hmm," I said.

"The girls can bunk together in Leia's room, but Alex has a guest room so you can stay over Christmas Eve. Then Jimmy can drive over in the morning since he's closer."

I looked up, surprised. "We're still invited to Christmas?"

Em stared at me, not bothering to hide the disbelief in her dark eyes. "Of *course* you are. Why, do you not want—"

"I do," I said quickly. "We do, of course we do. The way you said you wanted it to feel like home, I thought maybe it was a family-only thing."

"It is," she said. "And you're part of my family, so you better fucking be there."

The monsters were quiet, leaving me to fight back those weepy emotions all on my own. "I'll be there no matter what."

We'd driven to the cafe separately so Em could go to her photo session while I drove back to the studio to pick up the girls after their planning session with Mike. It was nice, since I had a few minutes to feel cautiously cheerful after my chat with Em. I mean, it all still sucked, but we were going to make it work. We weren't family, but we were *family*.

It left me feeling pretty good, to be honest. But that all changed when I walked into the studio.

Here's the thing about Leia.

She was a great kid. A really great kid. People loved her. Adults loved her, kids loved her, even the grumpiest grumpy fuck in the world—a.k.a. Mike—loved her. She might not have a father, but she had an abundance of male role models in her life. Alex was one, of course. He had been her guitar teacher, but he was also very much her father figure, ever since he and Em had gotten together. I guess that role becomes less complex when there's no one in it to oust in the first place, but he'd slipped into it so easily and smoothly that his role in Leia's life was unquestionable.

Then there was Jimmy, the fun uncle, the man who got to spoil her rotten and treat her like a princess and set the standard of what she should expect to be treated like by a man when she was older. He was a teacher too, in a way: he was there to show her how to make mistakes and how to fix them. How to have fun and go on adventures and live life in a way that meant something.

Lastly, at least for the men in the room at that moment, was Mike. The grandpa figure. The curmudgeon who had a soft spot for Leia's particular brand of zest and excitement and doted on her relentlessly. Which was great for Leia, I'm sure, since Mike was a good person to have on your side, what with all the connections and apparent badassery.

But it sucked for Baylee.

Granted, it wasn't solely Mike's fault that I walked in to see the three men showering attention on Leia while my daughter sat in an office chair. *All* of them were at fault for not seeing Baylee's expression as she sat there. Baylee wasn't the type of child to hide her feelings; she didn't seem to have an inside voice, and neither did her face.

She watched longingly as Alex laughed, showing Leia how to do something or the other on a small guitar. Mike sat nearby looking pleased as punch, a stack of posters abandoned on a nearby desk as he leaned forward to scold Alex jokingly. *Jokingly.* The old bastard was *laughing* about something. Jimmy was grinning, too, watching as Leia giddily strummed, then squealed.

On top of that longing was jealousy, though I recognized the way she was trying to cover that up. There was sadness, and loneliness, and a sense of exhaustion, the kind that someone gets after they've tried and tried and finally given up. And beneath it all, confusion, and not the kind I could explain away.

My little girl sat there, hurt and dejected, wondering why she was the sidekick in her own life, wondering what her best friend had that set her apart and made her more remarkable, more lovable, more worthy of attention than she was.

And that pissed me off.

"Hi, sweetie," I said loudly, interrupting whatever it was they were doing.

Baylee perked up, relief washing across her face. "Mom!"

"Kelsie!" Leia said happily. "Look what Mr. Mike got me! He got it special made!"

A new fucking guitar made just for her.

"Hey, Kelsie," Alex said. "We'll be done in a few minutes."

"I don't have a few minutes," I said.

I thought I said it politely, but my face didn't seem to have an inside voice, either. Jimmy glanced from me to Baylee with a look of concern. Alex looked stunned, and Mike's brow furrowed as his face sagged back into its usual irritable state.

"Baylee, Leia, let's go," I said.

"I'll, uh, go get the case." Alex gently took the guitar Leia was clutching. "Back in a sec, honey."

"My backpack's in Mr. Mike's office," Baylee said quietly.

"I'll go with you to get it," Leia volunteered, sliding off the stool she'd been sitting on.

"Just as well," Mike said as the girls left. "Had to talk to you anyway. Called in a few favors and managed to track down some Taylor Swift tickets. They're pretty decent seats."

"Wonderful," I said stiffly. "How much do I owe you?"

"Don't worry about—"

"I'd prefer to pay. How much are they?"

I wish I could have blamed that stupid, stupid statement on one of my inner monsters, but it wasn't them. I was the proud one, the one who was angry and frustrated with the man sitting in front of me, the one who had it in her head that she didn't want to be indebted to the grouchy old fuck. Selfishly, I wanted to take credit for the gift. I had it in my head that I was proving a point, though I had no idea who I was proving it to. Myself, maybe. Daniel. Mike.

It didn't matter. Mike hesitated, then shrugged, and told me a number that nearly made me sick.

"Sounds great," I said instead of vomiting all over him. "Is it okay if I pay that closer to Christmas?"

"Yep," Mike said gruffly. "Whenever's convenient for ya. I'll give Em the actual tickets so you can wrap 'em up for the kid or whatever."

At least I had that much. It gave me some wiggle room, some time to… well. Daniel wasn't an option, so that meant taking extra shifts at work. I started doing the math in my head. I was sure Em would babysit. I could tell her I needed to help at work a bit more since we were ramping up for the holidays. And then there were the Saturdays that Baylee would be with Daniel. Working six days a week for a while wasn't that bad. I might be able to swing it. I mean, just barely, but it was theoretically doable. And that meant I didn't have to admit my failings to Daniel or Mike.

The only thing was that Em would probably wonder why I was working more, which meant the selfish, proud little monster inside of me would be forced to admit it was too expensive. And Em would be understanding, but that meant she might tell Alex, who might tell Mike, who... well. I just couldn't tell Em. I would tell her we were short staffed. That I was doing my boss a favor.

I hated to lie to her, but I would think of something.

Lini poked her head in the room a moment later to tell Mike about a problem in one of the studios. Sighing, he stood and grumped his way out of the room, leaving Jimmy standing there staring at me.

"Don't," I asked as he opened his mouth.

"Don't what?"

"Don't ask me what's wrong." I folded my arms. "I don't want to talk to you right now."

"Me?" He looked surprised. "What did I do?"

I shook my head silently. Jimmy waited, then folded his arms in return.

"Seriously? You're gonna act all pissed about something and not even tell me what I did?"

"Yep."

A hint of anger escaped in the form of a dry laugh. "Didn't think you were the type to pull that shit."

"Didn't think you were the type to make my daughter feel like shit, but here we are."

"What?"

The stunned look on his face was so disgustingly ignorant that despite saying I didn't want to talk to him, I couldn't stop myself.

"A new guitar," I snapped.

"Uh... yeah," he said. "Mike got it custom made by—"

"He got her a new fucking guitar and gave it to her in front of my kid. Leia got a new guitar and Baylee got ignored."

"That's not—"

"That's *exactly* what happened." I glared at him, my heart hammering in my chest. "The three of you didn't even notice her sitting there, did you? Baylee never shuts up. You know that. Other than me and Em,

47

you're the adult who's probably spent the most time with her. She talks constantly. She smiles constantly. She—"

My voice caught and I swallowed, tearing my eyes away from him before I started crying.

"I walk in here to see three grown-ass men doting on Leia while my daughter sat quietly to the side, so fucking upset that she was completely silent. You know how often that happens? And not *one* of you thought to check on her? Not one of you thought 'Hey, maybe spoiling one little girl in front of the other little girl is unfair'?"

I'd never seen Jimmy look quite so stricken or quite so ashamed. "I'm sorry. We didn't think—"

"I don't want to hear it." I tried to swallow back the words, but now that I was talking, everything seemed to pour out at once, and I was stuck desperately trying to assign my anger to *something*.

Apparently, that something was Mike.

"Every time I bring her here, Mike acts like it's some goddamn miserable obligation to even treat her like she's human. She's just a kid. She's not Leia, but she's a kid. I don't know why you all act like he's King Shit of Turd Island, but I've never once seen anything from him that makes me think he's deserving of that kind of idolization."

"He might seem kinda... you know. But he does a lot of, like, charity work and shit. He's a good guy," Jimmy said.

"Oh, sure." I rolled my eyes. "He's such a good guy. He makes up for the way he treats my kid by, what, making everyone else around him plan this stupid fucking concert? Pretending like he's *so* good because of all these charities he supports?"

"Kels, come on. Don't be like this."

"I'm the one who has to go home now and try to make my daughter understand that she's just as special and just as talented and just as good as Leia because the three of you spent the afternoon tearing that away from her without even thinking about it." A tear spilled down my cheek.

"Like I get it, she's your niece and Mike's stand-in granddaughter, and she and Em are moving in with Alex so he's basically her fucking dad now, but that doesn't mean Baylee deserves to be treated as 'less than.' Is being considerate of her feelings too much to ask?"

He frowned. "Wait, Em's moving in with Alex?"

I didn't know that Jimmy still didn't know. Even still, I hadn't meant to let that slip. But before I could respond, Alex chose that moment to return. Jimmy looked at him, then back at me.

Before anyone could say anything else, I decided I'd had enough and left the room.

Six

KIDS HAVE THE DOUBLE-EDGED sword of inherent simplicity.

Up to a certain age, things are very black and white to a kid. Baylee was smart as fuck and picked up on far more than I expected sometimes, but she was still a child. She might have understood the injustice and heartache of the situation, but to her, the problem was the men in the room.

Walking away from them meant the problem was solved, at least in her eyes.

I worried about it, late that night after poking my head in her room to make sure she was fast asleep. God only knew what the fallout would be, what sticky bit of trauma would follow her from that defining moment, what deep-seated lesson she had learned that would manifest in some strange way later in life. But Baylee didn't blame Leia for it; on the contrary, she couldn't stop expressing her excitement as I drove the two of them home.

"It looks so *cool*!" she declared in the car.

"It'll make songs lots easier to play," Leia said. "So I can learn them faster and you can sing along with me sooner!"

Baylee clasped Leia's hand eagerly, childish exuberance filling the back seat. "I can't wait for you to play it more. Maybe I can be on your YouTube with you one day!"

They giggled and chattered and I kept my eyes focused on the road, wondering with pride and shame how my daughter had ended up so selfless when she had selfish parents like me and her father.

I expected Em to be pissed that I'd spilled the beans to Jimmy and had resolved to own up to it when she came to pick up Leia, but she already knew what had happened.

"I lost my shit on Alex," she said as soon as she walked into my house—without knocking, of course, because we didn't bother with those kinds of formalities anymore.

"Sorry," I said.

"Don't be." She walked to the fridge and grabbed two beers. "Put the popcorn on. I'm starving."

I grabbed a bag of microwavable popcorn from the pantry. "I mean I'm sorry for... I didn't know you hadn't told Jimmy. Was he mad?"

"Oh, that?" She snorted and rolled her eyes. "Of course not. If he wasn't pissed when he found out Alex and I were fucking, he wasn't going to be pissed about us moving in together."

I smiled in spite of myself. Jimmy's discovery of Alex and Em's relationship coincided with my discovery that Jimmy had grown up and matured a *lot*. He'd overheard me and Em talking about the fact that not only was she sleeping with his boss, but with the guy who had ruined his career, and that they were the same guy. Both of us had cringed, waiting for Jimmy's trademark anger to show, and for him to storm off to find Alex and lose his mind on him.

But Jimmy just laughed, called Alex a fucker, and declared he was going to ask for a raise.

"He was concerned more than anything," Em continued as she opened the beers and passed me one.

"About what?"

"You."

I laughed, startled. "What? Why?"

"Well, aside from feeling awful about the whole guitar thing, he wanted to know who was going to bring Baylee to school and watch her and stuff."

"I hadn't thought about that yet," I lied.

"We'll figure it out," Em said. "Anyway, that was his major concern. Then the guitar thing was... well."

"It's... she's fine."

"Clearly," Em said, indicating the off-key way my daughter was singing along to Leia's off-beat guitar playing.

"I'm probably more upset than she is," I admitted.

"For good reason." She sipped her beer. "I don't know whose asinine idea it actually was, but Alex took the blame for it. He said he should have told Mike to wait until Baylee wasn't there, but Mike was apparently crazy excited to give her the guitar."

"I wonder what that must have looked like," I muttered. "Giddy as a schoolgirl, that one. Probably pulled a muscle trying to smile."

She burst out laughing. "You know how he gets with Leia."

Oh, I sure did.

"None of them thought it through," she continued. "Alex had the balls to ask how it was any different from a kid's birthday party."

"Fucking seriously?!" I blurted. "Because it's not her birthday and—"

"—a kid understands how birthdays work but not necessarily how random fucking custom guitar gifts work," she finished. "I know."

"Asshole."

"That's what I called him."

We paused, sipping our beer.

"And what did Mike say?" I asked.

The shift was subtle, but there. Em tapped her beer bottle against the kitchen table.

"Well, I didn't talk to Mike," she said. "And, um..."

"What?"

She sighed. "Alex doesn't want Mike to know about it. He said he'd make sure nothing like it happened again, but... I don't know. Mike's kind of sensitive about Leia and I guess he's got some other stuff going on right now." She looked at me, dark eyes pleading. "I know it's not fair to ask, but—"

"Yeah," I said. "Whatever. I won't mention it."

"Kels—"

"Whatever, Em." I grabbed another handful of popcorn. Of course we were trying not to offend Big Mike's delicate sensibilities. Of fucking *course* we were. "Look, maybe it would be best if Baylee didn't hang out at the studio for a while."

"Don't take away something she loves because you're mad at Mike," she said. "I *know* it was a shitty thing to do, but—"

My mouth dropped open. "You think I would do that?"

She had the self-awareness to realize she'd crossed a line and the decency to look ashamed. "No, I... that came out wrong."

Sure it had.

"I wouldn't," I said. "I meant... I just—"

"I know," Em said. "If Baylee isn't... I mean, if she really doesn't want to spend time there, we can make sure the girls have somewhere else to hang out. This is all Alex's fault, remember? So he can figure something out for them. But if she does want to, I'll make sure they... it's going to be different."

"She's going to know if they're pandering to her," I said. "She's not stupid."

"It's not pandering." She looked at me, earnestly fierce. "Jimmy felt like shit. Seriously. You know he adores both of the girls."

"Sure. But Leia is his niece."

"Doesn't matter. Jimmy loves Leia, and Leia loves Baylee, and Jimmy feels as protective over Baylee as he does over Leia. He's spent so much time with the girls that... I mean, he cares about you both a lot, Kels. More than you know."

Something tugged in my chest as she said that. I sucked lightly on my lip ring but didn't say anything.

"He felt awful," she said. "I don't remember the last time I heard him sound so upset with himself. He's not going to let something like that happen again."

"If you say so."

"I do say so."

The words stuck in my mind long after Em and Leia left. Long after Baylee had her bath and crawled into bed and let the memories of the day wash away. Long after I should have been asleep so I could wake up early and take advantage of the numbered days I had left with childcare in the morning.

Long after I should have let it go, I held onto that flutter, the terrifying comfort I'd felt when Em said Jimmy cared about me and Baylee.

Seven

LIES.

All of it was lies.

Lies, trickery, untruths, and fabrications. Straight up fucking delusional bullshit.

I cursed them all. I cursed Em. I cursed the day that brought them into my life. I cursed Alex for instigating the whole thing. I cursed the inventor of the goddamn thing. I cursed Mike just fucking because.

All of them. Curses on *all* of them.

Especially that fucker Jimmy.

I don't know how he convinced Em he cared for me. A master of straight up deceit, that one. His actions weren't the actions of a man who understood what he was doing to me.

Although I had to give him credit. He did care for Baylee. That much was clear the second he put that cursed instrument in her greedy little hand and taught her how to play it.

A tambourine.

He gave my daughter a fucking *tambourine*.

I would be haunted until the day I fucking *died* by the jingles and the jangles and the palm-slapping pounding of an eight-year-old girl's hand on the head of it. And yes, those were proper terms for parts of the tambourine, as Baylee so kindly informed me fifteen fucking times.

The thing was, I had been right. The day after the new guitar debacle, I brought Baylee over to Em's house to get ready for school like I always did. And like always, Em was in the kitchen, blearily brewing coffee and tucking Fruit Roll-Ups into Leia's lunch bag.

And like sometimes, Alex was there, sipping coffee at the kitchen table as he flipped through some guitar magazine.

"Morning, Em!" Baylee said cheerfully.

"Morning, Bay," Em replied. "Leia's in her room. Go see if you can drag her out of bed, okay?"

Baylee dropped her bookbag and kicked off her shoes. "You got it!"

"No 'good morning' for me?" Alex teased from the table.

The sunshine on Baylee's face flickered and my heart broke.

"Morning, Mr. Alex," she said politely.

He caught the subtle shift just as clearly as Em and I had, but smiled anyway.

"Hey, before you run off, I was thinking. Your mom says you're pretty good at art, right?"

She brightened cautiously. "Yeah, sort of."

"Well, Em and I were talking and we could use some help with the posters for the concert. What about if you and Leia came by the studio after school today and helped us make some? We could get Lini to print them so we can put them up around town."

"Oh," Baylee said. "Um, maybe we could draw the posters at my house and then you can give them to Ms. Lini for us?"

Alex nodded casually. "Sure, kid."

"I didn't say anything to her about not going to the studio," I said to Em as soon as Baylee rushed down the hallway to wake up Leia. "This is the first I'm hearing about it."

"I believe you." Em glared at Alex. "And I told *you* to give it some fucking time."

They were still squabbling as I left for work and when I picked the girls up after school, neither of them mentioned going to the studio or drawing posters for the concert. Instead, they shut themselves in Baylee's bedroom for what I was told was a Very Important Secret Project. I heard giggles and whispers and the occasional gasp of laughter accompanied by words like "boyfriend," "married," and "in love." Before I could shit myself in panic at the fact that my eight-year-old was talking about boys, I heard a murmur about planning to "trick them into a date" and realized they were talking about setting up someone else.

That was a relief. I mean, they were *eight*. I told Em about it when she came to pick Leia up and we laughed, though we both cracked a beer and clinked the bottles together, silently grateful that we weren't the parents of whichever kids they were trying to set up on a date.

A few days after that, I had to work late and asked if Em could take care of pick up. And that was where I fucked up.

The silvery rustling of the rattling jingles slapped me in the face as soon as I opened the door to pick up Baylee after work. I didn't make the connection at first; loud and strange noises weren't all that alarming on their own, not when I had a boisterous kid with a rambunctious best friend. It could have been some game they made up—Shake The Pennies Inside A Metal Can Because Of Reasons, for example—or a craft Em had invented to keep them busy—Put These Pennies In A Metal Can To Scare Away Bears Or Something, maybe.

No, what made it alarming was that I looked into the living room to see Jimmy sitting beside Baylee on the couch, grinning as she tapped and shook and struck the tambourine in her hand while Leia looked on excitedly.

"Mom!" Baylee said. "Look, Jimmy taught me to play this!"

"Did he?" I asked, trying to sound like I was something other than devastatingly horrified.

"She's pretty good," he said.

The cynic in me wanted to roll my eyes at him, assuming that he was being tongue-in-cheek at best and facetious at worst. I was halfway to giving him one of those "I know what you're doing, asshole" looks, but I couldn't.

The look on his face was so genuine and bright and *proud* that I just... I couldn't.

"Of course she is," I said instead, and Baylee beamed.

"Mom, watch!" she demanded. "I already know how to do, um... this thing."

And she did a thing that featured rattling the tambourine and also hitting the tambourine. I guess it was good because Jimmy's face glowed with pride.

"Impressive," I said when the jingling faded.

"It is," Jimmy said. "It's actually—okay, so, I have to double-check, but I think... I mean, if it's okay with you, Kels, but you know the Poplin Family Jug Band?"

"I... yeah," I said.

"Okay, right." He was talking fast and motioned toward the tambourine. "Ethan Poplin makes instruments and stuff. He made this as sort of a test thing, I think. But he was saying he wanted to incorporate some tambourine into their songs and asked if I knew anyone, and I said no but clearly I hadn't heard Baylee play yet." He looked at me imploringly. "What would you say if Baylee maybe came to the studio to practice with the Poplins a couple of times? Then we could ask Ethan if she could play at the concert with them?" He glanced at Baylee. "Only if you want to, of course."

Well, there was no question about it. She nearly jumped off the couch, her fist tight around the tambourine in her hand, her eyes wide and wild and eager and full of a passion I'd never, ever seen in her before.

"Mom, please?" she asked breathlessly. "Please, please, please, can you ask Mr. Poplin?"

And how could I say no?

"No," I said.

Her face fell.

"But you can," I continued. "If you want to play the tambourine for the Poplins, you can ask Mr. Poplin if that would be okay."

Both Baylee and Leia *shrieked* with delight, and honestly, I had a feeling that Jimmy wanted to squeal right along with them. I sent Baylee to get her backpack out of Leia's room and as soon as the girls raced down the hallway, he stood from the couch.

"Is this because of the other day?" I asked before he could say anything.

The almost-wholesome excitement on his face faded. "Not even a little."

"Okay."

"I wouldn't do that," he said almost angrily. "Ethan gave me the tambourine and I thought the girls might like it so when Em asked me to watch them, I—"

"Wait, Em's not here?"

He shook his head. "She had a client tonight. Alex said he'd cover shit at the studio if I could watch them until she was back so..." He shrugged. "Anyway, I brought it over and Baylee saw it. It had nothing to do with... with that."

"Right," I said. "Okay."

He glanced at the hall, then lowered his voice. "But I am sorry, Kels. I fucked up. I'm sorry."

"Thank you," I said.

His jaw twitched and hurt flashed in his dark eyes before he looked away from me, nodding resignedly. "Okay. I understand."

Déjà vu poured over me. There was a clamping sensation in my chest, guilt seizing me as I didn't give him the response he was hoping for. For half a heartbeat, I saw Daniel, and I braced myself for the inevitable gaslighting, the subtle nudges to direct me to do what he expected, the deprecating ridicule until I was the one apologizing for making him feel bad.

But that never came.

Of course it didn't. Nothing about Jimmy was anything like Daniel.

"Jimbo," I said.

His mouth twitched and he looked back at me, one eyebrow flicking upward.

I spread my arms. "Come here."

The twitch turned to a full smile and he stepped forward, wrapping his arms around me as I pulled him in for a hug. Beneath the warmth of his body, I could feel the relief pouring off him, the gentle sigh as his tension slipped away.

"We're good?" he asked.

"We're good," I replied. "On that, anyway. The tambourine, on the other hand..."

He snorted, but before he could say anything, the sound of two eight-year-olds giggling in the hallway interrupted us. We parted to see Baylee and Leia standing there, grinning.

"Hi, Uncle Jimmy," Leia said loudly.

"Uh... hey?" he replied, confused.

They stared, then giggled again.

"Right," I said. "Baylee, you ready?"

"Yes, Mom."

She started towards the door, then stopped and rushed across the living room. Jimmy barely managed to get his arms open before she was hugging him.

"Thank you," she whispered, just loud enough that I could hear it, and that strange little flutter started in my chest again.

Eight

THE NEXT FEW WEEKS weren't hell, but they were pretty close.

The only saving grace was that I was working six days a week, plus grabbing overtime hours wherever I could, so that meant I got a bit of reprieve from the sound of my beautiful, talented, determined daughter playing her tambourine at all hours of the day.

She loved the fucking thing. Loved it. If I'd let her, she probably would have slept with it like it was a teddy bear. Before school, she was playing her tambourine, and after school, she was playing her tambourine, and when bedtime rolled around, it was a struggle to get her to relinquish the goddamn thing. Everything in my life was done to the beat of the tambourine: washing dishes became an exercise in rhythm, I swept and mopped and cleaned in time to the ever-present tintinnabulation, and even taking a shit became a musical number.

Of course, working that extra time meant one less day a week to spend doing all the other things I was supposed to take care of in my life. Casual nights with Em dwindled as exhaustion and obligation began to take over. The saving grace there was that Ethan Poplin had enthusiastically agreed to let Baylee play tambourine for them at the concert, so she was spending more time at the studio practicing and even performing with the Poplin Family Jug Band. Alex sorted it out so that he could pick the girls up from school those days and do some "official" guitar lessons with Leia while Baylee was practicing, which meant I could pick up a few extra hours here and there.

In a sick way, I was proud of how well I was covering up the stress I was going through. It gave me a sense of self-reliance, despite the fact that I was relying on other people heavily to help me. But each hour I worked was an hour closer to being Mom Of The Year in the category of Providing Basic Necessities And Bitchin' Christmas Presents Without Asking Her Squalling Turd Of An Ex For Help.

Which was something.

But the delusion that I'd been doing a good job handling it all came crashing down one Saturday night after I finished work.

The Poplins wanted Baylee to perform with them at some community thing, Em said, and the girls wanted to have a sleepover after, and would I mind if they had the sleepover at Alex's place so Leia could start feeling like her room there was *her* room?

And that made sense, so I said yes, of course, and when I got home from work, Jimmy was sitting on my doorstep.

"What are you doing here?" I asked as I slammed my car door shut.

"Bringing you food."

There were two large bags sitting beside him on the step. I glanced at them, then back at him with raised eyebrows.

"Why?"

"'Cause you need a night to yourself," he said. "That's why Em decided the girls were having a sleepover. She knows you've been working your ass off, but that you'd never ask for a break. So she decided you were getting one and I said I'd bring dinner over for you."

I eyed the overstuffed bags as I stepped past him to unlock the door. "How much do you think I eat?"

He followed me into the house, trapped behind me as I stopped to put my purse down and take my work boots off. "Well, I was pretty hungry, so..."

"So you figured you'd crash my night to myself?" I teased.

He grinned. "Nah, I was gonna grab some to go, but I mean, if you're offering..."

"Don't let me ruin your wild and crazy night," I said, straightening up as I tucked my shoes onto the mat. "Besides, I haven't showered or anything. You don't have to subject yourself to my stinky after-work smell."

The way my house was set up, the entryway was pretty cramped. It was barely wide enough for Baylee to squeeze past if we entered the house at the same time, which meant a tall, fully grown man like Jimmy didn't have a chance to get past my dump truck ass. That could have easily been solved by me doing something sensible, like moving out of the way, but when Jimmy caught my eye and leaned forward, all semblance of thought just... stopped.

There was half a smirk on his face and his dark eyes seemed to sparkle. Before I could even think to react, his face was to the side of mine, and I heard him inhale.

"You don't smell bad," he said, his voice low. "Kinda uh... flowery. Like candles."

I almost shivered, but rolled my eyes and slapped his shoulder. "It's like I work at a candle company or something. And stop sniffing me, you creep."

He burst out laughing and pulled away. "Go do what you gotta do. I'll get dinner on the table and then if you wanna kick me out, I'll go."

"Don't go," I said before I even thought the words. "Hang out with me."

I didn't quite know what to call the look on his face, but I liked it.

While Jimmy got dinner sorted out, I showered quickly, though I still gave myself enough time to overthink everything while I was at it. How I felt like I didn't deserve this kind of kindness. How I was embarrassed that everyone had noticed what I thought I'd been hiding so well. How easily I'd been swayed into letting him stay, and how delighted I was that he'd wanted to.

You know. Just your standard overthinking that had become a part of my personality after years and years of dealing with an ex that seemed to require it. Nothing entirely out of the ordinary, and once I was done, I debated putting on jeans and a nice top before shrugging on an old grey sweater and my comfiest leggings.

I mean, who did I think I was trying to impress? It was just Jimmy downstairs. And after I'd left Daniel and his Wardrobe Regulations For A Proper Wife, I'd sworn that the next time I dressed for a man, it was going to be when they put me in my coffin to go see Jesus. Or if I really, really wanted to get laid, but that would be *my* choice, not someone else's.

The point is that my outfit was both a blessing and a curse when I trekked back downstairs and into the kitchen.

It was a curse in that I was almost blind-sided by the man in my kitchen. And I mean *blind-sided*. When I'd gone upstairs to shower, I'd left Jimmy—young Jimbo, Em's baby brother, fun uncle to my kid's best friend, notably younger than me by a not-insignificant amount—in the kitchen to set the table and dish up the Chinese takeout he'd brought over for dinner. When I returned, I saw... well.

My outfit was a blessing because it was still Jimmy standing in my kitchen, but it was Jimmy in a way I wasn't supposed to be looking at him.

I don't know why it all hit me at that precise moment. Maybe it was the context: we'd been alone together before, but not... not like that. Not to have dinner and hang out and... you know. Be in each other's company or whatever.

Or maybe it was the subtle shift in his demeanor: the maturity that seemed to make him stand up straighter and exude a quiet confidence instead of a screaming cockiness.

Or maybe it was that I'd never seen him in anything other than concert t-shirts and ripped jeans, and now that his jacket was off, he was standing there in dark jeans and an unbuttoned plaid shirt overtop of a plain t-shirt, the sleeves casually rolled up to his elbows as he struggled to open a bottle of wine.

In any case, I was grateful I was dressed like a complete slob rather than in something that made me feel like I could have had a shot with him because *that* would have been even more problematic than the fact that he was opening a bottle of wine.

Or, as I said, struggling to open the bottle.

He didn't notice me right away, which was good, because it gave me a moment to watch and let that strange feeling pass; the more he twisted the corkscrew, the more I saw of the Jimmy I was supposed to know, until I wasn't sure I'd seen anything else at all.

"Need a hand?" I finally asked.

He looked up, his face turning red. The corkscrew was stuck, jammed into the cork at an angle. I pressed my lips together, trying not to laugh, and he shifted slightly as he cleared his throat.

"I thought I'd try to, you know. Class it up a little," he said. "But, uh..."

"First time?" I teased.

He laughed. "Yeah. I've never even had a glass before."

"Really? You've *never* had wine?"

He shook his head and I smiled, stepping into the kitchen. Without saying anything, I reached for the bottle. He passed it to me and I undid all his hard work. Once I had the corkscrew out, I flipped out the little lever thingie, re-screwed it into the cork, and put the lever thingie in place. As I pulled the cork out in one smooth motion, he groaned.

"It's that easy?"

"Sure is, Jimbo."

He'd put out two wine glasses and I poured a small amount into one, then slid it across the counter to him. He raised an eyebrow.

"That's it?"

I made a tsk-ing noise. "This is how the pros do it. I pour you a small amount, you swirl it around and sniff it and shit, then you take a little slurp." I put some wine in the other glass and showed him the steps, then lifted it to my lips and took a sip. "Then you say, 'mmm, that's quite lovely, is that from the Provence region of Italy? It tastes of smoked oak and ripened juneberries. That, along with the smoothness of the body, suggests the grapes were likely grown on a north-facing bush and harvested in early July. And do I detect a hint of tannins?'"

Jimmy stared at me, then frowned down at his glass. "Damn. I didn't know you knew all that shit about wine. I got this because the guy at the store said it was good." He shook the glass a bit, then took a sip.

And he tried. He really tried. And I tried not to laugh. But he was able to keep his face neutral for all of a moment before his mouth twisted down and his nose wrinkled.

"Hmm," he said, his voice higher pitched than usual, and I completely fucking lost it.

"Not a fan?" I managed to choke through my laughter.

Jimmy's cheeks turned red, but he grinned bashfully and set the glass down.

"Maybe it'll grow on me," he said. "But, uh…"

"Would you like something else instead?" I asked. He nodded gratefully and I started laughing again, motioning towards the fridge before I poured more wine for myself. "Help yourself."

He grabbed a beer and we moved to the table, which was teeming with Styrofoam containers holding what appeared to be every dish the Chinese food restaurant made. The sweet and sour scent of overly sauced pork and greasy noodles made me realize how very hungry I was.

"How'd you learn all that stuff about wine?" Jimmy asked as I started heaping my plate full of food. "All I tasted was, like... wine."

"Oh, I'm completely full of shit," I said. "None of that was true."

He laughed, his face turning pink again. "Oh."

There was a lull; an awkward silence made worse by the fact that I couldn't decide if I was regretful or relieved by it. Mostly relieved, I told myself, since the level of comfort I was feeling with him was... well. He was my best friend's younger brother. Emphasis on "best friend's brother" and on "younger." I swallowed hard and piled chicken-fried rice on my plate.

Still, the awkwardness was... well, awkward.

"This is awesome," I said, hating the fake tone to my voice. "You managed to get all my favorites. How'd you know?"

He chuckled. "Baylee was *very* specific."

"Baylee was in on this?"

He looked like I'd caught him with his pants down. "Sort of. She maybe said very pointedly that you deserved a nice dinner and spent a good ten minutes telling me what you liked."

"She's nothing if not thorough."

We chatted superficially over dinner. Easy things, unnoteworthy things, safe things about our day-to-day lives and shared connections. And that was good; it was right. But even as we cleared our plates and heaped them up again with far, far too much Chinese food, I could see Jimmy was holding something back.

And that was terrifying.

But whatever it was, he didn't say anything about it. He told me about work and joked about the "young punks" he had to give tours of the studio to, kids from nearby high schools who were barely younger than him. And he told me about his side projects; bands he was playing songs with at gigs so he could keep performing now and then, songs he was writing in his spare time that he hoped Alex would help him with, even a new guitar he'd had his eye on that he was pretty sure he was going to treat himself to.

It was refreshing listening to him talk. Those mindless things, those hopeful things, those things that were real and right and normal for a twenty-one-year-old to be dealing with. Things I couldn't relate to, not having had the chance to experience them myself, since I was married to a monster at that age.

Things that I so loved hearing about.

When we finished eating, Jimmy put the leftovers away as I cleared the dishes. Then, instead of doing something useful like sitting around and finishing his beer, he made it even harder for me to not have more of those thoughts I wasn't supposed to have by helping me wash and dry the dishes.

When we were done, we each grabbed another drink—more wine for me, water for him—and moved to the living room as easily as if we'd done it a million times before. I didn't have room for a full living room set, not that I'd ever needed one, so we had no choice but to sit side-by-side on the saggy old couch.

A silent beat went by and just as I was about to propose watching an episode of whatever trashy reality TV show happened to be on that night, he cleared his throat.

"So, uh, I wanted to talk to you about something," he started.

It took everything in me not to look up at him in alarm. Instead, I stared at the darkened TV in alarm.

"What's that?" I asked.

He cleared his throat again. "It's, uh, something I'm not sure you know. But it's... well. I know it's kind of big and give me a chance to explain, okay? 'Cause I think... I think it's important. I've wanted to bring it up for a while."

Oh, *God.*

"Okay," I said hesitantly, trying to keep my hands from shaking.

Jimmy took a moment to steel his resolve, then took a deep breath and looked at me earnestly.

"Baylee would be an awesome drummer," he said.

Nine

THERE IT WAS.

That was why Jimmy was here, all dressed up, trying to make a good impression. He thought my daughter would be a good drummer and now he was looking me in the eyes, his face earnest and serious and pleading, and I was staring back, disappointed.

No.

No, that wasn't right.

That was not allowed to be right.

I was staring back, *relieved*. So relieved.

And then dismayed.

"Surely you're fucking with me," I said.

"I'm not fucking with you. And don't call me Shirley," he said, proving yet again that he was Em's brother, and I groaned as he grinned. "Look, I know no one wants their kid to be a drummer, but Kels, she's just... she's got it."

"I... are you trying to kill me?! I've already put up with the tambourine at all hours of the day and now you want to introduce *drums*?"

He held his hands up defensively. "I'm not saying you have to, but she's a natural. Like, she just gets it. She's fantastic."

"How would you know?" I asked. "She's never played before."

He hesitated and I groaned.

"When?"

"I'm sorry!" he exclaimed. "I showed them to her at the studio one day and it was like she just *knew*."

"You're killing me, Jimbo," I muttered. "I live in a townhouse. The neighbors will kill me. I'm already dead. Tell Jesus I'm on my way to the grave right now."

"At least it'll be soundproof," he said.

As hard as I tried to keep being overdramatic, I couldn't keep a straight face. Jimmy grinned as I started laughing.

"Just think about it," he said. "She'd be so good."

"Why drums, though?" I whined, flopping back on the couch.

"Probably because it's the perfect balance for her." He shifted again, reaching for the glass of water he'd left on the coffee table. "She's loud and out there, but she's not like Leia who can just immerse herself in the music and feel it, you know? Percussion gives her enough structure to let loose and work through stuff the way she needs to." He paused to take a sip of water. "I used to play with a drummer who said it gives people the guidance they need to embrace their chaos."

For a moment, I had no idea what he was talking about. But even as I opened my mouth to express my confusion, I pictured my daughter. The little girl who was too much, too loud, too unabashedly herself, who understood too much and nowhere near enough. Who saw her best friend get things that she didn't and understood why at the same time that she understood nothing at all.

And I knew what he meant.

"Man, I'm doing a bang-up job," I said. "Giving her all that chaos to embrace."

It was meant to be a joke. Or, well, it was meant to sound like it was a joke. One of those jokes that wasn't a joke, just a statement I said like it was a joke because I wanted Jimmy to laugh so the realization hurt a little less.

Apparently, though, he didn't get it.

"What d'you mean?" he asked, frowning.

I made a sound that was supposed to be a laugh. "Oh, you know."

An annoyed look crossed his face. "No, I don't."

"It was a joke, Jimbo."

"It didn't seem like a joke."

"Oh, now you're insulting my joke-telling skills?"

His scowl deepened. "You know that's not what I meant."

Of course I did. And of course he wasn't letting it go. And of course he was scowling his trademark Jimmy scowl, which had absolutely no effect on me whatsoever, except that this time it did.

"She's got way more baggage than a kid her age should," I said, hardly aware I'd made the decision to speak. "I mean, between me and her dad, she... she's not getting the normal childhood experience. I haven't been able to give her that. And that's why she's... you know." I laughed shakily again. "Full of chaos."

I was looking at his hands, for some reason, but from the corner of my eye, I could see him studying me.

"It's not you, Kels," he finally said. "You know that, right?"

I didn't say anything.

"Kelsie," he said firmly. "You know it's not your fault, right?"

"I mean, it is."

"Wha—are you serious?"

I could feel heat rising up my neck as I stared at Jimmy's hands, needing something to focus on and hating that I'd chosen that particular thing. A creeping, crawling, nagging sensation was working its way up my spine, a coldness that was built on instinct, a warning in a calm, collected, hauntingly familiar voice to be quiet, woman, shut your fucking mouth.

But that voice wasn't Jimmy's voice, and that man wasn't here. And try as I might, I couldn't shut my fucking mouth.

"It is my fault," I said. "I wanted her so bad. So I brought her into the world, knowing damn well what kind of person she would have as a father. And when I finally figured out that she wasn't gonna get a normal childhood with... with how he acted, I took her away from a secure life to one where I can't—didn't, I mean, didn't know if I could make it paycheck to paycheck."

If I was someone else, a tear might have rolled down my cheek, but I wasn't. I was me, and I was focused on Jimmy's hands as hollowness filled my chest and my voice.

"I was selfish and now she's paying for it. No kid has a completely perfect childhood, but she's going to figure out how much more fucked up hers is."

"I don't even know what to say," he said.

I smiled wryly. "That bad, huh?"

"Your take on it? Yeah, it's fucking awful."

I was stunned enough to look up at him. There was a hardness in his gaze, but it softened as his eyes met mine.

"You wanted a kid. That's pretty normal. You had a piece of shit husband. That's less normal, but not your fault. *He* was the fucked up one, not you."

"If I'd just—"

"If you'd just nothing. You got her out of there. You put her before yourself. That's literally the *opposite* of selfish."

"You don't get it, Jimbo." I laughed again, mostly to cover up that hollow upset still ringing through my voice. "She's my kid. I love her. I want the best for her. Which means I know she deserves better than the shit parents she got."

"Not true. She's got a great mom."

"She's got a shit mom."

"You're not a shit mom."

I should have caught the aggravation behind his insistence, but I didn't.

"I am," I said frankly. "I can admit that, okay? Just because Daniel's horrific doesn't mean I'm not a shit parent, too."

"You know I fucking know what it's like, right?"

The fire in his voice shocked me in a way it shouldn't have. Jimmy had always had a bit of a temper; not a scary one, not the kind that made him lash out or get physical, but even though he was far calmer and more settled than he used to be, that anger was still there.

And he had a good reason for that anger, which I'd known. Apparently, though, I'd been so focused on myself that I'd forgotten why he harbored so much anger.

But Jimmy wouldn't ever forget. He *couldn't* ever forget.

"You know what my parents were like?" he continued heatedly. "You know. There's no way Em hasn't told you. You know I didn't know parents weren't supposed to scream at their kids constantly? Or that kids get presents on their birthdays? Or that people were supposed to eat three meals a day? You know they could've gotten us killed? You know they almost *did*? Or that they could've let CPS take us away, but then they wouldn't get their cut from the government, so they made sure they did the bare minimum to keep us at home? And you know how fucking low that bar is?"

"I—no," I said softly.

"It's low." His voice wavered, not quite a crack but nowhere near steady. "I *know* what shit parents are like. I know what it's like when someone treats you like nothing. Like you're a nuisance. Like you're not even a person. And I know Em tried her fucking best with me, and I know she feels like she fucked up and maybe she did, but she *tried*, Kels. I wasn't even her kid and she tried. By your definition, that makes her a shit sister. D'you think she was a shit sister? 'Cause I don't."

I shook my head, my lip trembling. "I'm sorry."

"Don't be." His cheeks were red, but some of the ferocity in his words began to fade. "Don't apologize. Just don't say you're shit, okay? You know how much would've been different if either of my parents cared about me the way you care about her? You know what I'd give to have someone like you in my life?"

I hated that he said it.

I hated the way his voice wavered and the earnest, heartbreaking honesty in his voice. I hated the yearning, the regret, the way it was so clear he felt like he'd missed out on something and the knowledge that it was true. I didn't know Jimmy's parents, but I hated that they'd done that to him, that here he was, years later, not sure why he'd had to go through the shit he did. Why he'd been so unlucky, why he hadn't been loved unconditionally the way that any and every child should.

And I hated, I fucking *hated* that it had the effect he'd intended. That the thought of how much worse I could be as a parent offered an undeniable comfort. That as chaotic and precarious as Baylee's life was, she would always know she was loved.

He wasn't looking at me. I don't think he could bring himself to. I glanced at his hands again. They were in his lap, fists clenched, knuckles white, and I couldn't stop myself from reaching forward and putting my hand over one of his.

A beat passed, just a heartbeat, but a beat nonetheless. There was an inevitability to the way his hand relaxed, to the loosening of his fingers and the twisting of his wrist so he could clasp my hand.

"I dunno why she didn't want me." There was no question who "she" was. His voice was gravelly, covering a brokenness that I knew he'd live with forever. "Wasn't worth it, I guess."

I squeezed his hand. "You were. You *are*. I don't know why or even how anyone could not want you around, Jimbo. I mean, sure, you've completely ruined my life, but at least my daughter will be a damn good drummer."

It made him laugh, which was the intention. And it made him look up, which wasn't necessarily intended, but wasn't unintended either.

But it also made his eyes meet mine, and that made him pause. Another heartbeat passed, and then another, and then he kissed me.

And that was not intended. Not at all.

And the fact that it wasn't unwelcome, well... that was a problem.

For that first heartbeat, I didn't react. I froze in my uncertainty, my mind swirling blank. His breath was warm and his lips were soft, enticingly sweet in a way that sent a rush of electricity through me, and I closed my eyes.

On the second heartbeat, I kissed him back, and he took it as a sign. His other hand left his lap and found the side of my face, calloused fingertips touching my skin and grounding me, confirming that it was happening, that it was all too real. I let the feel of him wash over me, that moment of *yes*, that sensation of something that felt so right, so real, so needed.

And so wrong.

Oh God, was it so, *so* wrong.

That didn't stop me from selfishly indulging in him for one more heartbeat. It didn't stop me from parting my lips for him or letting my tongue touch his. He deepened the kiss and I let him, I encouraged him, I almost lost myself completely and threw myself at him.

Almost.

"No," I breathed.

"Hmm?" he asked.

I grimaced, my eyes still closed. "Jimmy, no. Stop."

His hand fell away from my face and the spot where his lips had been was suddenly cold and empty. He was still close; too close, closer than he should have been and farther than I truly wanted him, but he stopped. I opened my eyes to see dark ones looking back at me, hungry but hesitant, almost innocent in their confusion.

"Kels?" he asked.

The innocent confusion made the guilt truly surge. I remembered wearing an expression like that, once upon a time. I remembered that feeling far, far too well.

What the fuck was I thinking?

"I can't do this to you," I whispered.

Confusion turned to a haughty sort of indignation. "You're not doing anything to me. I'm the one who kissed you."

"I shouldn't have let you."

"Why?" he demanded.

"You're not thinking clearly. It was a heated conversation and—"

"And I've been thinking about this for months. Years, actually, but I've wanted to do something about it for months." He sat back, his face earnest and stubborn. "You think I haven't thought this through? Give me a reason we shouldn't be together. Any reason."

I gaped at him, then laughed dryly. "Fine. I'm too old for you."

He'd obviously played this conversation over in his head because he answered before I even finished speaking. "You're not that much older than me."

"If you honestly think that, you're too young for me."

He shook his head. "It's an excuse and you know it. The age gap between Alex and Em is longer than I've been alive. This is nothing compared to that."

"You're not Em," I said. "And I'm not Alex. Not to mention Em's my best friend. She'd lose it."

"She'd understand. I mean, she slept with my boss *and* kept doing it after she found out he ruined my career."

"It's different when you're my best friend's brother!"

He shook his head. "She wants what's best for us. She wants us both to be happy. We could be happy together."

"It's different. Friends don't do that to each other. And you need a girl your own age."

"You don't know what I need. Or what I want."

"You've spent all night telling me what you want." My voice caught painfully. "I'm a single mom with an eight-year-old. You want to be on the road, playing music, writing songs, traveling the world. Those lifestyles do not mesh."

That seemed to catch him off guard. "I'd make it work."

"You shouldn't have to. You shouldn't *want* to. I'm past that point in my life. You deserve someone who can have those experiences with you."

"And what if I'd rather be here? With you. And Baylee. And—"

"You're twenty-one. You say that now, but—"

"Don't talk down to me like I'm a child. You're not that much older than me."

"I'm old enough to recognize that you're acting like a child," I said before I could stop myself.

His mouth opened, but nothing came out. I had won, it seemed, even though it didn't feel like much of a victory. A lump settled at the base of my throat.

"You... you should probably go," I said.

His throat flexed as he swallowed back his anger. Quietly, he stood and started towards the door. I hesitated, then for some God-forsaken reason, I followed him.

"I know where the door is," he said coldly. "I don't need an escort."

The *sass* of this boy.

I wanted to snap at him, but the retort faded as he turned and I caught sight of his face. He was scowling, sort of, but it wasn't his trademark scowl. The moodiness was there, but it was trying to hide the genuine pain in his eyes.

Pain I'd put there.

And that fucking killed me.

"I'm sorry," I said.

He chuckled, though he clearly didn't find it funny. "For what? You don't want me. I get it."

I bristled at that. "That's not—"

"Just say it," he said, his voice harsh. "That's what it's all about, okay? We can talk around it. You can give me every reason under the sun why it was a mistake and all that shit, but I know, okay? Just say you don't want me."

I tried to. The problem was, I couldn't lie to him.

"I can't," I said.

Annoyance flashed in his eyes. "For fucks' sake, Kels—"

But he didn't get a chance to finish. I took a step forward, grabbing the front of his shirt. His expression changed, his mouth still half-open with frustrated words still poised to fall from it.

And I kissed him.

Before a heartbeat could even pass, I was pressed against him. His shock melted, dissolving away like strands of spun sugar in the rain. A low noise rumbled in his throat as he kissed me back, something heady and deep that I felt surge through me.

I wanted that kiss to last. I wanted to be selfish more than any other time in my life.

But I couldn't.

"I *can't* want you," I said against his lips. "It has nothing to do with 'don't'."

My eyes were closed, so I couldn't see his face, but I felt the shift between us. He finally understood, I think, or at the very least, he resigned himself to understanding. Instead of pulling away from him like I should have, I let him wrap his arms around me and steal one more kiss, a lingering, yearning kiss that wanted to be so much more.

Then he did what I couldn't: he let go and stepped away, eyes meeting mine as we both processed the moment.

"Are things gonna be weird between us now?" he asked.

I smiled, then nudged his arm playfully. "Things have always been weird between us. We're a couple of weirdos. That's our thing."

It made him smile, which was the intention, but there was still worry behind it.

"Yeah, but is it going to make things awkward?"

I smiled back as reassuringly as I could.

"Only if we let it, Jimbo."

Ten

WE LET IT MAKE things awkward.

I mean, of course we did.

Maybe if I hadn't been stupid enough to kiss him again, we could have salvaged something. If I'd let him walk away thinking I didn't want him, it would have broken his heart, but with time, maybe it would have been okay.

But I made my choice. To paraphrase one Ms. Taylor Swift, I played a stupid game, and lo and behold, I won a stupid prize.

Still, I did the best I could to make it look like things weren't weird between me and Jimmy, which I was apparently not very good at.

"Are things weird between you and Jimmy?" Em asked me outright.

We were sitting on the floor of her kitchen, surrounded by half-packed cardboard boxes and piles of miscellaneous kitchenware that Em was sorting into piles of "Keep," "Give Away," and "I Don't Fucking Know, Put It Over There And I'll Decide In A Bit." Despite my attempts to convince her she didn't need to put *anything* in the Keep pile since Alex had his own kitchen filled with his own miscellaneous kitchenware that was arguably better quality than hers, Em had insisted she wanted to bring her own things.

Part of me was convinced it was because she was panicking, since now that the fundraiser concert was over and Christmas was looming on the horizon, the move was real and happening and terrifying. And by part, I mean the part that was literally all of me because it was so damn obvious. The problem was that I'd been working constantly and had barely had time to see Em, so all those real and terrifying thoughts she was having were going unchecked until there was no way for me to talk her through them.

That was how I ended up sitting on the kitchen floor helping her pack instead of working, even though it was Daniel's Saturday with Baylee.

"Please, Kelsie," she'd begged. "Can't your boss give you just one Saturday off? This way we can focus on it. I'll get Jimmy to watch Leia and Pepper and we can knock out a bunch of packing all at once."

I'd done the math in my head quickly and decided that I could still afford the Taylor Swift tickets even if "my boss" gave me one Saturday off, so of course I'd agreed.

Though I was somewhat regretting that as she turned the conversation to her brother.

"Weird?" I repeated. "Why would you think things are weird?"

She examined the slightly deformed plastic bowl she was holding before handing it to me. "This one's a Keep. And I don't know, it just seems like you're both sort of 'proper' towards each other, if that makes sense."

"Not even a little," I said, even though it totally did.

She laughed and grabbed another bowl, this one smaller than the first one. "Maybe it's just me."

"Probably that," I agreed.

"Keep," she said, handing me the smaller bowl. "Or maybe it's Jimmy that's weird right now."

I put the bowl in the Give Away pile. "Weird? How?"

She shrugged. "He seems kind of... I don't know. Not depressed, just... resigned. Alex said he started noticing it after the concert so I thought maybe he wasn't sure what to do with all his extra time or something, but it hasn't gone away."

Concerned guilt surged through me. "Really? I hadn't noticed."

Except I totally had.

I had seen Jimmy at the concert, but unlike all the other times I'd seen him after That Night, we didn't talk to each other because we couldn't and not because we were avoiding each other. When he wasn't running around catering to Big Mike's every whim, he was on stage, and when he wasn't doing either of those things, he was watching the show with a sense of accomplishment and pride that made him glow.

Not that I noticed the way he was glowing or how good he looked when he smiled the way he was or the careful carelessness he'd styled himself with, his lean body complimented by the dark jeans and well-fitted t-shirt and... well, like I said. I didn't notice.

Not even a bit.

In any case, he was there and he was busy, so I didn't have to force myself to pretend like things weren't weird between us. That was good, because I was focused on Baylee, who was walking on sunshine somewhere near cloud nine for the entire day.

She wasn't on stage long; just for the set with the Poplin Family Jug Band, but that was more than enough time for me to see what I had dreaded seeing.

"She loves it, doesn't she?" Em had asked.

I watched Baylee's blonde hair bounce to the beat as she played her tambourine, skinny hips swaying in time to the music. If I thought Jimmy had been glowing, Baylee was the embodiment of light. Her face shone with joyful exuberance as she played and I knew.

I just fucking knew.

"Looks like it," I replied as evenly as I could.

Knowing me as well as she did, Em caught the thickness in my voice. Hiding as much as I was from her, she mistook it for one of those emotional Mom moments where I was overcome by pride and excitement and astonishment at how fast my little girl was growing up rather than a moment of worry and fear and a sense of abject failure knowing I couldn't foster Baylee's passion the way I wanted to.

Jimmy, on the other hand, seemed to figure it out from his place across the room. As Em wrapped a comforting arm around my shoulder, his eyes met mine, dark and deep and understanding.

I don't know what he was trying to say with that look, but it was more comforting than Em's half-hug. Hating myself, I smiled back at him thankfully, then tore my eyes away and watched my daughter live her best life on that stage.

All too soon, it was over. I met Baylee at the side of the stage, catching her as she hurled herself into my arms.

"Mom, did you *see* it?!" she asked breathlessly. "Did you see me play?!"

"I saw, sweetie." It took some effort, but I managed to lift her into the air as I hugged her, and she squealed with delight. "You did so good. I'm so proud of you."

"Quick, look here!" Em said, and I turned and smiled in time for her to snap a picture. Behind her, I saw Jimmy watching us, but by the time I put Baylee back down and looked in his direction again, he was onstage, guitar slung low as Leia played yet another set.

She was onstage for most of the concert. I wasn't sure whether it was funny or sad. I don't think anyone thought she was a child prodigy. I mean, she was okay, but she was a kid. But instead of giving her the space to learn, they'd pushed her onto a stage to perform long before she was ready. And instead of giving her room to make mistakes, Jimmy was playing along to each and every song, so poor Leia thought all the cheers and hollers and hoots were because she was doing *so* well when it was all a charade.

It seemed unfair to me. I mean, my personal feelings on the whole situation aside, Leia worked her ass off learning to play guitar. But I'd seen the nerves on her face the very first time she'd performed. She hadn't been ready, and instead of letting her discover the skills and confidence she needed, they were lying to her. Like, what was the point? I still wasn't sure about the whole drum lessons thing for Baylee, but if I was going to suffer through listening to her practice, it wasn't going to be for nothing.

But it wasn't my place to tell Em that, so Baylee and I watched the rest of the concert together, and I tried not to think about how good kissing Jimmy had felt every time I looked at him.

When the concert was done, Alex took everyone out to eat. I caught Jimmy's eye once or twice, but each time he started towards me, I noticed someone else in the room that I'd been meaning to talk to and was gone before he reached the place I'd been standing.

And I was pretty sure that it was that, above all the other things, that twisted him into the subdued version of himself.

"I thought maybe it was a girl," Em said, breaking me out of my thoughts in the worst possible way.

"Like he's seeing someone?" I asked.

"Or was seeing someone and it didn't work out." She shrugged and handed me another bowl. "Give Away. Or maybe he actually is pissed about me moving in with Alex."

"I don't think it's about you," I said. "Have you, um, asked him about it?"

"Yep."

"Like, about you moving?"

"Yeah, and about why he's acting so weird." She shrugged again. "He said he's not and that it's none of my business. God, it was like having a flashback to when he was a teenager. I'm dreading when Leia goes through that phase."

"Tell me about it," I said, relieved that Jimmy hadn't told Em anything about us.

"What about us?" she asked.

I raised an eyebrow. "What about us what?"

"Are things weird between you and me?"

"I... what?" I asked.

She put down the bowl she was holding and studied me. "Well, I thought you were avoiding me for a bit."

I swallowed hard. That was sort of true, but it had mostly been because I'd gone through a few days of all-consuming paranoia that she would figure out I kissed her brother. Then, since I was trying to avoid Jimmy, there'd been a time or two or more than I could count that I'd come up with some excuse not to hang out if I knew he'd be around.

"Things are crazy at work right now," I said. "There were some quality issues with our new line of stress-relief candles spontaneously igniting so we had to do a recall and, you know, with the holidays coming up it's just... it's a lot."

"Right," she said, unconvinced.

"Em, come on." I picked up a beat-up looking wooden spoon and added it to the Give Away pile. "You were busy with the concert planning stuff and getting ready to move and raising your kid and sucking your boyfriend's dick, probably." She couldn't hold back a laugh and I smirked at her. "This time of year is always busy for me at work, and then I was also driving Baylee to, like, rehearsals and performances and shit with the Poplins."

"That's no excuse," she said sternly, moving the spoon from the Give Away pile to the I Don't Fucking Know pile. "How busy could you have been? You didn't even have any dicks to suck."

I feigned offense. "Bitch."

She laughed again, though the smile faded quickly. "Maybe I'm just worried."

"About what?"

She looked up at me, eyebrows furrowed in one of those rare ways that reminded me she was a good few years younger than me, even if it didn't seem like it most of the time. "You're my best friend. I don't want that to change because we're moving. I thought maybe you were avoiding me because it would make it easier when we leave."

"That's not true at all," I said, which was the truth because it wasn't why I was avoiding her. "If it was, d'you really think I'd come here and help you pack?"

And give up an entire day of pay that I could use for Christmas presents, I thought, but didn't add that part out loud.

She spotted the bowl I'd put in the Give Away pile and moved it to the Keep pile. "'Help' me pack is questionable."

"Not my fault I suck at packing. I warned you."

"You did not."

"Not my fault you didn't think to ask me if I was any good at packing."

I had to admit spending the day with her was nice, despite the active role I was taking in making my life more difficult. It had been a while since Em and I had spent time together, just the two of us, no kids and no dog and no Alex or Mike or Jimmy or whoever else happened to be around.

At the same time, it was almost strange, simply because it felt like it *had* been so long since we'd just hung out. I thought it was me, at first, knowing I was hiding something from her like kissing Jimmy, but as the day wore on, I started to think maybe Em was right.

I didn't know which of us was most responsible for it, but maybe things were kind of weird between the two of us.

In any case, neither of us acknowledged it. I did my best to hide the nagging feeling as the day wore on, laughing and talking as we finished packing up the kitchen and moved on to the living room, which went much faster. In fact, it went so quickly that instead of ordering pizza for dinner like Em planned, she suggested going out to an actual restaurant.

"My treat," she'd insisted, though based on the cost of the place she'd suggested, I assumed it was actually Alex's treat. Part of my pride wanted to decline, but the place she wanted to go was renowned for their seafood and I fucking *loved* shellfish, so I swallowed that pride along with enough shrimp to start a unique ocean ecosystem in my stomach.

We'd just finished eating when my phone went off and I nearly hurled it all back up.

I realize I'm early, but I assumed you would be home, read the text message from Daniel. *Will you be much longer? Baylee has to use the washroom.*

"Fuck," I said.

"What?" Em asked.

"Daniel's back early."

I didn't need to say anything else. Em grabbed her purse and beelined for the bar so she could pay the bill as I texted him back.

I wish you would have let me know. I went out for dinner with Em. We'll be back in 15 minutes, I replied.

We were walking out of the restaurant when my phone rang.

"Where's the spare key?" Daniel asked without saying hello.

"Why do you need the spare key?" I asked as Em and I rushed to her car.

"You may not be aware of this, but you locked your front door," he said. "Which means she can't use the washroom, unless you've installed an outhouse in the yard. Where's your key?"

"We will be there shortly."

"She says she can't hold it that long," he said. "I don't see why you can't tell me where the key is."

My face turned red. "Seriously, Daniel? Because I don't want you in my house. Why didn't you stop at a gas station or something?"

"Seriously, Kelsie?" Daniel mocked. "You'd rather our daughter urinate in a gas station bathroom instead of letting me know how to let her into the house? Is there something you don't want me to see?"

"That's not the point," I said.

"Mmm. Sure."

Em started the car and there was a long moment of tense silence over the phone. The truth was that yes, there was something I didn't want Daniel to see: my house. The entire thing. He had never set foot into the townhouse. It was *my* house, my space, a place that he hadn't tainted with his presence and where I was safe and secure and happy. Its dated design and old appliances weren't going to be featured in any home and garden magazines, but it was reasonably clean given that I had an eight-year-old and worked six days a week.

But was keeping Daniel out of my space worth keeping Baylee holding her bladder uncomfortably until I got home?

I gritted my teeth, then sighed as Em pulled out of the parking space.

"There's a fake rock buried in the left corner of the flower bed," I said. "You can let her in the house and wait outside the door."

"Sure," he said again, his tone flat. "God forbid I wait indoors where it's warm."

"It's not my fault you showed up early. I'll be home shortly."

"See you soon, my dear."

"I'm not your fucking dear," I muttered, not that it mattered since I'd already hung up on him.

"Are you okay?" Em asked.

"'Course I am." I fidgeted with my phone and looked out the window.

She drummed her fingers on the steering wheel. "Do me a favor and text Jimmy to let him know he can bring Leia home whenever?"

I got that she was trying to distract me, but texting Jimmy was about the least useful way to do that. Still, I couldn't tell her that, so I did as she asked and didn't reply after Jimmy responded, confirming he'd head over and asking if everything was okay.

Em parked in front of her house when she pulled up since Daniel's car was parked in front of my house. Even as she parked, I could see that he wasn't standing outside the door.

"That fucker," I hissed.

"Go," Em said simply, and I was halfway across the street before the door even finished swinging shut behind me.

As angry as I was, Daniel not waiting on the doorstep was something of a blessing. It meant that Em didn't have to see the effect Daniel had on me.

She'd never met Daniel. No one had. I didn't want them to. I didn't need anyone knowing that I was one person outside his presence and a very different person when he was there. It wasn't that I was pretending to be someone else or anything like that. Deep in my heart, I knew that my authentic self was the version I was before Daniel had gotten his hands on me. That was the me who had been in Em's car: all colorful hair and fun piercings and unabashed statements. The one who was a little too bawdy, a little too abrasive, a little too to-the-point, and a little too unapologetic.

That person theoretically should have been able to stand up to Daniel. That person had the strength to leave him, though it had taken her quite a while. She had the strength to avoid his bullshit every month, to firmly enforce the court's orders about what he was and wasn't allowed to have.

Sometimes, at least.

The problem was that Daniel had fucked with me and that, no matter how hard I tried, that would never fully go away. The person that I was outside of him faded when he was around for no other reason than that he terrified me.

Even years later, he terrified me.

And I was ashamed of letting anyone ever see that.

Eleven

HE'D BEEN WATCHING FOR me.

I was halfway up the sidewalk when my front door swung open, warm yellow light spilling past the dark figure standing in the doorway and splashing along the concrete steps. I steeled myself as I glared up at him, though my aggravated march towards the door became instinctively more hesitant.

"I said wait outside," I snapped.

"Baylee asked me in," Daniel said simply.

There wasn't enough room for me to squeeze past him into the house, so I stopped in front of the door and folded my arms. "Well, now I'm telling you to leave."

"Do I not get to say goodbye to my daughter?"

My jaw trembled as I clenched it. "Say goodbye, then."

He turned back towards the house. "Princess? Your mom says I need to leave."

"Okay, Dad!" I heard Baylee respond.

"Can I have a hug?"

I couldn't hear her response that time, possibly because she hadn't said anything, but I watched Daniel crouch and open his arms. From my spot on the sidewalk, I saw Baylee's arms go around his neck and the top of her blonde head poke out from over his shoulder.

"Thank you for my new shoes and my stuffie and playing laser tag with me!" she rambled. "If Mr. Poplin asks me to play tambourine for them again, I'll tell you and you can come and you can bring Grandma if you want!"

"I hope so. Did you have fun today?"

She hugged him tighter. "Yep! Did you?"

"Of course." Her arms loosened and he stood up. "Bye, princess. I'll miss you."

"Miss you too."

I'm sure his intent was to upset me, which he did, but I pretended none of it bothered me as he turned around and stepped outside. The front door swung closed behind him and the yellow glow of light was gone, leaving me and Daniel enshrouded in the cool evening light.

"You didn't have the right to—"

"—enter your house without your permission, I know," he finished. "What would you have me do? Tell Baylee you said I couldn't stand inside? You know I don't actively *try* to make you seem like the bad guy, right?"

It was bullshit, but I couldn't call him on it.

"Next time you plan on being early, you need to let me know," I said.

"Of course. I wouldn't want to interrupt your date again," he replied coolly.

My face turned red. "I wasn't on a date. I was out with Em."

Daniel's eyes trailed down, taking in my outfit. "Clearly."

I tried not to retch. "Right. If that's everything..."

"Actually, I brought her back early because I needed to speak with you."

Of fucking course he did.

"What do you want?" I asked.

He gave me one of his Looks, which I pretended didn't have the same effect on me as it did when we were married. "I don't *want* anything except to know why you've been working so much."

My mouth dropped open. "What?"

"Baylee informed me you've been working a lot," he said patiently. "All week and even Saturdays, she said. That's fairly unusual, Kelsie. Is there something we need to discuss?"

"Of course not," I snapped. "My job is busy this time of year and I'm helping my boss out by taking a few extra shifts."

"Hmm," he said. "Interesting."

"It's not that interesting."

"It has nothing to do with the Christmas present you've insisted you can take care of yourself?" he pressed.

"Not even a little bit."

"Mm. Or the fact that Baylee wants to take music lessons?"

My face turned red. "She hasn't asked to do that yet."

"Because she thinks it's too expensive." He folded his arms. "Is that the kind of thing you want her worrying about at this age? The *cost* of things? Because you're too vindictive to give me a bit more time with her?"

My mouth was dry. "I'm not."

He smirked. "You know that Baylee said she wished I would have come to see her play at the concert? What was I supposed to say to that, that you wouldn't let me attend? That you didn't even *tell* me? There's only so many times I can be the bad guy, my dear. Eventually, you need to admit you're trying to keep her from me."

"I'm following the court order," I said. "That isn't keeping her from you. That's what the judge said—"

"Then perhaps we should ask the courts to reevaluate our agreement. Or perhaps we could discuss it between us since I imagine that would work out a bit more favorably for you, considering you're now bringing in extra income that wasn't accounted for on our last review of the child support payments."

My mouth dropped open, but nothing came out. Daniel flicked one eyebrow up, a look on his face like he knew he'd cornered me.

And he had, hadn't he? The extra shifts were technically extra income and I hadn't made that connection. He had, of course, because he was constantly looking for *anything* that would allow him to get his way. And sure, working six days a week to get that income wasn't ideal, but with the right lawyer—which Daniel could afford and I couldn't...

"What do you think, my dear?" he asked.

And for once, I got lucky.

Or unlucky.

Or both.

In any case, I didn't have to respond because we were interrupted by a timely and unfortunate arrival.

"Hi, Kelsie!" Leia called as she raced up my sidewalk. "My mom said Baylee's home. Can I see her? I wanna show her a new song Uncle Jimmy showed me today." She stopped, apparently noticing Daniel for the first time, and looked up at him. "Oh. Who are you?"

"I'm Baylee's dad," he replied. "You must be Leia. Baylee has told me a lot about you."

Leia nodded, her exuberance fading slightly. "Nice to meet you." She turned back to me, eyes wide. "Can I go see Baylee?"

"I—uh, yeah. Go on in," I said, stammering only because as I responded, Jimmy walked up my sidewalk. He waited for Leia to run to the front door before speaking.

"Hey, Kels," he said casually, though he was looking at Daniel. "Sorry, Em didn't mention you had someone over. This a bad time?"

"Yes," Daniel said, his voice notably colder. "But it's fine. I was leaving." He turned to me, eyebrows raised. "Let me know when you need me to get that gift and when you'd like to discuss new agreement terms. I'm willing to be reasonable, Kelsie."

Like hell he was, but I couldn't bring myself to respond as he walked down the sidewalk and brushed past Jimmy. Both of us watched as Daniel got into his car, silent until his headlights flicked on and he drove away. Then, Jimmy looked back at me.

"What happ—"

"None of your business." I turned and started towards the front door.

The suddenness seemed to stun him and I was opening the door by the time he reacted. "Kelsie, wait."

"I'll send Leia back out, one sec."

"Goddamn—Kels, stop, *please*."

I don't know why I did. I don't know why his words were as effective as if he'd grabbed my arms and held me in place. Part of me wanted to blame it on the state of mind Daniel always seemed to leave me in, that facing the man who had controlled me for so long left me vulnerable and scared, not that Jimmy knew that so it's not like he could be blamed for it. Or maybe even that Jimmy had snapped, that his tone was angry and demanding and had frozen me in place.

But it wasn't. Those were the explanations I wanted, not the ones that were true.

The truth was, it was the way he said "please."

It wasn't desperate or needy. It wasn't spoken in frustration or anger. It wasn't even that it was a request.

It was just the way he said it. The sadness behind it, the regret, the resigned understanding of a yearning plea that he knew was too much.

And I couldn't keep moving.

Yellow light was spilling on me as I stood inside the entryway. From above, I could hear Leia and Baylee giggling and playing music, oblivious to the turmoil happening beneath them. A heartbeat passed, and then another, and then the hesitant shuffle of Jimmy's footsteps came up behind me.

"You said we wouldn't make it awkward," he said. "But it's been fucked."

"I'm sorry," I replied. "It's just... it's hard."

"I know. But can we talk? Just a quick talk. Please?"

The answer had been written the moment I'd frozen in place, but I nodded all the same and stepped forward so he could follow me into the house. I turned to face him as he closed the door, then looked up at me and swallowed hard.

"What do you want to talk about?" I asked.

He opened his mouth, then closed it, then opened it again. No words came out and he frowned, then sighed.

"Honestly, I wanted to ask if we could pretend like that night didn't happen and go back to how things were because I fucking miss you," he said, his voice mindfully low as we listened to the girls upstairs. "But now I... that was him, right?"

I couldn't say the words, so I nodded again.

"Em said he showed up out of nowhere and let himself in. She wanted to make sure you were okay. Are you?"

"I'm fine," I said.

"You're not."

"Of course you would know better than me," I snapped. "Why'd you even bother asking if you were so sure of the answer?"

"Because I don't know how to handle this," he said. "I don't know how to handle *you* and what... what happened between us. And I don't know where that leaves us, so I don't know how to tell you I wanna be here for you."

"It's not your problem," I said. "You don't have to worry about—"

"I want to, Kels!" His voice was a low hiss as he looked at me imploringly. "I *want* to make sure you're okay and I want that, even if it's just as your friend. So yeah, I haven't stopped thinking about you since that night and yeah, I still want you more than you'll ever fucking know, but I want to make sure you're safe more than I want anything else."

And for some reason, that was what broke me. For some reason, hearing his concern in that rumbling whisper touched part of me, shattered part of me, opened a part of me to him that shouldn't have been opened. I had a million theories ranging from being starved for someone to care about me to simple adrenaline coursing through me after Daniel's visit, but the truth of it was that it didn't matter.

He said those words, and I *felt* those words, and instead of laying out my fears and frustrations in words of my own, I kissed Jimmy again.

Twelve

IF JIMMY WAS SURPRISED I kissed him, I couldn't tell.

He didn't so much as gasp when I pressed my lips to his and his arms wrapped around me immediately, as if holding me would keep me from pulling back and realizing my mistake.

It didn't. I knew damn well it was a mistake from the moment I touched him, but he didn't need to hold me in the hopes I wouldn't stop. I had turned away all semblance of logic the moment he called out for me.

A groan rumbled against me as I slipped my tongue into his mouth. His tongue flicked against mine before teasing the piercing in my lip. I whimpered, the sound muffled against his face, and his arms tightened around me.

"The girls," he murmured. "What if they...?"

I shook my head. "Just don't be loud."

I saw a question flash across his face, probably something about what we'd be doing that he'd have to keep quiet for. But he didn't need to ask, not when I kissed him again before grabbing his hand and bringing it to my breast.

He exhaled softly, hesitating for a moment before cupping my breast. I sighed against his mouth and ran my hand up his arm and to his shoulder before tracing my fingers along his neck. Beneath my fingertips, I felt him shiver before he shuffled closer to me, and then closer, and then used his hips to guide me towards the wall.

I let him only because he made the move first; had another few heartbeats gone by, I probably would have done the same thing, only pressing him to the front door instead of him pressing me to the wall in the front hallway. It didn't matter which of us was pressed where. Both of us were trapped in a moment we weren't supposed to share and there was nowhere, fucking *nowhere*, we'd rather be.

I knew that because as he held me against the wall, I could feel the effect it was having on him. And while my body didn't have quite the same physical indicator as his did, I knew damn well the effect it was having on me.

A soft moan escaped my lips as he pushed his hips against me, one of his hands moving to the wall so that he was towering over me, using his height and his body to make me feel so small and so safe. His lips worked against mine as he fondled me through my shirt, the taste of his mouth and the warmth of his breath making me dizzy as I tried to get my fill of him.

It wasn't until I let my fingers trace back down his arm and to his waist that he made that beautiful, rumbly groaning sound. I touched his body delicately at first, growing bolder only when I heard his breath quicken. He reacted so openly, so honestly, so unabashedly, and apparently I was super into that. My skin felt like it was tingling as desire washed over me and my heart began to race so fast that when he slipped his hand beneath the hem of my shirt, I was sure he would feel it pounding.

If he did, he didn't say anything, probably because he was a bit distracted sliding his hand into my bra and groaning as that enticing bulge of his grew even more. The pad of his thumb brushed across my nipple and he inhaled sharply.

"Fuckin' knew it," he breathed against my lips before toying with the piercing there.

I squirmed as he did, a suddenly jolt of pleasure shooting through me. My nipples had always been sensitive, but the piercings had heightened that to a point where the slightest touch set my whole body on alert. Pressing my lips together, I attempted to muffle the high-pitched noise I made. Hopefully it was enough to keep it from travelling up the stairs because Jimmy most certainly heard it. I felt him smirk before he did it again, his smile widening as I failed to keep quiet once more.

"Fuck," he breathed. "You're so hot, Kelsie. I've thought about this so many times."

The girls being upstairs was both a blessing and a curse. It was a curse for obvious reasons, not the least of which was that we didn't want to be discovered. It was a blessing because it gave us a firm and unyielding reason to be quick, so the amount of teasing he could subject me to was limited.

And trust me, I was *very* grateful for that.

It hadn't taken much to get me wet. Between the adrenaline and fear left behind after Daniel's impromptu visit and the relief at finally indulging my feelings for Jimmy, every single one of my senses seemed heightened. The way he was playing with my nipple was setting me on fire, that deep place in the pit of my stomach aching with need as he explored me. His body was driving me mad, the way his cock was both there and not, hidden beneath layers of fabric instead of buried inside me where I wanted it.

And oh God, did I want it.

But I also knew that was dumb as fuck. I mean, it just wasn't possible. Baylee's bedroom was across the hall from mine, so sneaking upstairs so Jimmy could fuck my brains out was asking for trouble. And sure, the living room was right there, but the couch was fully visible from the stairs and that meant there was a very real risk of the girls stumbling on me fucking Jimmy senseless.

So that left us trapped in the front hallway with Jimmy using his hips to hold me in place as he held my breast in one hand and undid the button on my jeans with the other.

I swallowed hard, shaking in anticipation as his long fingers pushed past the waistband of my jeans. He wasted no time slipping them into my panties, though he did take some time to explore my mound and trace the lips of my pussy. He was still kissing me, or at least making an attempt to; it was hard for him to keep his lips on mine when he was smiling like that. Pure, relaxed exuberance shone on his face as he touched my pussy, his genuine enjoyment of my body almost wholesomely bewitching.

But it wasn't doing anything for that ache of desire in my stomach.

"Please," I gasped quietly.

His mouth twitched as he fought back another smile. "Please what?"

I made an aggravated noise and he laughed, but kept his fingers away from where I wanted them.

"Please what?" he repeated.

I tilted my head back, resting it against the wall as I squeezed my eyes shut. "Jimbo, stick your fingers inside me right now or I swear I will kick you out and do it myself."

He muffled his laughter by nuzzling his face against my neck and I could still feel little jolts of amusement as he thrust a finger inside me.

Truth be told, I was laughing too, but the noise was swallowed by my own hand as I pressed it to my mouth. I kept that hand there to muffle the gasping little moans I couldn't hold in as he began to move his hand, though it almost wasn't enough to keep in the noise I made when he added a second finger to my pussy.

"*Fuck*," he groaned again as he slipped his second finger inside of me. "How are you so fucking wet, Kels?"

"You have no one to blame but yourself for that," I whispered.

He made another soft noise, kissing the side of my neck. "So fucking wet for me. *Fuck.*"

I shivered as he spoke. He did too, I think, his hand trembling as he worked his fingers in and out of me. His lips moved against my throat, gentle kisses and soft bites adding to the sensations rushing through me. I pressed my one hand even harder against my mouth and grabbed Jimmy's shoulder with the other, clutching him like I might collapse if I let go.

And there was a damn good chance I would. The way his hand was turned, the base of it was brushing against my clit each time he shoved his fingers inside me, and that was more than enough for the tremors of an orgasm to start making themselves known.

I felt my mouth move against my hand as that pleasure built. What I was saying, even I didn't know, but I assume it was some sort of request for Jimmy not to stop because his breath came heavy against my neck as his fingers moved a touch faster. His hand left my breast, steadying me, grounding me, keeping me still as the promise of release pooled inside me.

It took everything in me not to cry out when my orgasm hit, and I mean *everything*. I wouldn't doubt for a second that my fingertips left bruises on his shoulder and part of me worried I was going to break his wrist as my hips bucked against his hand. He persevered, though, and even as white light and intense pleasure took over, I could feel him holding me steady, his hands and body and lips keeping me on Earth while my body and my mind were in heaven.

When I came back down and caught my breath, I could still hear Leia and Baylee playing music and singing obliviously upstairs. Jimmy seemed to sense that some of my consciousness had returned and the fingers that had been stroking my slit stilled, though he kept his hand in my panties for a few moments longer to cup my mound before pulling it out.

I leaned heavily against the wall as he straightened up and looked at me. Still in the process of catching my breath, I looked back at him, waiting for his inevitable request for his turn.

But it didn't come.

"You okay?" he asked instead of asking me to jack him off or spread my legs or suck his dick.

It took me a moment to respond, partly because I was embarrassed by my shock and internally scolding myself for projecting my own insecurities onto Jimmy.

"Yes," I said. "Yeah. I... yeah."

He smiled. "Good."

Another heartbeat went by and that time, I was sure he was going to ask. I mean, he wanted to; both his eyes and the stiff bulge in his jeans were telling me he was desperately turned on and in need of relief. But he didn't.

He just waited.

And God, if that alone didn't say so much about him.

"Jimbo," I finally said.

His mouth twitched. "Yeah?"

I licked my lips and glanced down. "Do you want a hand with—"

"Yes," he said immediately, then cleared his throat as redness touched his cheeks. "I mean, uh... fuck."

I was too busy laughing to make fun of him, but he didn't seem to mind as I brought my hands to the waistband of his jeans and began working on his belt. In fact, he seemed to mind so little that he leaned forward to kiss me as I worked the buckle open and moved on to the button of his jeans.

His face being pressed to mine meant I got to feel his appreciative sigh as I unzipped his jeans and heard the soft noise of happiness as I moved my hand into his boxers to find some happiness of my own.

It also meant he felt my face change the moment I wrapped my fingers around him and realized that there was a *large* amount of happiness filling out those boxers.

"Jesus, Jimbo," I murmured as I felt every inch of him, a sense of regret washing over me as I remembered I wasn't going to be shoving it in my pussy. Not that night, and not any night, since my orgasm had already cleared my mind enough to start screaming that this could never happen again.

I mean, it couldn't. He was Em's brother. It shouldn't have even been happening now.

But since it was, I'd be damned if I wasn't going to enjoy it.

His lips twisted, a smirk interrupted by pleasure as I handled his cock. He groaned, eyes closed as he forced a steady breath while I stroked him. Pre-cum was already leaking from his tip and I spread it along his shaft, though I couldn't stop myself from wondering what he tasted like.

Daniel had hated blow jobs.

I know. It makes him seem crazy, which he was, but his reasoning for it was based in logic.

He loved control. And whether that was control of my wardrobe, my mind, or my body, he wanted it. So it was no surprise that he wanted to be in control when we had sex. Fucking my pussy meant he could stay in control, as did fucking my ass.

But fucking my mouth?

That meant I maintained some control, since he had no actual way of stopping me from moving my jaw. And Daniel understood how cruel he was; despite having broken me, he wasn't about to put his dick between one of the few weapons I had left.

Not that I particularly enjoyed thinking about Daniel while I was with anyone else, but wondering what Jimmy's cock tasted like was a reminder of something Daniel had tried to keep from me. Contrary to popular stereotypes, I *liked* sucking cock. I loved the taste of it, the feel of it, and—especially after leaving Daniel—the control I had while I was doing it.

And since I was already breaking all the rules by touching Jimmy's cock in the first place, I figured there was no harm in indulging a little more.

He didn't realize what I was doing at first. With one hand still down his pants, I used the other to nudge him until he took one confused step backwards, then another. Carefully, I guided him to the other side of the tiny front hall until his back was pressed against the wall.

That's when I stopped stroking his cock, but only because I needed both hands to work his jeans and boxers down past his hips.

And that's also when he realized what I was doing.

"Oh my God," he whispered.

I met his eye and showed him a smirk of my own before kneeling in front of him.

His cock was lovely. I mean, it was seriously gorgeous. It was unfair how nice his cock was considering I was still telling myself this was the one and only time I was going to see it. Thick and hard, it jutted out proudly from the dark curls at his base. And he was definitely blessed, size-wise, though it wasn't so big as to be unmanageable. There was already more pre-cum collecting on his swollen head and before another thought could cross my mind, I stuck my tongue out and licked it off.

He made a choked noise when I did, adopting the same position I had with his hand covering his mouth. His other hand stayed beside him until I wrapped my lips around his tip and began shoving him to the back of my throat, taking his length as deep as I could. That was when he had to stifle another groan and he moved his other hand to my head, carefully brushing his fingers through my hair.

He didn't pull or shove my head down on his cock, which was good because as much as I loved sucking cock, I wasn't particularly skilled when it came to deep throating and he had a *lot* of cock to work with.

Instead, he played with my hair, holding it out of my way as I bobbed and sucked and licked.

I could feel his eyes on me, but as much as I wanted to, I didn't dare risk a glance up. I had a feeling that would be too much, seeing the look on his face as I worshipped him. Instead, I closed my eyes, listening carefully to make sure I could still hear the girls singing upstairs before focusing on the feel of his throbbing cock on my tongue and the strained noises he was making as I brought him closer and closer to the edge.

It didn't take long to get him there. Before I knew it, his stomach was twitching and he was panting, his fingers tightening almost imperceptibly in my hair.

"Kels," he finally whispered. "Can I please come in your mouth?"

That got me to look up. I'd never had anyone ask if they *could* before; usually I got a split-second warning before my mouth and throat were flooded with cum.

I met his eyes, which were dark and intense and pleading. I wasn't quite sure how to answer his question; I didn't want to take his cock out of my mouth and nodding wasn't all that easy given the aforementioned cock in my mouth, so I made what I hoped he understood was an affirmative noise with a slight jerk of my head.

He got the message and another soft noise escaped his lips. Before I could tear my gaze away from his, his hands moved to either side of my head. He didn't hold me in place or anything, just silently asked me to keep looking at him.

The truth was, I couldn't have torn my eyes away if I tried.

When he came, I was looking up at him, his cock buried in my mouth and his eyes studying me until he was forced to squeeze them shut. The flavor of him filled my mouth, hot and slightly salty and so intimately perfect, and despite forcing himself to remain quiet, the look on his face said *everything*.

I could have watched him do that again, and again, and... well.

I didn't take his cock out of my mouth until he leaned back heavily against the wall, sighing that telltale, conclusive sigh. Carefully, I sat back, swallowing and wiping my mouth on the back of my hand as he put his cock away. When I moved to stand, he caught my elbow, helping me up before pulling me into his arms and burying his face against my neck.

It should have been a beautiful moment, but guilt surged through me.

"Jimmy," I murmured. "We—"

"Don't," came the muffled response, and he held me tighter. "I know. Just... just lemme be selfish for a sec. Please."

I pressed my lips together, then closed my eyes and relaxed against him. Just for a moment, I told myself.

Just a heartbeat.

Thirteen

It was nine days before Christmas when I found myself sitting in my car in the CVS parking lot with my phone clasped between my icy cold fingers, wondering if there was a market for used panties worn by a thirty-something-year-old mom with a fat ass.

I mean, there was a market for everything, right? And selling used panties was basically harmless, right? And theoretically, the capital needed to start a used-panty-selling business wasn't super high. I could probably skip lunch for a couple of days and then raid the sale bin at Victoria's Secret. Wear a pair, throw an ad on Craigslist or something, and bam. Profit.

Right?

I wouldn't have even had to consider it if it wasn't for Jimmy. Despite now having an intimate knowledge of what his cock looked, felt, and tasted like, I'd held out hope that things would be less weird than they'd been before.

You know, after we'd kissed, but before I'd sucked his cock.

Because somehow *that* made sense.

Part of me assumed that the allure of it all would evaporate for him, but that was a heavily flawed theory. I didn't give Jimmy enough credit, which I was well aware of. I couldn't apologize for not giving him the benefit of the doubt, not when I had someone like Daniel in my past, but I at least understood enough about myself that I could recognize my instinctual suspicion wasn't entirely founded.

Even knowing that about myself, though, I still underestimated Jimmy constantly. In my mind, he'd got what he needed out of me: he'd had his moment to fulfill the Hot (In His Opinion) Older Woman Slash Possible Exploration Of Some Mommy Issues fantasy and he could hitch up his jeans and move on.

I wanted it to be true as much as I didn't want it to be true. I refused to entertain the possibility that I wanted anything more from him, but it certainly would have made things easier if all we'd needed to get past all of this was for him to indulge in his fantasy and get over it.

It was also easier to blame the whole thing on Jimmy, even though it was objectively not *entirely* his fault.

Most of it was Mike's.

And Alex held a good amount of the responsibility, too.

"What's this?" Em had asked as he handed her an envelope.

It was not quite a week after That Second Night. We were all standing in her mostly empty kitchen: me, Em, Alex, and Jimmy, of course. Somehow, Jimmy and I had managed to avoid being alone together, probably because every time it seemed like it was about to happen, I found some excuse to go check another room of the house.

Aside from Em's bed, Leia's bed, the associated bedding, and the overnight bags Alex had insisted they pack so they didn't have to dig through their boxes to find the bare necessities the next morning, everything else was neatly stacked in cardboard boxes in the living room, waiting ominously to be moved into the U-Haul the next day. The girls were playing amongst them, pretending they were a fort or a castle or some shit, and Pepper was whimpering as he tried to figure out what in the fuck was going on.

"Why are you asking me?" Alex replied. "Open it and find out."

She eyed him suspiciously before sliding her finger beneath the flap of the envelope. Out of the corner of my eye, I saw Jimmy looking at me instead of watching his sister, which made me eye *him* suspiciously since I figured it probably meant he knew what was in the envelope.

And of course he did.

"What the fuck, Alex?" Em gasped as she withdrew the paper inside.

"Surprise," he said.

"But the U-Haul—"

"Canceled. I hired movers." There was a lightness in his voice that didn't quite cover the worry in his eyes. "I thought we could celebrate us, you know, officially being... you know. A family. And then everything'll be set up and unpacked when we get back."

Em didn't like having Alex make decisions without telling her. That was fair, in my opinion; she wanted the same amount of say in their relationship as he had. It was one thing to spoil her with a surprise trip to Mexico as a gift, but it was quite another to change her entire moving plan after she'd spent weeks preparing for it.

And for a moment, I thought Em was going to tell him that. An expression of annoyance flashed across her face before she took another look at the piece of paper, the realization hitting her at the same time it hit me.

Because she'd told me, of course. It wasn't common knowledge, but she'd told me what had happened to Alex's family two and a half decades earlier. His wife and his young son, both gone in a flash, cruelly torn out of the world by a truck driver who picked the wrong moment to be distracted and smashed into their little car.

A little car, which had been full of all their worldly possessions.

Because they were in the process of moving.

So yeah, of fucking *course* he was having a bit of trouble with the whole situation.

"It's perfect," Em finally said, struggling to hide the emotion in her voice. "This is a great idea. And Leia's gonna love it."

Alex's shoulders relaxed, the relief on his face obvious as he grinned. "I figure we can grab dinner and then head out. Should only take about an hour to get there."

"Where are you going?" I asked as lightly as I could.

Em glanced up as if suddenly remembering both that I was in the room and that the next day was Saturday.

"Shit," she said. "You're working tomorrow." At Alex's confused look, she rolled her eyes. "I'm supposed to watch Baylee."

I tried to smile. "Don't worry about it. I can... I'll figure something out."

"Maybe the daycare can take her?" Alex suggested.

I was surprised he said it. I mean, given that he was probably quite aware that the daycare situation was a point of contention between me and Em. She'd been shocked a couple of days earlier when I mentioned I'd found a lady who ran a daycare in her house that could take Baylee after school.

"Wait, so you're not picking the girls up anymore?" she'd asked, looking alarmed.

It had taken me a moment to respond, mostly because I was stunned. "Uh... I mean, I can't, Em. I have to drop Baylee off in the morning. I won't finish work in time to pick them up."

"Oh," she said. "Shit. I didn't... I wish you would have told me."

"I thought you knew," I replied, half-insulted. "I mean, I figured when we talked about the girls not being dropped off together anymore..."

"Right." She shook her head. "I should have figured it out."

I snorted. "Good thing you're pretty, hey?"

And see, that kind of banter was normal for me and Em. At least, it used to be. Instead, that time she'd stared at me, then laughed somewhat awkwardly before changing the subject.

In any case, I assumed that Em told Alex everything, which meant it was weird that he brought up the daycare thing. Em apparently thought so too, because she laughed that same sort of awkward chuckle she had when I'd jokingly implied she was stupid.

"She's closed on the weekends," I said. "But it's fine, I can, um…"

And there were only so many ways I could end that sentence. Em was my go-to person. I didn't have family—at least, not family that lived nearby or, more specifically, that I associated with—and I didn't have that many other friends. So I could either not work, or I could call Daniel.

"I can watch her."

Ah, fuck.

I looked at Jimmy, trying to remember what kind of expression I made when I looked at someone gratefully so I could hide the cringing dread I was actually feeling. "Don't *you* have to work tomorrow? If Alex is away?"

"You do," Alex said to Jimmy before looking at me apologetically.

"I think this is a higher priority," Em said bluntly. "It's not fair to Kelsie."

"Don't worry about it," I said.

"What if I watched her in the morning?" Jimmy asked. "I have to be at the studio, but I don't have anyone to play for until the afternoon, so I could watch her there. I know it's not all day, but…"

But it was better than nothing.

I swallowed my pride and forced a smile. "Look at those problem-solving skills, Jimbo. Your boss should give you a raise."

"His boss is gonna go broke if he keeps giving him raises," Alex muttered.

"Maybe his boss should stop doing things that require him to step in to save his boss's ass," Em said pointedly.

Baylee and I went to leave a short while later so Em and Alex could leave for their little getaway weekend, which included some fancy spa package for Em and a trip to the North Pole Village for Leia. Just before we left, Em pulled me aside.

"Kels," she said, and a second later, she started crying.

I didn't know what to do. "Girl, don't cry."

"I can't help it." She sniffled and threw her arms around me. "I'm going to miss living here. I'm going to miss living by *you*. You've been so understanding through all of this and I—" She stopped to sniffle again. "I'm sorry about tomorrow. And thank you. For everything."

I blinked back tears of my own as I hugged her back. "Stop talking like we're never gonna see each other again. You live across town, not in a different dimension. And you know damn well those girls of ours aren't going to let us drift apart."

Her laugh was watery, but it was still a laugh as she pulled away and wiped her eyes. "True. It's just... change, you know?"

"I know." I squeezed her one last time before letting go. "But it's all gonna be okay."

And wouldn't it have been nice if that were true?

Jimmy had offered to pick Baylee up the next morning but given what had happened last time he stopped by my place, I opted to drop her off at the studio myself. If circumstances had been different, her excitement would have almost been sweet. As it stood, the constant chatter of "I wonder what me and Jimmy are gonna do today!" and "I never get to hang out with Jimmy by myself, it's gonna be so fun!" and "Mom? Mom. Are me and Jimmy friends or am I s'posed to call him Mr. Jimmy 'cause he's a grown up? Or Uncle Jimmy like Leia does?" as we drove was more exhausting than anything.

She was practically vibrating when we got to the studio, doing a skipping sort of run ahead of me and yanking the front door open. By the time I grabbed the coffees I'd bought and made it inside, a still-not-quite-awake-yet Jimmy had met her in the foyer.

"—the drum set again maybe, if you want to?" Baylee was saying. "Only if you want to though, 'cause if not my mom said I can read my book and she sent me some coloring stuff too. I know that sounds kinda silly 'cause coloring books are for babies but my dad got me these ones. They're really fancy and complicated and I have special markers and—"

"Baylee, give him a sec to catch up," I said, holding one coffee out. "Here. Figured you'd need this."

"You are a literal angel," he said gratefully, taking the coffee.

"Consider it a thank you for watching her," I said, hoping the implication of 'and nothing more than that' was clear.

He grinned. "Don't need to thank me for hanging out with my buddy Baylee here." He turned to her. "What was that you were saying about the drums?"

Baylee had beamed when he called her his buddy, but glanced at me almost nervously. "I was wondering if maybe you could show me more of the drums today, if that's okay."

"Hell yeah," he said. "Why don't you drop off your stuff in... uh, use Alex's office today, since he's not here."

She nodded eagerly and started towards the office without so much as a glance at me.

"Bye, sweetie," I said loudly.

"Bye Mom!" she hollered, still racing the other direction.

I rolled my eyes and turned to Jimmy, who had his lips pressed together to hold back a laugh.

"She seems excited," he said.

"Hasn't shut up about it," I muttered. "Anyway. I should be back by two at the absolute latest. If you have stuff you need to do or need a break from her or whatever, give her a chair and a desk and she'll amuse herself for a while. She's got books, coloring stuff, her headphones and music—"

"Kels—"

"—a bunch of snacks and a lunch, so don't worry about feeding her, she'll eat when she's hungry. Oh, and some of her homework if she somehow manages to get *that* bored, but I won't hold my breath. And if you need—"

"Kelsie," he said more firmly. "This isn't the first time I've babysat."

I knew that. And he knew I knew that. And we both knew that I was rambling because it was awkward and weird and we were both probably thinking about that time his dick had been in my mouth, or at least I was thinking that and he probably figured it out because I couldn't quite look him in the eye.

"Right," I said. "Okay. I'll see you later."

"Wait." The lobby was fairly deserted, but he glanced around anyway. "Do you have a sec to talk?"

Ah, *fuck*.

"I have to get to work," I said.

He sighed, something between frustration and discouragement on his face. "We need to talk about it, Kels. Ignoring what happened isn't going to make it go away."

"No, but refusing to acknowledge it might," I said. "I'll see you at two-ish."

I don't think he meant to laugh, but I heard him chuckle as I walked away and I thought maybe things were going to be okay. Awkward, sure, and a complete betrayal of my best friend's trust because giving your best friend's brother a blow job in the front hallway of your house is still a questionable thing to do, but maybe Jimmy and I could go back to the way things were.

And God, wouldn't it have been nice if *that* were true?

Part of the reason I said I'd be back at two is because that's when Jimmy said he had to play for the band that was coming in to record. From what I understood, that was most of his job: whenever someone needed a guitarist, he stepped in to play. He did other things, too, as Alex relied on him more and more, but most of his days were spent playing on other people's albums.

So it worked out well, since I figured if I timed it properly, I'd pick up Baylee just as Jimmy was getting ready to work with whatever band needed him, and that meant I wouldn't have another awkward moment where Jimmy insisted we needed to talk about things.

Except I didn't time it properly because this particular band was apparently going through some shit. When I arrived at quarter after two, they were in the lobby, screaming at each other about creative differences as Big Mike stormed up looking grumpier than was healthy for a man of his age.

He didn't seem to notice me as he laid into the band members, which was fine. I slipped past the commotion and wandered down to where I knew the offices were. It was much quieter over there, save for the sound of my daughter squealing excitedly from one of the other rooms—the break room, I realized.

"—ask her for me, really?" I heard her say.

"I'll talk to her about it," came Jimmy's response. "But you're gonna have to ask yourself, Bay. You want this, you gotta go after it."

"I gotta go after it," she repeated. "D'you think maybe you can be there when I ask her? To help me if I need it?"

"Yeah, kid," Jimmy said after a brief pause. "But you won't need me. I'm sure about that."

It didn't take a genius to figure out they were discussing drum lessons. Or maybe it did take a genius and I should've applied for fucking MENSA or something. Either way, I was certain that's what they were talking about, which... well.

It was a problem for another day.

"Sorry I'm late!" I said as I walked into the break room. "Traffic was crazy."

Both of them turned towards me, Jimmy with a hint of guilt on his face.

"Mom!" Baylee said excitedly. "Guess what I did today?"

"Hmm," I said. "I bet you did *all* of your homework and were having so much fun, you started working on next week's homework, too."

"Ew," she said. "No."

"Darn," I said. "Well, go grab your stuff so we can go home and start working on it."

She grumbled, but then glanced at Jimmy and brightened up. "Mom, I gotta ask you something."

"Sure, sweetie," I said. "You can ask me in the car. Jimmy's already late to start work, so we should let him get to it."

No one said being a mom was easy, but the moments like that—the ones where it felt like my stomach was about to fall out of my ass and my heart was aching with shame as she tried to hide her disappointment, thinking I didn't know what she wanted to ask instead of knowing that I was purposely trying to avoid the conversation—reminded me how hard it could be. There was an echoed whisper in my head, a familiar and haunting voice reminding me I was too selfish to be a good parent, but then Baylee nodded and slid off the chair she'd been sitting on.

"I'll go get my bag," she said.

Before I could respond, she scurried out of the room, leaving me with Jimmy.

Fuck.

"Well, don't let me keep you," I said as conversationally as I could.

"I can't stop thinking about you," he replied.

Fuck.

"That's not—"

"I hear your concerns, okay?" He stood up, clearing his throat, and it was obvious he'd practiced saying this probably a thousand times before.

"But I disagree with them. And I know it's not just up to me, but I don't understand why you think it's not worth *trying*. 'Cause I think it is."

I sighed, glancing at the door. "I don't have time to tell you all the reasons again. If you've heard my concerns, you already know them."

"Is that what you want, then?" he asked bluntly.

I frowned. "What?"

"You want to give up what might be a good thing because you're worried how my sister might react and—"

"You are too goddamn young for me," I hissed. "And even if you weren't, your sister is my *best friend*. Chicks before dicks, even if the dick in question is really nice."

He opened his mouth, but whatever he was about to say was lost in a smirk. "You think I have a nice dick?"

I took a deep breath because if I didn't, I would have burst out laughing.

"That, right there," I said. "That is why you're too young for me."

He looked bewildered, then annoyed. "Because I'm funny? Come on, Kels. You're grasping at straws here."

"I am not."

"You realize how ridiculous this is, right?" The frustration in his voice was barely hidden. "I fucking like you and you like me. Why—"

"Because I don't want to steal these years from you!"

My voice was shrill enough that he paused. Or maybe it was because my voice cracked. Or maybe even the tear that broke free from my eye and spilled down my cheek.

"You know I know what it's like, right?" I asked, my voice wavering. "You know someone took those years from me? My ex-husband was—You know I've never kissed someone in their twenties before you? I can't take these years from you, Jimbo."

"What if I want to give them to you?"

"You don't. You can't." I looked at him imploringly. "I don't want to be the bad guy, Jimmy. Don't make me do something that puts me on his level."

"But I..." He trailed off, looking down as he fell silent.

"I'm sorry," I said. "I am, Jimbo. You deserve a girl who's gonna make you happy. I'm going to make you miserable."

He lifted his eyes, almost offended. "That's not—"

But of course, that's when Mike swaggered into the break room.

"Thought I saw you sneak past," he said to me gruffly, then glanced at Jimmy. "Shit's sorted out with the band. They wanna start in five. I told 'em if they so much as give each other a dirty look, they're banned for life. Then it's all 'oh no, Mr. Acton, please don't ban us.'" He rolled his eyes. "Fuckin' babies. They cause any trouble, end the session."

"Sure," Jimmy said.

Mike turned to me. "Been meaning to talk to you about those Swift tickets. I know I said you could pay closer to Christmas but—"

And see, this is why all of them were to blame.

If Alex hadn't decided to surprise Em with a last-minute weekend getaway while he rightfully avoided the trauma of his past, I wouldn't have been there.

If Jimmy hadn't offered to babysit Baylee, then distracted me so I couldn't leave right away, I wouldn't have been in the break room.

And if Mike hadn't brought up Taylor fucking Swift and the goddamn money I owed him when I was *already* raw and emotional and embarrassed about who I was as a person in general, I wouldn't have said what I did.

And if I was a better person, I wouldn't have blamed any of them since I was the one entirely at fault for the whole thing.

"I know, Mike," I snapped. "I will get you the money. Jesus, if I'd known it was such a big deal, I wouldn't have asked."

Mike raised a bushy eyebrow. "Lady, you're the one making it a big deal."

I didn't need a mirror to know my face was *red*. The sudden dizzy rush that ran through me was more than enough of a hint.

"I will have it for you next week," I said stiffly. "Excuse me, Baylee and I should go."

"Kelsie, wait," Jimmy said, but I was too busy marching past Mike with what little dignity I had left to acknowledge him.

It wasn't the first time my pride had gotten me into trouble, and it certainly wouldn't be the last. It wasn't even the last time that week. I wish I could explain it; I wish I could tell people I knew how infuriating it was, my inability to admit that I was in over my head and that I needed help. I wish that part of me wasn't intrinsically broken. That I could just explain how I had an unrealistic need to prove myself so badly that I was willing to put myself through the hell and high water I could have avoided simply by telling the truth.

I wish I was the woman I wanted to be. The woman who was strong enough to stand up to her ex. The woman who was open and honest and willing to ask for the support I so desperately needed.

It's just that, the last time I did that, I ended up with Daniel.

And I couldn't risk something like that happening again.

Fourteen

I spent the rest of the weekend finally giving in and letting Baylee decorate the house for Christmas. We put up the ugly-ass Christmas tree and put cartoon-y window clings on the living room window and listened to way too many Christmas carols accompanied by Baylee's fucking tambourine. But it was wonderful, and magical, and everything I needed to get through the next week.

Monday brought an experience I hadn't had in years: seeing Em at school drop-off. I couldn't remember the last time both of us had been at the school for drop-off; maybe when the girls were in kindergarten. But kindergarten drop-off had been very different. Back then, we'd walked the girls to the door to meet their teacher and make sure all their little possessions made it into the neatly labeled cubbies and coat closets.

Now, drop-off involved a parking lane and idling cars, students letting themselves out of the backseat and rushing past the supervisors to find their friends so they could line up to go into the school together.

So while I saw Em, she was in her car and I was in mine, and we managed little more than a quick wave at each other before a supervisor gave me a very pointed gesture to keep the line moving and the car behind Em honked.

It felt wrong, so I texted her after I got to work.

How was your weekend getaway? Come over for popcorn and beers tonight?

I didn't see her response until I went on my lunch break a few hours later.

ahhhhh I wish. Tomorrow maybe? I have to go grocery shopping tonight. Alex apparently has no idea how to feed an eight-year-old.

But on Tuesday, I was so exhausted that I fell asleep on the couch after dinner, even though Baylee was practicing her tambourine in the same room.

Wednesday, Em had a client in the evening. Thursday was Leia's guitar lesson. No matter what we proposed, it seemed like one or the other of us wasn't available since it was no longer a matter of a quick jaunt across the street. It wasn't until the weekend, when Em had promised to watch Baylee again, that I finally saw her face to face. And considering that, aside from the time she'd been away with Alex, Em and I used to see each other every single day, it... well.

It was hard.

"I feel like I haven't seen you in ages," Em said as I entered the coffee shop we'd agreed to meet at after I finished work.

"Right?" I sighed heavily and collapsed into the seat across from her, my feet and back aching as I tried to cover my exhaustion. "God, I miss you."

"We're gonna have to get better at this." She slid a cup of coffee across the table at me. "But that's a problem for later. We've only got an hour before the Girl Scout leaders realize that planning a Scouts-only Christmas party was a terrible idea and beg us to take the girls back."

I snorted and grabbed the coffee, taking a long swig in the hopes that the caffeine would kick in sooner rather than later. "Okay, tell me everything new. How was your weekend getaway? Did you suck Alex's dick more or less times than when you were in Mexico? I was betting on less because Leia was there, but then I thought maybe more since like, clandestine hookups while she was distracted."

She burst out laughing. "You're awful."

"You love it." I sipped my coffee and raised my eyebrow. "So?"

It sounded like a lovely little getaway. While Em had spent time getting massaged, pampered, and facialed in the not-fun way at the spa, Alex had taken Leia to Santa's Village for what basically amounted to a "dad-and-daughter" day.

"I almost sobbed," Em said as she recounted Leia's excited retelling of her day out with Alex. "I just... she loves him so much and he..." Her voice caught and she shook her head, then laughed. "Look at me. I'm turning into one of the mushy Live-Laugh-Love moms."

"That's a deal-breaker for me," I said. "Friends off."

She laughed again, but took a moment before she could speak again. "I just... it sounds so stupid to say it out loud, but I think I finally found her dad."

Cynical though both of us could be, I don't think either of us actually thought it sounded stupid.

"What about you?" she asked. "How are things with, um, Daniel?"

That was unexpected.

I stared at her, the wheels in my mind cranking and groaning as I tried to figure out why, exactly, Em had felt the need to bring Daniel up out of nowhere. At no point in the history of our friendship had she asked about him like that. At no point in the history of *ever* should she have thought it was okay to bring up someone that we'd only ever talked about in hushed voices, surrounded by empty beer bottles and the yellow glow of lights in one of our kitchens. And there I was, so stunned and so tired that I couldn't even muster up a response.

"I just mean after he showed up that... that one day," she continued hurriedly when I didn't answer.

"Of course," I said, but it didn't sound like my voice. "Um, they're fine, I guess? He's... he's still Daniel."

"Right, yeah." She nodded. "Can I ask you something kinda personal?"

That should have been a red flag. At no point during our friendship had we ever felt the need to ask permission to ask something. That wasn't how our friendship worked.

But I didn't catch it.

"Sure?" I said uncertainly.

She toyed with her coffee cup. "Why didn't you tell me about him asking for two weeks with Baylee?"

I swallowed hard. "How did you—"

"Jimmy mentioned it. Just in passing, after he ran into him that night he brought Baylee back early."

My head felt light. "Did he?"

"Don't be mad. I hounded him to make sure you were okay when he got back."

I tried to gauge if that was *all* he'd told her about after That Night. She wasn't raging angry, so either Jimmy was right and she was way cooler about shit than she had any right to be, or he hadn't told her about the whole feeling-each-other-up-in-my-front-hallway thing.

"I had to, Kels," she said. "They were gone for longer than I thought and I was so freaking worried that something had... well. He finally said you were shaken up and just wanted to talk, so he'd sat with you while you calmed down. He didn't tell me anything else. He said that it was between you and him and I could ask you if I wanted, but I didn't know if..." She sighed. "Sorry. This is coming out wrong."

"It's fine," I said.

"You're just usually so unflappable," she said. "So to know you were that upset, I just... I felt bad that I hadn't come over myself. I'm sorry."

Oh, God. And now she was apologizing to *me*.

"It's okay, Em," I repeated. "Really."

She took another deep breath. "Okay. Here's the thing, though, because it's not okay."

I felt frozen in place. "Why?"

She looked at me, her eyes a strange mix between hard and sympathetic. "Things have been so weird lately and I couldn't figure out why. You've been working like crazy and when Jimmy told me Daniel asked for two weeks, I had to wonder why, you know? And then Alex said that you and Mike had an argument last weekend about the Taylor Swift tickets, and I realized Daniel asked for the extra time around when Mike got the tickets for the girls and—"

"Em, stop," I said, my voice shaking.

"Please don't tell me you've been working yourself sick over this."

I tried to answer. I tried to say I wouldn't tell her that. But my mouth went dry and there was a thick lump blocking the base of my throat. Fortunately or not, that seemed to be answer enough.

"You're joking," she said. "Seriously, Kelsie? All of this has been about the... I mean, you went to Daniel—you went to your fucking *abuser*—and asked for more money just for some stupid *concert tickets*?!"

Shame burned through me, flashing as bright and hot as the anger that followed it. Because on one hand, she was right: I'd put myself in this position for fucking Taylor Swift tickets. I didn't even *like* Taylor Swift.

But my daughter did. And she wanted to see that concert more than anything. And I wanted to give her those things, to be part of those memories, to have those moments she would look back on for the rest of her life.

And that meant it wasn't *stupid*.

"Jesus, I can't believe this. I can't believe *you*," she said, her voice full of anger and hurt.

"Do you want to stop yelling at me for being in a shitty situation?" I asked coldly.

"I'm not yelling at you," she shot back. "But no, I'm not going to stop being pissed. We're supposed to be friends, Kelsie. You're supposed to tell me when you're going through shit. Instead, now I get to feel like a total jackass for making you miss work and not knowing you were struggling."

"Right, because this whole thing is about you."

"You know damn well that's not what I meant." She sat back in her chair, glaring at me with a look that was far too reminiscent of Jimmy's scowl for my comfort. "Why didn't you tell me?"

"You had your own shit going on," I muttered.

"What?!"

"You did," I said. "With Alex and moving and planning the friggin' concert and—"

"That's bullshit and you know it. You *know* I would have made time for you."

I made a scoffing noise, glancing to the side as I tried to collect my thoughts. "I didn't... I had it figured out."

"Did you? Did you really?"

"You can stop being a bitch about it any time."

"I'm not—"

"No, you are," I said, glaring at her as my face burned. "You're sitting here judging me just like you would've if I'd told you I couldn't..."

I trailed off as Em gaped at me.

"Do you seriously think that little of me? Do you *seriously* think I'd judge you for not being able to afford something?"

I didn't respond.

"Seriously?!" Her voice went high pitched and patches of pick appeared on her cheeks. "After all we've... I thought we were closer than that. I thought I was the person you could trust to lean on."

I didn't know if she was trying to manipulate me into feeling guilty, but that's what was happening. There was a familiar instinct, a deep-seated response made of fear and self-preservation that was trying to surface telling me to apologize, to tense my shoulders and tuck my chin so that when someone struck out at me, I'd be able to curl up in a ball and protect myself.

I don't think she intended it, but I wasn't in a place where I could control it. Rational thought didn't seem to exist in that place either, just shame and anger and the concept of fight or flight, of either bowing down and letting someone else win or of standing up and facing them.

And I'd let Daniel win far too many times.

"You're not," I said bluntly, and Em recoiled. I straightened up in my chair. "You're not the same person anymore. I don't feel like I even know you."

Her face crumpled. "This is exactly what I said I didn't want to happen when I moved. I fucking *said*—"

"Your move had nothing to do with it." I didn't intend to be cruel, but my words didn't seem to understand that. "You started becoming someone else the moment you and Alex got together."

"I did not!" she protested.

"You did!" It was a struggle not to shout at her. "You let him change you and you didn't even realize it."

"Oh, and you're just bringing this up now because...?"

I laughed. "Because what was I supposed to say? 'Em, you're not the kind of person who volunteers to put on a big charity concert'? Like I was supposed to question you doing good things?"

She stared at me, bewildered. "I... what?"

"And what about Leia? What was I supposed to say there? That you were *so* against her performing for so long, that you were *so* concerned about her being involved in the music industry because you knew what it could do to people, and then you fuck Alex once and suddenly she's a YouTube star performing with huge names in the music industry?"

"That's not—"

"It is. Don't you fucking deny that's what happened." I shook my head. "You would've *never* agreed to that before you met him. And now you're sitting here acting all self-righteous because you could afford the tickets and I couldn't."

The pink on her cheeks burst into red. "I am *not* acting self-righteous!"

"You've changed, Em."

"Well, so have you," she snapped back.

"No, I have—"

"Yes, you have. You can't just claim I've changed when you started acting differently around me. You apparently noticed all this happening for however long and said nothing? You went from the person who could tell me anything to someone putting herself through hell to avoid, what, admitting she needed help? The Kelsie I know wouldn't change who she is because of her fucking *pride,* like that means more to her than her friendships or her daughter."

Deep in my chest, I felt those words. I *felt* them hit me, strike me, gouge their fingernails through my skin. Some sane part of me knew Em hadn't meant to hurt me like that. It was the same part of me that knew she had a point and that her anger wasn't entirely unjustified, that I *had* acted differently and that the whole thing was indeed my fault, just like everything was.

But the rest of me, the little monsters that made up every inch of my horrible self, were screaming, wounded and rabid and angry. It didn't even matter that Em's face changed, that she realized what she'd said and was opening her mouth as though she could shove the words back in where they'd come from.

It didn't matter.

"Kelsie, I didn't mean—"

"I don't need this," I said, grabbing my purse and digging in it for my wallet.

"Wait, let me—"

"You know what, Em? I saved up the money. I put the work in. And yeah, maybe I originally hoped that Daniel would step up and be a reasonable person for once and just fucking help me, but he didn't and that's fine. I did it by myself. I didn't need him and I didn't need you. I can say I bought my little girl's Christmas present on my own and you don't get to take that away from me or make me feel shitty about it. I fucking *did* it." I found a few dollar bills and threw them on the table as I stood up. "Here. For the coffee."

She said my name again, and again, but I was already striding past the not-so-secretly enthralled customers and uncomfortable-looking coffee shop employees who had clearly overheard us. A lady looked at me sympathetically and I realized they'd heard Em say *who* I'd asked for the money from. I exited the shop with my eyes on the ground and my face beet-red, the chilled outside air almost painful against my overheated skin.

I couldn't pinpoint a time I'd been so angry, so riled up, so right and so wrong and so lost. All I knew was that I had to get out of there, that I had to get away from the eyes and from Em and from the horrible words I'd said and heard. Shaking, I got into my car, turned the radio on as loud as I could stand it, and started driving.

I was driving in the complete opposite direction of where I needed to go when I remembered I'd have to pick up Baylee, and more specifically, that I'd have to see Em when I picked her up. Because of course I would. Because of course I had to fight with my best friend and then see her while I was still angry, not even at the point where I was ready to grieve the loss of her, while I was still battling the contradiction of her blaming me for the situation I'd put myself in. Of course I'd have to see her while my heart was still raw, while I felt like my soul was crumpled and crushed and torn, while I was embarrassed and upset, whether it was justifiable or not.

I wasn't sure when I started crying, but I do know that it was sometime between flicking my signal light on so I could pull a U-turn at the next intersection and approximately thirty seconds later, when I noticed the brake lights flash red in front me just in time for me to wreck my car like I'd wrecked my friendship with Em.

My body jolted forward as I hit the back of the pickup truck in front of me, my seatbelt catching and throwing me back against the seat hard enough to make me gasp for breath. It happened so fast that the tear blocking my vision before I hit him was only just finishing its trail down my cheek, dripping onto my collarbone as I stared straight ahead until the hazard lights on the pickup started flashing.

"Fuck," I said to no one, and then I started *sobbing*.

That was how the driver of the pickup found me: arms folded on the steering wheel as I cried inconsolably. It wasn't until much, much later that I realized how alarming the sight must have been; all he would have seen was a shocking mop of pink hair and shaking shoulders, which is probably why he pounded frantically on the window before nearly ripping my door off the hinges.

I, of course, took that to mean he was angry.

"N-no, no, *no*," I squealed, jolting backwards and jerking away from the open door.

"Miss, are you—"

"Don't hurt me," I begged.

"Shit, do I gotta call an ambulance?"

I looked at him with wild eyes, fear and adrenaline coursing through every vein and artery until I managed to take a breath so oxygen could take its place and I could truly see who was standing outside my vehicle.

He was older than me, maybe Alex's age; mid-fifties, maybe sixty at a stretch. A black beanie sat on his head and a bushy mustache barely concealed the look of concern on his face. Wearing the kind of ski jacket that everybody's dad seems to wear, he couldn't have looked less threatening if he tried.

"Wh-what?" I asked.

"You said something about being hurt," he said. "Do you need an ambulance? Can you move?"

The adrenaline began to give way to yet another round of humiliation. "Oh, no, I'm not hurt, I said—" I stopped and shook my head. "I'm not hurt. J-Just shaken up. I... I'm s-sorry, it's been a hell of a day and I have to go get my daughter and—Are you hurt? Did I hurt you?"

A smile that almost looked condescending but was probably intended to be soothing filled the space beneath his mustache, and he extended his hand to help me out of my car. "Ma'am, if it weren't for the noise, I probably wouldn't've even noticed. Didn't feel a thing."

When I saw where I'd hit him, I understood what he meant. There wasn't even a single scratch on his vehicle. Mine, on the other hand, had a great big hole that was perfectly in line with the trailer hitch on his pickup.

"Shit," I said.

"Yeah, no repairing that," he said. "Gonna need a new bumper. But go ahead and pop your hood, lemme take a look and make sure you didn't put a hole through the radiator, too."

By some miracle, I hadn't—"Missed it by a quarter-inch at most, you lucky lady," he said—and by the time he closed the hood of my car, I'd gained enough sense to dig out my license and insurance info.

He took it from me, glancing down at the horrendous photo I had on my driver's license before glancing at the car.

"You got comprehensive?" he asked.

"What?"

"Insurance. Does it cover you if you're at fault?"

I shook my head. He took another long look at the front of my car and the back of his truck, then handed my license and insurance back to me.

"Don't need it."

"What?" I asked. "But I—"

"There's half a scratch on my trailer hitch and I didn't feel a thing," he said. "A new bumper's gonna cost you probably fifteen hundred, maybe two grand. All a claim's gonna do is raise your premium. You don't need that."

I stared at him in disbelief. "Are you sure?"

The man smiled and patted my shoulder. "Pay it forward one day, ma'am. Merry Christmas."

Before I could even think to ask for his name, he got back into his truck, turned his hazards off, and pulled away.

That was how I ended up in that CVS parking lot nine days before Christmas with a hole in my bumper and my phone clutched in my hands, wondering if anyone would buy my used panties.

I wish I could say contemplating selling my panties was what made me realize I'd gone too far. I mean, I wish I could say my fight with Em was what made me realize it, but that clearly hadn't happened, either. But seriously considering selling used panties online should have been more than enough to be a red flag.

Like yes, money had been tight, and yes, I'd been stressed and working my ass off to save up for Baylee's present. But I hadn't had to forgo any necessities or give up anything of significance. The electricity was still running. The bills were paid. Baylee hadn't had to miss a field trip at school or a Girl Scouts activity. There was still food on the table. Hell, there was still beer in the fridge, not that it was a necessity, but I'd still managed to treat myself a little.

No, the red flag wasn't considering selling my panties.

It was trying to decide whether skipping a few lunches was worth it if it meant I could start my half-baked used-panty-selling business because I'd need the money to buy spare panties to sell.

That's when I knew it was too far.

That I wasn't going to be able to buy the tickets.

That I couldn't do it on my own.

I'd managed to stop the tears when I'd been looking at the front end of my car, but I couldn't stop them from pooling in the corners of my eyes as I unlocked my phone and tapped the screen. Shivering, I took a steadying breath as the phone rang once.

Twice.

Three times.

And then he answered.

"I was wondering when you'd call," Daniel said pleasantly. "How much do you need, my dear?"

Fifteen

I TALKED HIM DOWN to a week.

"She's never been away from home that long," I said. "Two weeks is too much."

"This is her home, too," Daniel replied. "Or it would be, if she was allowed to spend any length of time here."

I bit back my instinctual response, which was to tell him to talk to the courts, since that probably wouldn't work in my favor anymore. "Let her ease into it. I'm not asking for me."

"Two weeks, but we can split it into one-week blocks."

I took a steadying breath and let it out. "One week and we'll see."

His tone grew colder. "I don't think you have quite the bargaining power you seem to think you do."

Another breath, this time through clenched teeth. "I'm not bargaining, Daniel. I'm trying to do what's best for our daughter."

"In exchange for money."

Breathe in. Breathe out. "One week."

"Hmm."

"It's the best I can do. One week. If it goes well and *she* wants to, another one a few months later."

"If she wants to?" he repeated.

"I'm not going to force her to do something she doesn't want to do," I replied.

"Right, my dear, but I just want to confirm that if Baylee *wants* something, you'll consider it?"

Breathe in.

Breathe out.

"I will consider it," I said. "But you'll need to consider upping your child support permanently."

"When?"

"When will I consider it?"

I could almost hear him roll his eyes. "When is my week with her?"

My stomach curled in disgust as I realized he was agreeing to it. "Send me the money first and then we'll pick a week."

"Absolutely not."

"Daniel, I can't pick a week right this second. I need to check her Scouts schedule and her school stuff and—"

"I don't think you understand, Kelsie. I'm not sending the money *until* I have my week with her."

"Then I guess you're not getting a week with her."

"Let me remind you which one of us called to ask for money, my dear."

There was no breathing in and out that time.

"Yeah, and I need it before Christmas, so either way, you're leaving me screwed," I snapped. "So I guess you don't get a week with her after all."

"Or you could just—"

But I didn't hear what I could "just" do, since I hung up on him.

I'd never hung up on Daniel before. I don't think either of us quite knew what to do. Half of me expected him to call back right away, raging mad, screaming and berating me for doing something so boldly disrespectful.

Or worse, maybe he wouldn't call. Maybe he would just come.

But he didn't call back. And it wasn't like I was home or he could magically just appear in front of me. Not that it mattered, since I figured either way, I was back to the used panties idea.

I was so certain that was the only option that I'd started checking the Victoria's Secret website and pricing out the cheapest panties I could find in my size while I was waiting for Baylee to come out after the Girl Scouts Christmas party. It was while I was in the process of adding a bunch of clearance panties to my cart that my phone buzzed.

I will transfer the money at the end of the week.

Holy shit.

I stared at the message, eyes wide.

I'd won.

Daniel had backed down on something and I'd *won*.

I mean, I had to give him a week with Baylee. So I hadn't completely won.

But still, something on this God-forsaken day had gone right. I might've lost my best friend and fucked up my car's bumper and gone crawling to my ex-husband for money and promised him way more time with my daughter than he would ever deserve, but damn it, at least I had... that.

It was small, but I had it.

And that was what got me through most of the week. That was what got me through seeing Em's car pull up behind mine while we each waited alone for the girls.

It was what got me through Baylee flinging the door open and asking if she could pretty-please go over to Leia's so they could play music together.

It was what got me through the crushed look on her face when I said no, not today, but maybe next weekend.

It got me through Monday, when I tried not to cry as I handed over all the money I'd managed to save to the body shop repair guy.

And Tuesday, when I got a text message from Em that I wasn't ready to read yet.

Wednesday, when she texted me again asking me to call, and then again telling me Leia wanted Baylee to come over and could we at least let the girls hang out.

Wednesday, when I texted her back a short message saying I agreed that the girls should hang out but that I honestly could not make it work that day.

Wednesday, when she texted me back a short *Okay. Sure.* that I knew meant she didn't believe me, even though I was telling the truth.

Wednesday, when I cried myself to sleep for the fourth time that week, miserable and lonely and so ashamed of myself that I could barely close my eyes.

Wednesday, when I both regretted my words and didn't.

Wednesday—well, Thursday, technically—when I sat near the window at two in the morning, staring out at the house across the street, a place now foreign yet familiar, where I used to sit with a woman who was more family to me than my own family ever had been.

When I realized Christmas was a few days away, and that we were supposed to spend it with Em and Leia and Alex and Jimmy, and the realization it probably wasn't going to happen and I was going to have to tell Baylee that.

When I was silently thankful that at least I'd gotten the Taylor Swift tickets from Em weeks ago so I didn't have to deal with *that* bullshit on top of bringing money to the studio for Mike.

When I realized Em not being in my life meant that Jimmy wouldn't be in my life either. When I tried to convince myself that was a good thing because Jimmy was not for me. That he was too young, that this was for the best, that it was going to be far easier to not be around him because we couldn't have had anything anyway.

When I couldn't stop picturing his face and the way he'd looked into my eyes as I'd knelt in front of him. The way he'd clutched me, his quiet voice pleading with me to give him a moment. The way his lips felt. The way his arms felt. The way his fingers felt inside of me.

When I told myself I needed help.

It got me through all of Thursday, that final day of school before Baylee's Christmas vacation started. It got me through work, even though I was running on barely three hours of sleep. It got me through telling my boss if I was leaving a little early because I wanted to pick Baylee up myself, since I didn't need to keep working crazy hours now that Daniel had agreed to give me more money, and also would she mind if I took the next day off, which she instantly agreed to. It got me through the now-familiar wave of nausea every time I remembered I'd let him buy time with our daughter.

Baylee didn't know I was planning on picking her up, so I parked my car down the block and walked up to the school to meet her at the doors instead of waiting in the parking lane. There was a handful of other parents milling about, hazy puffs of breath hanging frozen in the air as we shivered against the walls of the school. I rubbed my hands together, wishing I'd brought my gloves as I listened to the sounds of younger children enjoying the playground equipment while their older siblings finished up the school day.

It was a few minutes before the dismissal bell rang that my phone vibrated, which I felt because my hands were firmly shoved in my pockets in an attempt to stay warm. Almost hesitantly, I took it out of my pocket.

And then I nearly dropped it as I gaped at the notification on the screen.

Five thousand dollars.

An automatic deposit of five *thousand* dollars had dropped into my account from Daniel.

It had to be a mistake, I thought. One extra zero, maybe. Five hundred was less than I'd asked for but I wouldn't put it past him to split things into multiple payments in an attempt to give me less. Shivering, I took a screenshot of the notification and texted it to Daniel.

Is this a mistake?

He barely waited thirty seconds before messaging back.

I don't make mistakes, my dear. Enjoy.

Enjoy.

I gaped at my phone, stunned beyond belief.

Five thousand dollars.

It was more than enough for everything. For the tickets and the car and... I mean, shit, there was enough in there that I could have bought *regular*-priced panties from Victoria's Secret, plus a drum kit for Baylee if I really wanted to torture myself. But it was the first thing I was most concerned about; paying back Mike was the priority. Almost giddily, I dug into my purse to find my checkbook and a pen.

Yes, a checkbook.

Anyone who says checks have no place in the modern world does *not* have a child in school and various other sports and activities. Checks were far easier than dealing with a thousand and a half e-transfers and credit cards and shit. There was always some activity that needed money or some teacher that wanted forty-two dollars and fifty cents for a field trip fee, exact change or checks only. So yes, I had a checkbook, and yes, I used it regularly, and yes, I scribbled a check to one Mr. Mike Acton for the exact amount of the goddamn Taylor Swift tickets. I managed to resist adding "here you go, you grumpy fuck" to the memo section, signed it, and tucked it into my pocket with the full intent of stopping by the studio on our way home.

And then the final bell went off.

Excitement buzzed out of the school before the first throng of students even threw the doors open to rush home for the winter holidays.

It was electric, that energy, and despite my exhaustion and general inability to feel anything above dejection, I had to smile as I heard the joy and laughter behind the walls of the school.

The older kids made it out first, likely because the vast majority of them knew how to zip up their own jackets and tie their own shoelaces, save for the ones who were far too cool to stay warm in winter. They swaggered past the waiting parents, laughing and hollering and cursing simply because they *could*, because what was anyone going to do? It was Christmas, after all.

Most of them were gone by the time the younger kids started filtering through the doors. Rousing cries of "Mom! Look what Mrs. Vargas taught us to make today!" and "Moo-oooom! MOM! Can we stop at McDonald's on the way home?" and "Mom? What are you doing here?"

"Hey, sweetie," I said in response to the last one as Baylee shrieked and burst past the other kids. "Surprise!"

"I don't have to go to daycare today?" she asked, excitedly throwing her arms around my waist and making my heart melt in a way only she could.

"Nope," I replied, hugging her with one arm. "I decided we're going to have a girls' night. With hot chocolate and candy for dinner and Christmas movies for dessert. And I took tomorrow off too, so we can spend the whole first day of Christmas break together."

Her face brightened even more, somehow, and she danced a strange little jig, giggling and spinning and making me remember why, at the end of the long, long days, it was always worth it.

"Hi, Kelsie!" A second later, Leia came rushing up. "Are you picking us up today?"

Fuck.

"I, um, I'm not sure," I said. "I think your mom might be here to pick you up."

Leia frowned. "Really? But Uncle Jimmy's been picking me up."

Of fucking *course* he was.

"Right," I said. "Well, let's double check and make sure Jimmy isn't here yet because I didn't, um, talk to him before I finished work."

She looked towards the parent parking lane. "Oh. He *is* here. Probably 'cause I gotta go to the studio." She turned to Baylee, her eyes wide and sincere. "We're gonna hang out over Christmas break though, right?"

"Uh, *duh*," my sassy child said with an eye roll and a giggle.

"*Duh*," Leia repeated, and they both grinned as they embraced each other.

"See you later, Kelsie!" Leia said, then skipped her way towards the parking lane.

"C'mon," I said to Baylee. "I'm parked down the street."

She sighed heavily. "Okay, but can you carry my backpack? It's heavy."

"*Heavy*?" I repeated, taking the bag from her. "You think *this* is heavy? Maybe we need to start eating more broccoli for dinner so your muscles start growing."

"Broccoli doesn't make you stronger," she said.

"Sure it does."

"Nuh-uh. That's just a story they tell kids to make them eat more broccoli."

"Why else would people eat broccoli?"

"I don't know, Mom. They shouldn't 'cause it's gross."

I couldn't hold back a laugh as we reached the sidewalk.

"Kels!" someone called from behind us.

Well, I say someone.

I knew who that someone was.

And I ignored him.

"Hey, Kels! Kelsie!"

"Sir, you need to get back in your car," I heard one of the pickup supervisors say. "There's no parking here."

"I just need to talk to her real quick. Kelsie!"

"Sir, get back in your car."

"Jesus, lady, give me one goddamn second to—"

"Mr. *Reilly*, there are *children* around!"

"Mom, I think Jimmy's trying to get your attention," Baylee said quietly.

I swallowed hard. "Is he? I didn't see him."

"He's behind us. Miss Abernathy is yelling at him."

Though Miss Abernathy was trying to use her exasperated-fourth-grade-teacher superpowers to herd Jimmy back into his car, he was still standing beside said car waving frantically in my direction.

Which was perfect, actually.

"Wait here," I said to Baylee, putting her backpack beside her and striding towards Jimmy before she could respond.

He looked surprised to see me walking in his direction and moved around the front of his car, ignoring Miss Abernathy as she scolded him fiercely.

"Kels," he said as I reached him. "What the fuck happened with—"

"You're going to the studio right now?" I interrupted.

He frowned. "Uh, yeah, I have to work and—"

"Here." I withdrew the check from my pocket and shoved it at him. Instinctively, he grabbed it. "Give that to Mike. Tell him he's a grumpy old fuck from me."

"Ms. Bauer, there are *children*!" Miss Abernathy said in a tone so high-pitched that it was almost inaudible to anyone but the nearby dogs.

But it didn't matter. I was halfway back to my daughter before she even finished squealing.

"So, what kind of candy do you want for dinner?" I asked as I reached Baylee and grabbed her backpack.

She grinned maniacally. "Reese's Peanut Butter Cups. And Dino-Sours. *And* those bright green frogs that are really soft and chewy."

When we got to the CVS, I talked her down from half the candy aisle and convinced her popcorn was also a candy, then promised her she could pick out at least two of the Christmas movies we were watching, as long as we watched *How The Grinch Stole Christmas* at some point, too.

And no, not the classic cartoon. I fucking *loved* the Jim Carrey version.

"—pretty sure we've watched it a hundred times, Mom," Baylee complained as we got home.

"A *hundred* times?" I repeated, closing the car door behind me and grabbing Baylee's backpack again. "I'm pretty sure we watch it one time every Christmas. And you're not a hundred years old."

"I will be if I have to watch that movie one more time."

"Ouch," I said, but I was laughing as I unlocked the door.

"Okay, fine," Baylee said, following me inside. "But only if we get to watch *Rudolph* first, and then we need a break for more hot chocolate, and then—"

"*Shit!*"

I barely managed to catch myself after I tripped on the shoes in the front hallway. My wrist bent back painfully as I hit the same wall I'd pressed Jimmy against when I went down on him, a loud thunking sound doing nothing to drown out my shocked cry.

"Mom, are you okay?" Baylee asked, alarmed.

"Yes, Kelsie. Are you all right, my dear?"

I'd tripped on his shoes.

Why his shoes were in my front hall was less of a concern than why he was in my living room. Or rather, why he had been in my living room and was now standing inside the entrance to it, looking at me with mild concern for my well-being and strong distaste for the language I'd used in front of our daughter.

"*Dad!*" Baylee shrieked, kicking her shoes off and shoving past me so she could throw herself into his arms. "What are you doing here?!"

"Surprising my princess, obviously," he said with a warmth that didn't seem possible, given the cold look he was shooting at me above her head.

And it was cold. Cold enough to freeze me in place, to paralyze every inch of me from my mind to my vocal cords to my feet. It was like falling through the ice, the shock of him so sudden and all-encompassing that I could do nothing but stare as the air around me turned to liquid, filling my ears and my nose and my lungs.

"I'm so happy to see you!" Baylee was saying, and the only reason I clued in to her talking was because I saw her lips moving. "But—oh no." She looked up at me, her little forehead wrinkled with worry. "We were supposed to have a girls' night."

Daniel smiled tranquilly, his eyes trained on me. "That was part of the surprise, princess. Your mom didn't want you to know I was coming. But she made sure she put the spare key back in the exact same place so I could get in and wait for you to get home from school."

Baylee's face brightened. "Really?"

Someone nodded my head. No idea who it was, because I had no recollection of making the decision to do so, but my head moved up and down and that made Baylee happy.

"Really," Daniel said. "And that's not all. I have a very special Christmas surprise for you, too."

No.

Oh, *fuck* no.

"Daniel, please," I managed to choke.

He gave me a Look. "This is what we agreed to, my dear."

It wasn't, though. It wasn't at all what we'd agreed to. It was what he wanted and so instead of playing by my rules, he'd created his own. He'd sent the money by the end of the week, as he'd promised, and I'd been so stupid that I hadn't even realized he...

He was cashing in right away.

And he was doing it in front of Baylee so I couldn't say *shit* about it.

"What'd you agree to?" she asked interestedly.

Daniel bared his teeth in what was probably a grin. "Well, princess, your mom and I decided to surprise you for Christmas this year. How would you like to come spend Christmas with me and Grandma and Grandpa and your whole family, like you said you wanted?"

Her jaw dropped.

"For real?" she finally managed to gasp. "But I thought—"

She turned towards me, forehead creased again.

"Mom, how'd you know I wanted to stay with Dad at Christmas?"

I tried as hard as I could, but I couldn't stop the stinging sensation of tears in my eyes. My face twisted as I tried to smile.

"I just knew, sweetie," I lied.

Her little frown grew deeper. "And you don't mind? 'Cause I didn't want you to think I didn't wanna be with you at Christmas."

"Not at all."

The concern didn't leave her face. "What're you gonna do, though?"

I didn't come up with an answer to that one, but it didn't matter. A moment later, she slapped a hand to her forehead and grinned.

"*Duh*. You're staying at Mr. Alex's, right?"

"Mr. Alex?" Daniel repeated, eyebrows raised.

"Em's boyfriend," I whispered. "She j-just moved in with him."

"Right," he said, unconvinced.

"Yeah, it sucks," Baylee said. "'Cause that's Leia's mom and now they don't live across the street anymore, so we don't get to see each other as much. But that's okay 'cause she's in my class at school and Mr. Alex is her guitar teacher, so we get to play more music and he's got a studio at his house and everything."

"Hmm," Daniel said.

Baylee studied my face with far more intensity than a child her age should have been capable of, but not enough insight to know what she was seeing.

"Is Santa gonna know where to find me?" she finally asked. "'Cause if not, I should probably stay here."

Daniel raised an eyebrow at me. I looked at him, wishing I could muster up the strength to do anything but force the biggest smile I could.

"I'll make sure he knows where to find you, sweetie."

Sixteen

SHE PROMISED TO CALL me three times every day.

I didn't ask her to. Neither did Daniel, obviously. He tried to tell her that three times seemed like a little much because I might be busy or sleeping, but Baylee was insistent.

First thing in the morning, because if she didn't tell me good morning, I might not have a good day.

Around supper time, because every day at dinner we had to tell each other our favorite part of the day and we hadn't missed a single day of doing that in *months*.

And, of course, right before bed so we could sing our goodnights and "I love you"s and "sweet dreams" because we had a no-talking rule right before bed, but she had argued one day that no talking didn't mean no singing, and so every night we sang at each other for far longer than we should have but I couldn't bring myself to let the habit die because she was my little girl and one day she wouldn't want to sing at me anymore.

He promised she would be safe.

Even though he broke into my house and manipulated me into letting Baylee pack her things so she could spend an entire week away from me for the first time since he'd put me in the hospital, he gave me his word that she would be safe. And even though if you bought his word for a nickel, you'd get five pennies in change, I believed him.

I mean, I had to. I had no choice. But I knew he was telling the truth. He wouldn't dare risk anything more than he had; I might have been between a rock and a hard place, but he wouldn't push it any farther. At the end of the day, he might have been able to afford better lawyers than I could, but the records were right there in black and white. So he had to balance, to take what he could in a way that didn't allow me to fight back.

Because I had said he could have a week. And I had taken his money. And the only person who knew about any of this happening was our daughter, who could only see that her dad—the person she wanted to spend Christmas with—showed up to surprise her, and if I said she couldn't go...

Well, who would be the bad guy there?

He promised she would be back one week later, the day after Christmas, with her opinion of me intact and nothing but happy memories in her head. He promised he wouldn't play with her mind. He promised he wouldn't make her think badly of me.

But I wasn't about to bet my pennies on that.

After they left, I sat in the living room, watching the colours dancing on the wall. They came from the Christmas tree near the window, the one I'd put up with Baylee a few weeks earlier. It was an ugly thing, that tree, a cheap plastic one I'd bought at Target the very first Christmas that it was just me and her. I could barely afford presents that year—who was I kidding, I could barely afford *food* most weeks—but I wasn't going to let Baylee miss Christmas. It was her favorite time of year. I mean, she was a kid, so of course it was, and I was her mom, so of course I wanted to do everything I could to keep it magical for her.

Even if that meant she wanted to spend it with family. I couldn't give that to her, since I didn't have a family, but Daniel could, so… so it was important for her to be there.

Until then, I had been silent. My pain was beyond wailing, beyond screaming, beyond anything I'd ever felt before. I was a tree in a forest, falling with no one to hear me, breaking in a way I'd never been broken before, and considering how very, very broken I was, that was saying something.

I needed someone.

It still took effort to convince myself to go get my phone. I'd talk myself into it, then tell myself Em wouldn't want to hear from me. I'd tell myself that she'd laugh, that she'd take Daniel's side, that she'd berate me for letting him walk out of my house with Baylee in tow. She'd yell and scream and tell me I was a horrible mother, that I was probably never going to see my daughter again, that I didn't *deserve* to ever see her again.

But maybe she wouldn't.

I mean, she probably wouldn't.

When I finally convinced myself of that, I forced myself to go to the front hallway and get my phone. The selfish little monster inside of me tried to rear up. It tried to remind me of what Em had said, those final words and accusations, that I deserved to be told those hurtful things because they were true but that didn't mean she had to come out and *say* it.

But she'd been right, and I managed to convince that little monster that calling her *was* selfish of me, that Em had no reason to want to help me and yet I had the audacity to ask for it. And somehow that logic made sense, so I dialed her number.

It rang once.

Twice.

And halfway through the third ring, it disconnected.

I swallowed hard, then tried again.

Once.

Twice.

Three times.

Then it picked up.

"Hi, you've reached Em Reilly of Portraits by Em and Passion by Fire. I'm not available right now, but please leave a message or send me a text at this number if you're looking for an appointment."

Beep.

For a heartbeat, I couldn't say anything, and then I cleared my throat and tried to speak past the dryness in my mouth.

"Em, it's me," I said. "I... I know shit's been... I can't do this on a voicemail. Call me. Please. I need... I need help."

After I hung up, I sat there silently, then pulled up my messages. After all, maybe she was screening my calls. She'd have every right to.

You were right.

I sent it, then pressed my lips together.

Please. Please call me.

When my phone finally rang hours later, startling me out of a half-hazy doze I hadn't realized I'd fallen into, it wasn't Em.

"Gooooood evening Mom, did you watch the Grinch without me?" Baylee sang into the phone.

I laughed shakily and tried to sing back. "Don't worry sweetie, I wouldn't watch your favorite movie without youuuu!"

She groaned and then giggled. "Mom it's not my favorite movieee. It. Is. Yours."

Let no one say my daughter wasn't committed. She sang every single word as she told me all about how Daniel had taken her out to a "real fancy restaurant" for dinner that turned out to be the Olive Garden, which I'd never taken her to because the Olive Garden in Pueblo was right next to the Red Lobster and I fucking love shellfish, so that was where we went on special occasions. And she sang about how Daniel had set up an entire bedroom just for her that had a princess bed with a canopy and a fluffy pink carpet and a big window that looked into the backyard.

She sang about the Christmas tree at his house and how he said they were gonna go see Grandma the next day. And she sang about how the day after that, he was going to take her out to the North Pole Colorado that Leia had visited with Em and Alex a few weeks ago, since it wasn't too far from where Daniel lived, and that she'd try real hard but Daniel said there wasn't good phone reception near the mountains so she might be a little late calling at dinner.

And when someone said something to her that I couldn't quite hear in the background, she sang that she missed me lots and hoped I slept well and she'd talk to me in the morning.

"And I la-la-la-LOVE you!" she finished.

I hoped she couldn't hear the wateriness of my voice. "I la-la-la-love you too, little firefly. Goodnight."

"Night, Mom," she whisper-sang, and then the phone went quiet.

Em hadn't called back. Or texted. It hurt seeing that, but I thought... well.

Almost mindlessly, I got in my car and drove to Em's new house. Along the way, I rehearsed the things I wanted to say to her almost numbly, almost like I was making a checklist of transgressions and ways I'd fucked up.

I wanted to tell her that I was sorry.

That I was stupid.

That I was selfish.

That she was right.

That I needed her. That I was probably always going to be a little ashamed of asking for help but that I would try, I would really *try* to get better at it.

That I said things I shouldn't have and wished I could take back. That she hadn't deserved that. That I was so *fucking* sorry that I'd pushed her away and would she please, please forgive me?

And that Daniel had stolen Baylee from me for Christmas and that I knew it shouldn't have taken something like that to get me to reach out but if she could maybe find it in her heart to give me a hug and let me cry for a while, I would really, really appreciate it.

When I pulled up in front of Alex and Em's house, her car was in the driveway and I could see lights on through the front window of the house. Out of habit, I parked across the street; Alex had a garage full of cars far too expensive to park outside, so I tried not to block the garage in case he was out working or something.

As it turned out, it didn't matter.

I knocked on the door rather than ringing the bell. Leia was in bed, I assumed, since it was definitely past her bedtime. No one answered right away, so I knocked again, slightly louder.

Before I could knock a third time, the door opened and a heartbeat went by.

"Kels?" Jimmy finally said. "What are you doing here?"

Of course it had to be him.

"Can I talk to Em?" I asked.

"Uh, she's not here."

I stared at him blankly. "What?"

"She's... she and Alex went to the mountains for the weekend," he said. "I'm here watching Leia because..."

He trailed off. That was fine, since there was no reason for him to finish the sentence. He was watching Leia because Em and I had fought and so she couldn't ask me to watch Leia.

Because Em and I weren't friends anymore.

"Oh," I said, then swallowed hard. "Okay. Well, um, tell her I stopped by, if you don't mind, and that, um, I tried calling her and... and that's all, I guess."

"Bullshit, that's all," Jimmy said bluntly. "What's wrong?"

"Nothing's wrong."

"Kelsie."

"I'm fine."

"Yeah? You're totally fine?"

"That's what I said."

He raised an eyebrow. "So you dropped by after not talking to my sister or to any of us in almost a week because you're fine? You look like hell."

I laughed. I mean, it was a fake laugh, but I laughed. Or I made a noise of some kind. "Yeesh. You sure know how to flatter a lady."

"You know what I mean," he said, not laughing. "You've been crying. You're literally *still* crying."

I scoffed, wiping my hands across the wetness on my cheeks that I hadn't realized was there. "No, I'm not. I'm fine. It was good to see you, Jimbo. I'm gonna go and—"

"Kelsie," he said slowly, frowning as he looked past me. "Where's Baylee?"

I wasn't entirely sure if I managed to say anything intelligible, but whether I answered him or not, Jimmy's arms caught me and held me close as I fell to pieces, sobbing against his chest in the doorway of Alex and Em's house.

Seventeen

JIMMY REILLY USED TO be a rock star, sort of.

Jimmy used to drink too much, smoke too much, and blew too much money on drinking, smoking, and blow.

He used to have a temper.

I mean, he still did, but it used to be worse.

He used to be made of anger in a way that I both feared and understood. He had every reason to be angry after the life he'd had, but that didn't make it any easier to witness. I'd never been afraid of Jimmy, not really, but I'd feared the potential that anger had to poison him, to a man who guarded his ego fiercely because it was all he had and turn him into the kind of monster who realized how much power he had when he was in control.

That had never happened, though.

And it never would.

Because at his core, he was good. He knew right from wrong. He may have mis-stepped from time to time when he was—God, it felt so *wrong* to say "when he was younger" when he was still so fucking *young*—but he'd learned. He'd grown. He'd committed himself to doing better, *being* better, controlling the anger and pain that had followed him since he was younger than Baylee and Leia were now.

And that was the Jimmy I knew. That was the Jimmy that was making it so hard to stay away, that I was thinking about in ways I shouldn't because he was twenty-one and I was decidedly *not* twenty-one and was also his sister's—well. Used to be his sister's best friend, I guess.

The point was, the Jimmy I knew was more mature than he should have been. He was level-headed and sweet. He was funny and had a smile that had far more of an effect on me than his moody little scowl did.

So to see him lose control when I finally managed to tell him what Daniel had done was terrifying.

But not as terrifying as what he was trying to do.

"You *can't*," I hissed, lunging forward to grab my phone from him.

He pulled it away from me, standing firm. "Kelsie, he—are you fucking *serious*?! You can't be thinking straight here. He kidnapped Baylee! I'm calling the goddamn police."

It said a lot about how much I trusted Jimmy that I was comfortable enough to push past him and try to grab my phone again. The instinct to never put myself in a position where a man could shove me or hit me or throw me away was strong, but with him, it wasn't there.

But I wasn't capable of realizing that, not when I was embroiled in a hushed-but-intense conversation-slash-battle to get my phone back before he could make everything worse by calling the fucking police without waking up Leia and Pepper, who were sleeping in Leia's brand-new bedroom down the hallway.

"I'm not the one not thinking straight," I whisper-shouted back.

"He *kidnapped* your—"

"Stop saying that!" The pitch of my voice rose, since my volume couldn't.

His eyes seemed to flash with anger. "Then what did he do, huh? What do you want to call what he did, huh?"

"That—" I swatted at my phone "—doesn't—" I stumbled and he threw his arm out to keep me from falling "—matter!"

On the final word, I jostled his arm and my phone went tumbling to the ground. I meant to kick it out of the way so he couldn't grab it again, but I wasn't exactly steady on my feet and a sickening crunch came from under my shoe.

"Shit," I whispered.

"For fuck's sake," he muttered. He made sure I was balanced before letting go of me. "I'm going to get my phone. I'm calling the police, whether you—"

"Would you fucking listen to me for one goddamn minute?!"

It was loud enough that he froze, glancing wildly down the hall towards Leia's bedroom before looking back at me with indignant offense that I dare raise the volume of my voice during our argument.

"What do you think is going to happen if you call the police, Jimbo?" My face was burning as I struggled to lower my voice. "I agreed he could have a week. I took the money from him. And Baylee wanted to go."

"She... what?" he asked, confused.

"She wanted to go," I repeated. "She wanted to spend Christmas with her grandma and grandpa and all her family because sh-she doesn't g-get to see them and I d-don't have a family. She *wanted* to go."

My voice cracked and the next thing I knew, his arms were around me.

"I'm sorry," he whispered as I buried my face against his chest again. "Fuck, I didn't—I'm sorry, Kels."

"All calling the police will do is give him more ammunition," I choked. "S-So he'd be able to argue he should have c-custody because she w-wants to be there. Then h-he can take me back to c-court and I'll lose her."

"You won't lose her," he whispered, his arms tightening around me. "You're not losing her."

"Don't call the p-police. There's nothing we can do. He's won, okay? Just p-please don't call them."

"I won't," he promised. "I... I wasn't thinking about that. I'm sorry."

He calmed me again, just like he had the first time, consoling me when I was inconsolable until I'd managed to tell him what had happened. This time, instead of his anger ballooning and bursting when he found out what Daniel had done, he ushered me to the couch in the living room, settling me there with a box of Kleenex before bringing me my busted phone and going to the kitchen to get me a glass of water. When he came back, he found me with my head in my hands, elbows propped up on my knees. He sat beside me almost hesitantly, seemingly uncertain about what to do, but it was only when a tentative hand found my back and made gentle circles that I began to calm down.

That hand fell away when I sat up to reach for the water he'd brought, but he allowed himself to relax against the couch a bit as I wiped my face and took a steadying breath, then drank more of the water.

"What happened with you and Em?" he asked after I put the glass down.

I frowned, but didn't look at him. "What do you mean, what happened?"

"She didn't tell me."

I didn't say anything. After a moment, he sighed.

"I know you had a fight. I know Em went back and forth between being raging mad and devastated. At first I thought she maybe found out about, like... you know."

"Me sucking your dick?" I asked blandly.

He tried to stifle a laugh. "Uh, yeah, among the other things."

I felt the hint of a smile twist my lips, though it might not have been enough to even be visible. "Not as far as I know."

"I feel like if that were the case, she would've said something to me," he said. "I know it had to have been something big, but she wouldn't tell me. But with... you said you told Daniel he could have more time with

Baylee because he gave you money, and there was the fight with Mike and then the check..."

Of course he'd figured it out, too.

I waited for that moment of nauseated shame, for my stomach to curl and my face to burn and anger to surge through me as it tried to protect me from humiliation. But whether my emotions were completely burnt out or that the whole thing seemed like a relatively small turd compared to the most recent load of shit hitting the fan that was my life, that wave of embarrassment didn't happen.

Instead, I let out a resigned sigh and closed my eyes.

"I couldn't afford Baylee's Christmas present," I said. "The Taylor Swift tickets. So I asked Daniel to pay for them. And when Em found out, she decided it was her right to tell me how fucking stupid she thinks I am and I..." I cleared my throat. "I might've said some things I shouldn't have said, too."

A heartbeat went by. I couldn't see him, but I could almost hear the wheels turning in his head. "I don't mean to sound like a dick, but—"

"Because I was embarrassed," I snapped. "Because I can't give my daughter the same things that Leia gets and I didn't want to admit that to anyone so instead, I thought maybe her dad would help since despite seeming completely incapable of caring about another living creature, he cares about her. And then he wouldn't, so I tried to do it all myself because I didn't want to deal with Em and Alex and stupid fucking Mike judging me over it, just like I don't want to deal with you judging me right now."

"I'm not judging you," he said. "Not even a little."

I snorted, that watery tone returning to my voice. "You should be."

"Why?"

"Because I could have avoided this whole thing if I'd just said I couldn't afford the tickets," I said. "It's like Em said. I put myself in this position for... for concert tickets to friggin' Taylor Swift, of all people."

"So you think I should judge you because you reacted to a situation in a totally understandable way?"

I frowned again, opening my eyes. "What?"

"No one likes admitting they need help." I felt him shrug beside me. "Like, I've been there. Remember when I had to sit down and ask Alex for help after my career went to shit and..." He cleared his throat. "It fucking sucked. No one wants to admit they fucked up. I dunno if Em understands what that's like. She's got a different outlook on that kind of thing 'cause of what she used to do for work. Like, the modeling and stuff. But I imagine it's probably a lot harder when you're also dealing with a dirtbag like your ex who's waiting to jump on any little thing you might mess up."

After all of it, after everything I'd been dealing with, that was apparently all I needed to hear.

Before I knew it, I was telling Jimmy everything that had led up to my fight with Em. About the anger, the sadness, the fear. About how I felt like I barely knew her anymore. About working my ass off and losing everything I'd saved up.

And I told him about going to Daniel for help, about what I'd promised him and how he'd twisted it. And how I just wanted my little girl to have the things she wanted. Not all of them, of course. I didn't want to spoil her.

But I wanted her to be happy.

"I just want her to know her parents care about her," I said, wiping my eyes again. "Like, I know Daniel's a squalling turd, but whether or not I like it, he's her dad and he cares about her. I don't want her growing up thinking he doesn't and developing some fucking complex about it."

"You know, if he cared about her, he'd give her all this shit without asking for anything in return."

I opened my mouth to respond, then closed it.

"You know that, right?" Jimmy pressed. "Regardless of how he feels about you—and trust me, I don't understand how anyone could not fucking adore you—if he *really* cared about Baylee, he'd make sure she had everything she needed and wanted. Even if it meant you'd... I don't know. Look like you benefited from it or whatever."

I still didn't know what to say to that, so I latched onto the one thing I could and laughed dryly. "There's a lot of reasons people don't adore me, Jimbo. Like calling someone Jimbo even though they aren't a huge fan of it. Or calling out my best friend's parenting when I clearly am in no position to comment on anyone's parenting skills."

"Bullshit," he said. "Jesus, Kels. You're fucking awesome, you know that? You're so friggin' cool and hilarious and straightforward. You're unapologetic. And it doesn't hurt that you're hot as fuck, obviously, but—"

"Yeesh, laying it on a little thick, aren't you?"

"I am not," he insisted, and before I knew it, he had grabbed my hand and was looking into my eyes with an imploring earnestness I didn't know how to handle. "You are awesome. You *are*. And the thing that blows my mind about all of this is how someone like you ended up married to such a piece of shit."

"I was selfish."

Jimmy rolled his eyes. "That's not—you remember you told me how you ended up with him, right? That your parents... like, Jesus, Kels, getting a belly button ring doesn't mean your parents should've sold you to some guy who *groomed* you into thinking you couldn't do any better."

"They didn't sell me. He... he wanted me, so—"

"Fucking regardless!" His outburst came out louder than he intended and I saw him glance towards the hallway before lowering his voice. "That has nothing to do with you being selfish. You realize how fucked up that is? That your parents let some guy marry you because they found out you had a belly button ring?"

"They only found out I had a belly button ring because of my abortion."

I didn't say it loudly, but the words seemed to echo all the same. I didn't say it angrily, or shamefully, or regretfully, or any of the other emotions people assumed should be associated with an admission like that. I said it the same way I'd said it to Daniel the first time, long before he'd played with my mind and convinced me he knew me better than I did: matter-of-factly, quietly, owning up to every aspect of the decision that I'd made and what it meant.

Because even after everything, I still didn't regret it.

Jimmy paused, his head tilting to the side like some kind of adorably confused puppy stuck in some horrendous nightmare of a situation, stuck between wondering why I hadn't told him the whole story before and why it had happened.

So I told him.

Selfishness is what brought me to Daniel. My selfishness, and my parents' selfishness, and Daniel's selfishness disguised as generosity. My parents hadn't known how to deal with a teenage girl that loved loud music and multi-colored hair and sneaking out behind their backs. They screamed and yelled and lectured, they sent me to counseling at the church, they threatened and shook their heads and stamped their feet, but nothing worked.

Not until I got pregnant.

It didn't matter by who or how. That wasn't... it wasn't something I wanted to think about. I'd been a wild teenager because I'd had no other choice and I'd ended up in a situation where I had to make a choice.

And I made the right choice. The only regret I ever had was that it was what brought Daniel into my life.

I took care of it all myself. I made the appointment. I got myself there. I told no one and pretended I'd been skipping school that day so I had an alibi. I spent a ton of time thinking up the lie so that no one could question where I'd been.

It didn't end up mattering. Not when I was one of those rare but unlucky women who ended up having a rather nasty infection, so bad that my choice was to either risk dying or admit to my parents what had happened and ask for help.

They were more disgusted with me than they'd ever been in my life. Selfish, they called me, for choosing my life over a smattering of cells. Selfish for being lonely and afraid, for choosing sin over sin, for not facing the consequences of my own actions. For the shame and embarrassment I'd caused them. For never thinking of anyone but myself.

I discovered they'd been nice to me until then. All the counselors and programs and church groups had been the peaceful solutions. After making the choice I did, they felt I needed the big guns.

So they brought in Daniel.

I couldn't relive how he took me from the girl I was to the one I became. Not without thinking of his voice and the way he squirmed into my head. He was a wizard, in a way, a player of mind games, purposeful and hypnotic and charming in the worst possible combination.

And he liked me.

My parents rejoiced about that. It didn't matter that he was too old for me, that at eighteen, I was practically brainwashed into loving him. I was damaged goods, and so the fact that *anyone* could want me was good enough for them. It didn't matter that he stole my youth, that he stole my life, that I didn't get the chance to learn who I was because I was under his thumb. He wanted their tainted, baby-murdering daughter for some reason, so they gave me to him.

And I let them.

It took me a while to figure out why he'd wanted me, even though it should have been obvious. Sex was meant to be for one thing and one thing only, which I had been told for years I'd be perfect for since I had those big old child-bearing hips. So people in our church tended to marry young. They do that when sex is considered *such* a sin, you know?

So for Daniel to be in his thirties and unmarried was strange.

But that was the option he felt he had. That was the choice he made because he'd decided early on that he didn't want kids. And in the church, you didn't admit that you didn't want kids. Instead, he dealt with the side-glances and the whispers about him, even though it *killed* him to have people think he was anything but perfect.

So when someone brought a little baby-murderer to him for counseling, he thought that marrying her seemed like an excellent solution to all his problems.

The thing was that I did want kids. I always had. I just didn't want them *then*. I didn't want them before I'd had a chance to escape from the church and make my own way in life. I wanted to have a family with someone I loved, not someone I married as soon as I was eighteen because I wanted to get laid in a God-approved way.

And Daniel managed to convince me that I loved him.

I have no idea if my husband was a virgin when we got married, though I'd say he probably wasn't. He fucked me a lot. We didn't have sex as a couple. We didn't make love or enjoy each other's bodies or whatever. He would just fuck me. And I thought that meant we were trying to have a baby, but when a few years went by and I hadn't gotten pregnant, I asked him if we should see a doctor or something.

"For what?" he'd asked.

I'd been so confused. "To... to have a baby. I want a baby."

That was the first time he hit me.

Because yes, he was manipulative, and yes, he was horrible, and yes, he'd been emotionally abusive for years already, but he'd never hit me. And I was so shocked, so absolutely *stunned* when I'd ended up on the floor in front of him with pain shooting through my face that I'd sat there, staring blankly at his shins until he crouched down and took my hand.

"Kelsie, my dear, are you okay?" he'd asked, his eyebrows furrowed with concern.

Slowly, I looked up and met his eye. "I... what?"

"You fell, my dear. Are you alright?"

I stared at him, then like the pathetic excuse of a human being he'd turned me into, I nodded.

Eighteen

BAYLEE WAS UNEXPECTED, BUT she'd never been a mistake.

She wasn't planned, but she'd *always* been wanted.

At least by me.

I didn't tell Daniel about her until I was months along, long enough that he couldn't make me get rid of her, but he wasn't as angry as I'd thought he would be. Maybe he had resigned himself to it; maybe he was tired of the new whispers and side-glances at church, the rumors about him he'd hoped would go away when we got married and never quite did. Whatever it was, he accepted we were going to be parents, though I think he always hoped we would only have to have one.

And when bringing my squalling little turd of a daughter into the world nearly killed me, he got what he hoped for.

"No more babies," I told Jimmy. "Doctor's orders. They tied my tubes right after I gave birth. But I have her. And she was worth all of it."

He'd been silent as I talked, but he had kept his eyes on me the whole time. At no point had he looked away or shifted uncomfortably; he just sat there, listening, dark eyes studying me as I revealed every horrible, awful thing that had happened, the selfish choices I'd made and the consequences I told myself I'd deserved.

The problem was that he remained silent, even when I couldn't think of anything else to say. Desperate for something to do, I grabbed the glass of water and gulped it down, putting it back on a coaster. Still, Jimmy remained silent. When I couldn't take it anymore, I laughed, staring at the empty glass on the coffee table.

"Judging me now?" I asked.

He didn't say anything. He should have, but he didn't. Instead, he took my hand.

I didn't say anything. I should have. I should have very, *very* clearly said no, but I didn't, so Jimmy pulled me into his arms and kissed me.

There was a lot in that kiss. Sadness and sympathy, though not pity. Not even a little bit of pity, but plenty of that sorrowful anger I knew so well. His arms were steady and strong around me, holding me together in a way that no one really had before, at least not that I could think of in the moment. And his lips... fuck.

They were amazing, and it was unfair. It was so unfair.

I indulged a bit. I knew I shouldn't. I knew I was playing with fire, kissing him in Em's living room while her daughter slept down the hall. But on a day when everything in my life had shattered, he was what I needed, and he was there. So I kissed him, and I let myself be comforted by him and his closeness, and I tried to turn my mind off for a heartbeat.

Or two.

Or three.

He touched the side of my face, fingers caressing my skin before he stroked my hair. I shivered as he flicked his tongue against my lip, tracing it gently before toying with my lip ring. And when he slipped his tongue into my mouth, I indulged for a heartbeat longer, just long enough to feel that warm rush of energy travel through my skin and nerves right down to my bones, and then I put my hand on his chest.

He stopped, moving back just enough that his lips weren't on mine anymore. I could feel his breath against my mouth, his forehead resting against mine as his arms loosened enough that I could pull away if I wanted to.

"You understand now, right?" I whispered. "Why we can't... why *I* can't take these years from you?"

"You're not taking anything from me," he replied.

It was the most infuriating response I could imagine and I sat back, my face pained. "I *just* finished telling you—"

"That has nothing to do with you and me," he said. "Or my age. Or your age."

"Daniel took these years from me," I said. "He convinced me that no one else in the world would ever love me because I was broken and damaged and that I should marry him because he would love me no matter what. I went from being a teenager to being a wife. I didn't have time to fucking grow up and look at me now, just fucking... fucked. Just fucking fucked right the fuck up. He stole those years from me and I can't ever get them back and I don't want to do that to anyone else, ever, okay? I don't want to steal these years from you."

Whatever I was expecting him to respond with, it wasn't for him to smile wryly.

"I've been an adult longer than I was ever a kid," he said.

I opened my mouth, then closed it and frowned. He chuckled, shaking his head as he looked down.

"By the time I got kicked out and moved in with Em, I wasn't a kid anymore. I was fifteen, but it started long before that. When you're worrying about shit like where you're gonna live and if there's gonna be food on the table and—"

He stopped, then shook his head again.

"Em got out at a good time. I mean, as good as it could be considering. They got worse after she left. It's not her fault but... well, it wasn't her fault. My dad was—"

And again, he stopped, trying to stifle the anger in his voice. I bit my lip, my hand drawn to his by a force I couldn't control. My fingers brushed the back of his hand and after a moment, he turned his wrist, palm facing up so he could clasp my fingers.

"He was shit," he finally said. "Not like Daniel. He wasn't... I dunno, smart enough to be that manipulative or anything. But angry. Lazy. The entire world was out to get him, you know, only in his case it was true because he was just fucking garbage. And my mom should've never been a mom. She was such a fuckin' narcissist. I mean, when you say Daniel convinced you that you fell, I *get* that. There's shit I remember from when I was a kid that I'm still not sure is real and I'll never fucking know. I don't *want* to fucking know."

He looked up, eyes hard enough to break. "I was ten when I learned how to pay the utilities. Eleven when I started using my own money to do it because my dad whooped my ass when he realized I was using his credit card every month. I counted down the days to being able to leave and when they finally kicked me out, you wanna know why?"

I didn't as much as I did.

"It was 'cause I skipped school to busk at the corner so we'd have enough money for groceries. And only because I got caught skipping and the school gave them shit since it was the third time that week. I fought back and my dad nearly killed me. Mom said I had thirty seconds to leave or she'd let him push me off the balcony of the apartment and tell everyone I'd jumped." He paused, not looking at me, his eyes far away. "I think I made it out the door with about three seconds to spare. I'd wrenched my knee trying to get away from him so..."

There were no words. All I could do was squeeze his hand. He squeezed it back, then looked me square in the eye.

"I get why you're concerned, okay? Fuck, I might even agree with you, if I'd had a normal life. But you don't get to turn that part of you off when things get better. I don't get to have those years back. I tried to, sort of, when I thought I was gonna be the next big thing, but all I managed to do was become the same kind of asshole my parents were. 'Cause I don't *know* how to be normal. All I can do is move forward with what I've got. And I've got it good now. They'd be floored if they could see me now. I got a good job, I've got people I care about... It might not be normal, but it's fucking *good*."

His hand tightened around mine again, like he was trying to make sure I was paying attention, but I was already entirely captivated by his eyes.

"So you can't steal these years from me, Kels. They've already been gone a long, long time."

It wasn't like that was the perfect answer. It was heartbreaking at best, horrifying at worst. It didn't address so many of the concerns I had about being with him, though that list was growing smaller since Em didn't want to be my friend anymore.

But it was enough. And I was so tired. I was exhausted from fighting, from the constant kicks while I was flat on the ground, the never-ending spiral of shit that seemed to be whirlpooling around me. Wasn't I allowed to be selfish? Wasn't I allowed to give in once in a while, to do something for me, to follow what my heart was telling me it needed?

So I gave in.

His lips had consoled me; now it was my turn to kiss away his demons, to hold him in my arms and try to make him understand how very wanted he was. I touched his face, trailed my fingers along his neck, brushed the hair away from his face as he kissed me back, searching for more, and more, and more.

"Promise me something," he murmured, lips brushing against mine as he spoke.

"If it's one I can keep," I replied.

I felt his lips twitch into a smile. "Promise you're kissing me 'cause you want to. Not 'cause you're upset or feel bad for me or—"

I pressed my mouth back to his insistently, absorbing whatever that last fear of his was.

"I promise," I whispered, and it was the absolute truth.

I felt that smile, too, and the way the tension in his shoulders released. I felt the soft sigh of his breath and the tug of his arms, pulling me and guiding me until I was on his lap, legs on either side of his thighs as he kissed me again and again.

For a heartbeat, things felt right in the world, at least in the little space that was occupied by me and Jimmy. His hands wandered along my body, exploring my curves in a purposeful yet luxuriating way. I had a hand on either side of his face, holding it as he touched me and kissed me and comforted me, losing myself in the feel of him, forgetting the pain and heartbreak and stress for a moment.

Just a heartbeat.

A hand ended up beneath my shirt and immediately moved towards my bra. As it cupped my breast, I felt a twitch beneath me, excitement making itself known as he touched me. I couldn't keep myself from shifting, letting that burgeoning bulge press against the junction of my thighs, almost teasing myself as I thought of how good that would feel pressed against something a little more... internal.

He groaned and his bulge grew, as did my need to feel it. He slipped his hand beneath my bra, toying with my nipple piercing before running the pad of his thumb along the hardened nub. It was a sensitive spot, which he apparently knew; need *roared* through my body and I whimpered against his mouth.

"Kelsie," he breathed.

"I want you, Jimbo," I murmured, and somehow the way his laughter vibrated against me was the sexiest thing I'd ever heard.

It didn't last long. The laughter turned into a throatier noise as I let my fingers trail down his chest and stomach, moving back on his lap just enough that I could get my hands on the button of his jeans. I managed to unbutton it before he guided my hands away so he could lift my shirt over my head. Before I could resume working on his pants, he unhooked my bra, eagerly sliding it down my arms before stopping to look at my breasts with an expression of unwarranted awe.

I waited, amused, until he looked up at me.

"No, no," I said. "Take your time. No rush."

He smirked. "You know how long I've wanted to see your tits?"

"You saw my tits the first time we met."

He shook his head, moving his hand up to my left breast. "I saw the outline of your tits. All I had to go off of was a general size and shape and the fact that I was pretty sure you had pierced nipples. You know how long I spent trying to picture the real thing?"

I raised an eyebrow, shuddering as he passed his thumb over my nipple again. "How close was your imagination?"

He glanced up, a wicked look on his face. "My wildest dreams didn't even come close to how fucking sexy you are."

Oh, was he ever a charmer. But before I could respond with anything, he'd dipped his head forward and taken my nipple into his mouth.

It took everything in me to stifle a moan. When I'd decided to celebrate my liberation from Daniel by piercing every part of me that I could, I hadn't expected my nipples to become so impossible sensitive, but they had, and there was a reason they were my favorite piercings now. I was almost certain with the right touch, I could orgasm just from playing with them.

I never had, but not for lack of trying.

In any case, the sensation of Jimmy's tongue toying with my piercing before sucking my nipple lightly was as close to heaven as I could imagine. His eyes flicked up as I tried to keep quiet, sparkling in a mischievous and adoring way, and before I could lose too much of my mind, I moved my hand back between us so I could work his cock out of his jeans.

He sighed in relief as I released him, warmth brushing against my breast before he went back to playing with my nipple. His cock was rock hard, already throbbing and hot as I wrapped my hand around his shaft. A battle seemed to roar inside of me, part of me dead set on getting his wonderfully thick cock back in my mouth. A second part of me was determined to sit on it as soon as humanly possible so I could feel my pussy stretch around him. And there was a final part of me reluctant to do anything but stroke him so I didn't have to stop him from sucking on my tits.

Fortunately—or, far more accurately, unfortunately—I didn't end up having to decide.

"What the *fuck*?" came a disgusted voice from behind us, and I almost tore my nipple off as I whirled around to see a furious-looking Em and a stunned-looking Alex standing in the hallway.

And instead of answering, I made the very well thought out decision to belatedly cover my tits with my hands as every fear, worry, and nightmare came to life at once.

"Wait, I got this," Jimmy said, tucking his dick back in his jeans as he stood up. "Em, before you freak out, remember that time you fucked my boss and the guy who ruined my career and they were the same guy?"

"Uh, man, I'm right here," Alex said, but his voice was practically drowned out by the daggers Em was glaring at me.

"You've got to be kidding me," she said. "I have been freaking out trying to get ahold of you after getting a cryptic fucking phone call and for what? To come home and find you fucking my *brother*?"

"Technically we weren't fucking," Jimmy said, and I was torn between wanting to slap him for being a moron and slap myself for believing he was as mature as he thought he was.

Luckily, Em ignored him. "So what's this about? Payback? Is this why you called, to tell me you're going to hook up with my—Jesus Christ, Kelsie, he's *twenty-one*."

"Em, calm down for a sec," Jimmy said. "This isn't what—"

"I do not even give a shit what you have to say right now," she snapped.

"Maybe you should at least give Kelsie a second to put her shirt back on," Alex suggested, so level-headed it was almost timid.

"Maybe she shouldn't have taken it off around *my brother*!" Em shot back.

There was going to be no explaining.

There was going to be no understanding.

And given the shade of red on her face and the anger practically pouring off of her, there was going to be no chance of repairing our friendship.

That was okay. I'd kind of assumed that was the case. It just hurt a little more now that I knew I'd been wrong and there might have been a chance.

Jimmy and I had made every attempt to remain quiet since Leia was sleeping down the hall, which Em pointed out loudly a number of times as she ranted. She managed to hit all the notes: how disgusting this made me, how much of a betrayal this was, how she didn't think I was so petty that I'd pull some bullshit like this but she guessed that it made sense given how ridiculous I'd been about the concert tickets.

And he tried to defend me. His face turned the same shade of red as Em's, but she had the unique position of being both his sister and, at one point, his guardian. That meant an assault on Jimmy triggered the mama-bear response, regardless of his feelings on the matter, and there was no getting through the rage I'd managed to trigger in her.

Still, it was kind of nice that he tried, and the two of them turning on each other gave me an opportunity to finally pull my shirt on without everyone staring at me. Not that it mattered, since Alex was the only person in the room who hadn't seen my tits, but for some reason I was feeling a little self-conscious.

It wasn't until I stood up and grabbed my purse that Em took notice of me again, stopping halfway through a tirade directed at Jimmy to set her sights on me again.

"Where do you think you're going?" she asked.

Somehow, I managed to find my voice. "I'm leaving."

"Don't go," Jimmy said harshly. "Em, calm down for five fucking seconds and *listen*, would you?"

Em did not calm down or listen for five fucking seconds, instead ignoring Jimmy as she snorted her derision at me. "You're that selfish that you're going to go wake up Baylee in the middle of the night during a sleepover so you can storm out? Because somehow I doubt you're planning on coming to get her in the morning."

There was a beat of silence, a heavy sort of expectation in the air as I felt three sets of eyes bearing down on me.

"Em," Jimmy said miserably.

I swallowed back the pain and put my purse over my shoulder.

"Baylee's not here," I said, then walked towards the door.

"What?" Em said. "What do you mean, Baylee's not here?"

I ignored her, slipping my shoes on as I fought to keep from crying.

"Kelsie, tell me what the *fuck* you mean!" she demanded.

"Leave me the fuck alone," I snapped.

"Mom?" a sleepy voice asked from the hallway. "Why're you yelling?"

"For fuck's sake," Em muttered. "Leia, go to bed, please."

"Why's Kelsie here?"

Fuck if I wasn't asking myself the same question.

Before anyone could answer, I grabbed my jacket and shoved the front door open, golden light following me down the sidewalk until the door slammed behind me and I was left in the lonely silence, my life in ruins around me.

Nineteen

I SPENT THE NIGHT in a darkness that was void of movement, dreams, and emotions.

One night earlier, I'd barely slept, memories and fears and regrets blanketing themselves over my ability to sleep. And things had only gotten worse since then, so it would stand to reason that I was in for another sleepless night wrapped up in shrouds of angst and anger, grief and guilt, sorrow and shame.

But I slept. After leaving Em and Alex's, I got myself home, tracked down the old iPhone I'd had when I first left Daniel that still *technically* functioned, and put my SIM card in that. Then I plugged it in to charge, stripped naked, sat down on my bed, and woke up the next morning.

I suppose it made sense. There was only so much the human mind could handle before simply shutting down, and that's the point I was at. I mean, there was rock bottom, and then there was wherever the fuck I was. Hell, I supposed. It wasn't fair, nor did it seem reasonable, nor even fucking realistic for all this to happen to one person, yet there I was, surviving it.

At least I could say that.

I survived it.

Barely.

When I woke up the next morning, I panicked upon seeing multiple missed calls from numbers I didn't have saved on my phone, thinking I'd missed Baylee's call. Thankfully, before I frantically called any of the numbers back, the screen lit up and flashed Daniel's name at me.

Of course *his* number was saved on this phone.

Our call was quick and after I hung up, I took more than just a hysterical glance at the screen and realized I recognized both of the numbers I'd missed calls from. Well, I recognized them after realizing both numbers had also texted me.

Did you make it home? I'm sorry if you didn't want me to but I had to tell Em about what happened. She thought Baylee was dead or something.

Answer your phone please. Jimmy told me what happened and I'm sorry, okay? Let me help.

Shit. Your phone's broken. You probably can't see this.

Okay Jimmy also just told me that you broke your phone. On the off chance this goes through, head's up that I'm coming over to check on you now.

Kelsie. Let me in.

Please.

I couldn't tell when the messages had been sent, but it looked like they were from the night before. Not that it mattered.

I wasn't ready to let anyone in.

There were more texts from both of them, but I ignored them and got out of bed. I wasn't quite sure what I was feeling. Maybe partially numb, my emotions not recovered yet from the overwhelming ride they'd been on the day before. Or maybe just quietly resigned, having made it through the night. And maybe even better, in a way, now that I was removed from the chaos and drama. Now that I'd heard my daughter wish me a good day. Now that I knew where I stood with Em and where I had to stand with Jimmy.

Or maybe it was a mix of all three with a dash of delusion so I could try to protect my heart as it mended itself.

In any case, I bustled around my bedroom mindlessly, putting on my work uniform and brushing my hair, eyeing the roots that were creeping into the faded pink color and debating what color I should dye it next. Green seemed festive, but I'd done green before and it tended to fade to a gross-looking color.

Maybe blue, since it was about to be a blue, blue, blue Christmas for me.

My boss was surprised to see me but didn't say anything as I buried myself in work. There wasn't much of it, to be honest; with working all those extra hours and the fact that most stores were already overstocked with our product this close to Christmas, things were pretty manageable.

But there was enough that I kept myself distracted from the chaos that was my personal life for most of the day, though once three o'clock hit and I was faced with either going home or sweeping the warehouse floor for the third time, I decided it was time to leave.

"Have a good Christmas," my boss said as I collected my things from the office.

"You're off next week?" I asked.

She shook her head. "You are. Happy Holidays." I must have looked shocked because she laughed. "Hardly anyone was going to be here anyway since school's out, so I decided we're going to close for the week."

"But—"

"It's paid time off, Kels. Everyone's off for the week and trust me, you need the break more than anyone." She stood and walked around the desk, holding out a festive red envelope. "Your work this season wasn't unnoticed. Thank you."

I took the envelope and opened it, smiling at the sparkly-yet-generic card before laughing at one of the items enclosed.

"Red Lobster," I said, picking up the gift card. "You know me too well."

"That's for you to take out Baylee," my boss said. "The rest is your bonus and that comes with strict instructions to treat *yourself*, understand?"

I unfolded the second enclosed item, which turned out to be a check stub showing a bonus that had been deposited into my account. A *large* bonus. I looked up, eyes wide.

"This is—"

"—too generous, very kind, unexpected, blah blah blah," she said, waving her hand. "Don't get all gushy on me. Just take some time to relax, spoil yourself for once, and I'll see you after Christmas."

I almost hugged her, then hesitated, then decided fuck it and hugged her anyway.

On my way home, I stopped at the mall and put that bonus towards a new phone, which I figured met my boss's requirements since technically the shitty old iPhone I had still *worked* so it wasn't like a brand-new phone was necessary. And I got myself a cute new case for it, too, and stopped by the Chinese food restaurant in the food court and treated myself to an early dinner.

After all, she'd said the Red Lobster gift card was for me to take out Baylee, so I couldn't spend the entire thing on fried shrimp and biscuits, as much as I might want to be selfish about it.

When I got home a short while later, I was feeling alright. Not great, not outstanding, not even necessarily good, but alright. And that was something.

And then it was nothing.

"I thought you'd taken the day off."

I stopped on my sidewalk, staring at Em as she sat on my front step. She didn't look up at me, instead staring at the plastic rock in her hands as she idly fidgeted with it.

My spare key.

"Who told you that?" I finally managed to ask.

"Leia. She heard you tell Baylee when you picked her up at school yesterday." Em stood up and held the rock out. "You need to hide this better."

I took it from her hesitantly. "Why didn't you let yourself in?"

"Because I'm not a presumptuous asshole who assumed you'd be okay with me letting myself into your house."

I toyed with the piercing in my lip. "How long have you been waiting?"

"Long enough that I almost considered becoming a presumptuous asshole. Can I use your bathroom?"

My face twitched into an almost-smile. "Sure."

It was almost absurd, the way she followed me into the house both casually and not, like nothing should be different and yet everything was. It was stupid little things, like the familiar way Em rested her hand against the wall so she could slide her boots off juxtaposed with my memory of Jimmy pressing me against that very same wall. Or the way she led herself to my bathroom without a second thought, my house as familiar to her as her own had been, only to return to the kitchen when she was done and hover restlessly.

I had a choice to make, just then. I could choose anger. No one would blame me, not for a second. Not after everything that had happened and after what Em had said. Anger was practically the logical choice in all of this. And even if I didn't choose anger, Em might.

But anger wouldn't get me anywhere, and as I'd proved time and time again, I was inherently selfish.

So I chose to take the risk.

"Popcorn and beer?" I asked.

She hesitated, then grinned. "God, yes."

My almost-smile was a little harder to hold back that time, and I went to the fridge while Em found a bag of popcorn in the cupboard. Another familiar scene, followed by another awkward moment with both of us sitting at the table while the microwave did its magic, unsure of what to say and uncertain of who should break the silence.

When I couldn't take it anymore, I broke first. "How much did Jimmy tell you?"

"Most of it, I think," she replied. "But like, a high-level overview. Given how much there is to unpack anyway and the fact that he's my brother, I figured I could survive without the more gratuitous details."

I didn't even manage an almost-smile that time. "Right."

More silence, and then Em sighed heavily.

"Fuck this," she said. "Kelsie, I'm sorry, okay? I didn't realize all this shit you were going through and I said... I mean, that was the last thing you needed to hear and I blurted it out like it was nothing. I'm sorry I was a shitty friend and that you didn't feel like—no." She stopped and shook her head. "Not that you didn't feel like you couldn't talk to me. I'm sorry that *I* made you feel like that. I feel like shit about it. You didn't deserve any of it. At all. This fucking sucks and I miss you."

"I... thanks," I said, stunned by the suddenness of it all. "I'm... I'm sorry, too. For not telling you. And for what I said when we were at the coffee shop. And for..."

I didn't know how to finish that sentence. For not fucking her brother but trying to? For almost fucking her brother in her living room? For crossing a line I shouldn't have crossed involving, of all people, her brother?

Luckily, Em didn't seem to want me to finish it as much as I didn't want to finish it.

"I'll be honest, that was kind of shitty of you," she said bluntly. "Like, I keep telling myself that I know you're not the kind of person who would do something like that just to get back at me. But I..."

She trailed off and I gaped at her, torn between being understanding and being offended. Em glanced up at me, a pained look on her face.

"I hate that I have to ask," she said. "But just be honest with me. Was it—"

"No," I said, almost dumb from shock. "All of that started before we fought."

Based on the look on her face, Jimmy had not, in fact, told her most of it. "*What*?!"

Defensiveness crawled up my back and I felt my face turn red. "It wasn't about you. Ever. We... I kept saying we couldn't *because* of you."

"How long?" she asked with the same kind of horrified curiosity as someone watching a car accident.

I stared at my beer, desperate to take a sip only because my mouth was achingly dry but aware of how bad that would look.

"We kissed that one night the girls were having a sleepover at your place and he brought dinner over," I finally said. "And then we, um... also kissed the day Daniel brought Baylee back early. And then last night."

My euphemisms were not fooling her in the slightest, but she kindly didn't call it out. "I don't know if that makes it better or worse."

It took me a moment to process what she said. When I did, I looked up at her in disbelief.

"You don't know if me and Jimmy liking each other is a *worse* option than me fucking your brother as some sort of sick payback?" I asked.

"It was more the fact that you've been hiding it from me for literally... Jesus, that was before the concert," she said.

Oh. That made a lot more sense. So much sense that I couldn't think of a response and nearly dove off my chair when the microwave beeped to say the popcorn was ready, thankful for any semblance of a distraction. Em waited until I brought the bowl over and sat down before speaking again.

"Here's my issue," she said. "He's my kid brother. Like, legitimately. He's my brother but I raised him, too. So instantly, that means I'm always going to despise anyone who hurts him."

"I know, and that—"

"But you're like my sister," she continued, ignoring my interruption. "For a long time, you were all I had, and that means I'm going to instantly despise anyone who hurts you."

I wasn't ready for her to look up at me, her expression fierce but twisted with confusion and frustration and fear. I didn't know what to say, so I simply watched until she took a breath and continued.

"I had this whole big speech ready about all of this but knowing it's been going on longer than just last night, that's... it changes things. It wasn't some in-the-moment situation or anything like that. This is... like, you like him. And he likes you. This wasn't some one-time thing."

I fidgeted with my lip ring. "No. It wasn't."

She sighed. "I can't lecture you about being older than him because that makes me a gigantic hypocrite. Alex is basically twice my age. That's more than what's between you and Jimmy. And I can't ask you what you see in him or what he sees in you because I know exactly what both of you see in each other." She picked a piece of popcorn out of the bowl but just toyed with it before looking up at me. "Is this what you want?"

I knew what she wanted me to say, but I couldn't.

I wasn't going to lie to her.

"I don't know," I said honestly. "I don't want to hurt him and that's probably what's making this so much worse because I'm so fucking concerned about everyone else's feelings I can't figure out what *I* want. But I mean, that's also on top of everything in my life being an absolute shitstorm right now, so I don't think I've given it a fair amount of thought." It was my turn to look at her with a fierce expression of my own. "As much as I like Jimbo—and I do, okay, I'll be fucking honest about that because I really fucking do—if it comes down to having to choose between you and him, I'm picking you." A beat went by and I bit my lip. "At least, if all of this means we're friends again."

She raised an eyebrow. "So if we're still friends-off, you'd go after him?"

I shrugged apologetically. "If we're not friends, I care less about what you think."

Another beat went by as Em held my gaze and I held hers, and then she burst out laughing.

"That's fair," she giggled, grabbing a handful of popcorn. "For the record, we're friends again. If you're forgiving me, I mean."

I nodded, though I was suddenly nervous. "Does that mean you're forgiving me, too?"

"Yeah, of course." She shoved some of the popcorn in her mouth. "And I'm not making you pick between me and Jimmy. Just don't hurt him, if you can help it."

I nodded, but something was still nagging at me. "And what about what I said about... when we were at the coffee shop?"

She leaned back in her chair, fidgeting with the beer bottle.

"Well," she finally said. "I can't forgive you for that."

My heart almost fell out of my ass. "Oh."

Em looked up and I realized her eyes were wet. "There's nothing to forgive. You weren't wrong."

Oh.

Oh, *shit*.

"What's going on?" I pressed, scooching my chair closer to the table.

She smiled sadly. "I was pissed because you called out the exact things I've been feeling and was too... I don't know. Too scared, maybe, or too stubborn to acknowledge. Things have changed and I don't know if I like all of it."

"Have you talked to Alex?"

She shook her head. "No. It's like you said. How can I call out something that's doing good? Like, Leia wanted to be involved in a charity concert thing because that's something that Alex and Mike have done before. And what was I supposed to do? Tell her no, you can't help raise money for homeless children or sick dogs or whatever it was? But then it turned into this whole fucking thing and that was on top of the goddamn YouTube channel."

"I don't get it, Em," I said. "You were *so* against her performing and now—"

"I know. You're right." She ate a piece of popcorn and sipped her beer. "Like, I always knew she looked up to Jimmy. Her big rock star uncle who was *so* cool. And she wanted to play the guitar because of him and I thought, why not? Then I feel like I turned around for five seconds and suddenly she's all over the internet. And Alex and Mike keep pushing for her to do more and she loves it because she loves music but—"

"But she doesn't know if she loves it," I interrupted. "She's not even playing for real half the time. It's not about the music, Em."

Her mouth opened, then closed.

"Sorry," I said cautiously. "I—"

"You're right." She blew out a breath. "I have to talk to him. I was so... it wasn't all at once, right? Like, it was little things. A recital here. Then a concert there. And then a video because she wanted to show off her new song. And you're right, it's not Leia asking for it."

"She asks for a picture of the moon and Alex and Mike trip over themselves to bring her the real thing and all of the stars, too," I said.

"And Jimmy," she said. "You don't get to leave him out just because you're fucking him."

My face *burned* as she howled with laughter. "For the record, we have not actually—"

"TMI!" she said quickly.

"Telling you I haven't fucked your brother yet is TMI?" I shot back.

"Maybe not, but throwing the 'yet' in there was highly unnecessary."

For a long, lovely, wonderful moment, things were like old times as we struggled to stop laughing.

"It just needs to be dialed back a bit," I said when we composed ourselves. "Like, think of what Leia actually enjoys about it. Playing music with Jimmy, obviously, but she still looks kind of terrified every time she goes on stage. She loves messing around with Baylee. The two of them can spend *hours* dancing and singing and... I'd hate for her to lose that side of it."

"You're right," she said. "I'm gonna talk to Alex. It's..." She hesitated, then tilted her beer bottle at me. "This isn't a jab at you, so don't take it that way. It's just, this is why I wish you would've told me sooner. If I'm ever making you feel like you can't tell me things, please tell me. You mean too much to me to risk this happening again."

There was a lump in the base of my throat and I had to swallow a few times to clear it. "I promise, Em."

"I promise, too."

We clinked our beer bottles together and each took a sip. There was another silent moment, but not an awkward one. This one was comfortable, familiar, one of those silences between friends who have transcended friendship. I sipped my beer again, easing into that moment and knowing unequivocally that things were going to be okay between me and Em.

Then she had to go and ruin it.

"I don't know how to ask this so I'm just going to say it," she said. "What the fuck happened with Daniel?"

The mention of his name made my shoulders tense, my muscles almost groaning as any of the tension that had been relieved came roaring back.

"I thought Jimmy told you most of it."

"I mean, keep in mind that he told me most of it in the process of us screaming at each other in the living room while Alex tried to get Leia to go back to bed." Her face went red. "He was pretty upset with me. Rightfully so."

I toyed with my lip ring, not sure what to say to that, then sighed.

"It started with Taylor Swift," I said.

"I fucking knew it was her," she said. "I'm personally blaming Taylor Swift for everything from now on."

I laughed. Or at least, I tried to laugh. The tears were already threatening to start and there was a thick, tight feeling in my throat that made the sound come out choked and watery. Without saying a word, Em got up and grabbed the Kleenex box from the counter, bringing it back just in time for my regularly scheduled pre-dinner breakdown.

Slowly, I took her through everything that had happened. I didn't hold back a thing; everything from my inability to let my pride go for even a moment to the way I'd almost puked all over Mike's shoes when he told me the cost, but still insisted I could do it right up until I knew it was impossible.

From my first call with Daniel to my plan to work and work and work until I'd saved the money up myself. From the car accident to proving how incredibly stupid I could be when I thought I'd won after he transferred me the money.

And when I choked out that Baylee had wanted to go and that she'd been hiding it from me because she didn't want me to be alone on Christmas, she cried with me. She pulled me out of my chair and hugged me, taking part of my heartbreak on so I could try to heal, holding me up when I'd insisted I could hold myself up, and proving to me what a fucking idiot I'd been for not talking to her sooner.

"There has to be something we can do," she said, wiping her eyes as I finished speaking. "He can't get away with this. There's no way."

"He already has, Em," I said, mirroring her actions. "He made sure she wanted to go and that I found out when both he and Baylee were in the room so I couldn't even discuss it with her first. He knows what he can get away with and how far he can push without me being able to retaliate. I can't take him on."

She made some half-hearted suggestions, but there wasn't anything I hadn't already thought of. A short while later, Baylee called for her pre-dinner chat and discussion of the best parts of our day.

"Seeing Santa," she told me boldly. "At the North Pole. And I got to tell him what I wanted for Christmas and he said he was gonna do his best but he couldn't make any promises and I said if anyone could do it, he could, so I expect him to try really, really hard because it's not a present for me."

"It isn't?" I asked, amused. "What'd you ask for?"

"Mom. You know I can't tell you or it won't come true."

"That's wishes, sweetie. Not Christmas presents."

"Yeah, well, this is kinda a wish, too."

God, I hoped it wasn't the type of wish that involved her parents getting back together that all kids with divorced parents seemed to wish at one point.

I heard someone say something in the background and Baylee sighed.

"In a *minute*," she said, her voice just distant enough that I knew she'd moved the phone away from her ear. "I'm talking to my mom." There was a pause, and then she heaved the kind of heavy, dramatic sigh that only eight-year-old girls seem capable of. "*Fine*. Just let me finish." There was a rustle, then her voice was clear again. "Mom? I gotta go pretty quick. What was your favorite part of the day?"

I glanced at Em, who was pretending not to listen as she sat at the table.

"You know, sweetie, I think my favorite was getting to visit with Em for a while today," I said, who looked up as I said her name.

"Really? But you visit with Em all the time!"

"That's true, but it can still be my favorite."

"Okay." Another voice in the background and Baylee's voice went high-pitched. "I *know*! I'm talking to Mom!"

"It's okay," I said. "I'll talk to you tonight before bed."

"You mean you'll sing to me tonight before bed. No talking allowed."

"You bet. Love you, Bay."

"Love you, Mom." And then, just before the line hung up: "*Okay*, I'm done now, jeez."

It was because of Baylee's call that we realized how late it was. Seeing as Em hadn't had early bird Chinese food at the mall food court and also had a kid and a boyfriend to feed, she grabbed her things and started getting ready to head home.

Before she opened the door to leave, she turned to me.

"So, remember when you said you hadn't fucked my brother 'yet'?" she asked.

"Jesus, Em," I muttered. "I thought that was TMI."

"It's between TMI and Not Enough 'I'," she said.

"So exactly the right amount of 'I'?"

"Are you gonna see where things go with him?"

"I..."

"I'm not saying you have my blessing," she said. "'Cause that's a stupid thing to say. But if you and him are gonna be a thing, I'm not going to be against it. You said you like him."

I nodded again, swallowing back that lump in my throat. "I still don't know what I want."

"Understood." She slung her purse over her shoulder. "For what it's worth, he's miserable and thinks he doesn't even have a shot with you anymore. And I've never seen Jimmy so down about something like that before."

"Really?"

"Mm-hmm." She gave me a pointed look. "I'm not telling you what to do, but I know not hearing from you is torturing him. He likes you, Kels. He cares, probably more than he knows how to handle."

Long after she left, I let those words tumble through my mind.

The reasons I gave to Jimmy for not being able to be with him were, for all intents and purposes, completely addressed. Our ages didn't quite matter so much anymore, not when we were discussing the things that had forced each of us to grow up a little too early and a little too incompletely. And Em, well. She might not like the word "blessing," but that's basically what it had been.

Now, all that was left was fear.

After I left Daniel, I'd slept around. I mean, why the fuck wouldn't I? I'd freed myself from a marriage to a monster and for the first time in my adult life, I was single. So yeah, I fucked around, I had some fun and some orgasms and some reminders that sex was *amazing* when you weren't trapped beneath a guy who had zero concept of female pleasure, and that's where I left it. I had never met anyone I wanted as anything more than a good time.

So Jimmy, young Jimbo, twenty-one-year-old brother of my best friend, would be the first, if that's where things went.

And that was as terrifying as it was somewhat distressing.

Terrifying and exhilarating, in a way, especially because I had been telling the truth. It might have been the first time I said it out loud, but I did really like Jimmy. Up until then, it had been a serious problem with a simple solution: it wasn't possible.

Now, though. Now it was possible, which meant I had to make a choice.

I didn't know if I could ever get over my anger at Daniel for ruining the girl I'd been. I tried to find that girl again after I left him, but she'd been gone for a long time. Sure, she'd been stupid. She'd been a rebel, though at least it was with a cause. She drank and smoked and did stupid shit like most girls her age did, but most girls her age didn't have parents who subscribed so thoroughly and so mindlessly to that horrific level of indoctrination.

So she'd rebelled against that and in the process, trapped herself even further.

He'd taken everything that made me *me*, bit by bit and piece by piece. Some of it I knew was a sin to begin with; the church was very clear about drinking and smoking and premarital sex. But other bits of it were broken away by Daniel: the love of music, of bright colours, of piercings and tattoos and wild hair. Things that represented any level of independence, of individuality, of the girl I wanted to be.

I rebuilt some of those things when I left him, but I couldn't rebuild it all. I could dye my hair and pierce every flap of skin that was safe to put a needle through, but I couldn't give myself back those years of discovery, those vital times when everyone else was learning who they were.

To be so far removed from those years when the man I wanted was smack dab in the middle of them... Part of me wanted to mourn for what I'd never get back, and part of me was afraid that not having that experience meant there would always be something missing.

Specifically, that something would be missing between me and Jimmy.

So now it was up to me to choose. I didn't have the excuse of "you're my best friend's brother" or "I'm too old for you." All I had was a fucked-up life and the question of whether or not it was right for me to drag Jimmy into that.

Especially knowing that it wasn't the life he'd dreamed of.

It wasn't even the life I'd dreamed of.

I told myself I didn't have to choose right away, that Jimmy would understand and so would Em. With everything happening right now, it was perfectly reasonable for me to put off making that choice. I could probably have even texted Jimmy to tell him that.

But I didn't.

Instead, after Baylee called me to sing her goodnights, I hung up the phone and changed into my pajamas with tears in my eyes, miserably missing my daughter and seething at the disembodied voice in the background that belonged to my ex-husband, urging her to hurry up and finish so she could go to bed.

And as I wiped those tears from my eyes, I made my choice.

Twenty

"I'M ONLY GOING TO say this once, so listen carefully."

"I will. I am."

"Okay. You will always be too young. You—"

"We already talked about—"

"Jimmy, shut the fuck up. I said listen."

"Fine."

I took a deep breath. "You will always be too young. You will always be my best friend's brother. That's never going to change. And I'm always going to be too fucked up. I'm never going to understand what these things are supposed to be like.

"I've never had a normal relationship. Never. I don't know how and I'm past the point where I think I can learn. And dealing with that wouldn't be fair to anyone, least of all to you. Not when you can do so much better."

"Okay, hold up, that's not—"

"Let me finish."

"I'm not going to sit here while you say—"

"For fuck's sake, let me fucking finish. This is hard enough, okay?"

He sighed miserably. "Fine."

"I'm not telling you all this because it's fun, okay? I need you to know all the shitty things about me. I need you to know that I'm scared of hospitals. And that it took sleeping with probably three different guys after I left Daniel for me to realize I was having problems getting off because I was so used to being hurt during sex that it felt like something was missing. And that there's a pretty good chance there are more things I just don't fucking know because my frame of reference includes a goddamn monster.

"I'm going to cry. I'm going to fall back into my bad habits and let my pride get the best of me. I'm going to try not to, but I know I'm going to fail. I'm going to get scared and I'm going to bring up the same things again and again, even when I know better. There's going to be days when I get paranoid and I'm going to make choices that don't seem to make sense, even if they make sense to me.

"The best thing for you would be to find someone else. Someone your age who can give you more of themself than I can. Someone who doesn't have a psycho fucking ex-husband to deal with. Someone who can put you first. I have a daughter. She is always my priority. With me, you can't come first. You just can't.

"I'm telling you all this because I need you to know I'm selfish, Jimbo. Because even having said all that, I want this. I want you. I'm telling you all this because if we do this, if you decide you still want me, you deserve to know about all of this first. And if you still want—"

"Yes."

"I'm not done."

"Doesn't matter. There's not a single fucking thing you can say to make me change my answer."

I sighed. "This isn't a joke. If this is seriously something you want, then—"

"Come here."

I frowned. "What?"

He laughed. "I said come here."

"To... where? To the studio?"

"Nah. To your door."

I turned on my heel, eyes wide as I glanced towards my front door. "What... are you... seriously? I thought you were working."

"I left when I got your text," he said. "Em told Alex he had to be on call tonight in case you smartened up after you talked with her earlier. Now would you come let me in? It's fucking cold out here."

I stormed to the front door, my phone still pressed to my ear as my face turned red. Flinging it open, I saw Jimmy standing on my front walk, a shit-eating grin on his face as he took his phone away from his ear and slipped it casually in his jacket pocket.

"Hey," he said.

"You're a presumptuous little jackass," I said.

His grin widened. "Yeah, but you like me."

Well, he wasn't wrong.

I'd done what I had to do. What I needed to do to absolve myself from all the reasons I shouldn't want him. I'd warned him. He knew my deepest secrets and my biggest fears and even still, even with all that knowledge, he was standing in front of my door, wanting to come in.

Wanting to be part of my life.

Wanting to be with me.

And I wanted to be with him.

I barely had time to put my phone in my pocket before he was in front of me, taking me into his arms as I reached for him. His body guided me back into the house as he dipped his head, making me melt with his warm lips and squeal as his ice-cold nose pressed against mine.

"You're *frozen*," I gasped, and he laughed as he let the door swing shut behind us.

"Completely," he said. "Warm me up?"

Before I could answer, he boldly moved his hands to my hips and slipped them beneath the hem of my shirt. I shrieked, writhing as icy fingers met skin that had been the perfect temperature seconds earlier.

"Jackass!" I said as he tried to hold his hands against my stomach.

"Yeah, but you still like me," he said.

"True." I shoved his hands out of my shirt. "I like you so much that I won't even insist you get undressed like I was going to. You know, since you're so cold. I wouldn't want you to get any colder."

He smirked and grabbed at me again. "Oh, don't worry about that. I can brave the cold if you want to see me naked."

I slipped out of his grasp, blinking innocently. "It'd be irresponsible of me to let you do that, Jimbo. I'll have to find you some mittens. Maybe a parka. And one of those full ski masks that goes over your entire head."

"You wouldn't," he said.

"Wouldn't I?"

He reached for me again and that time, somehow, he managed to catch me. Probably because I very, very much wanted him to catch me. He pressed me against the wall, his hips holding me in place as he captured my lips again.

"You wouldn't," he repeated. "And besides, it's just my hands that are cold. The rest of me is nice and warm. Too warm, actually. Might need to lose a few layers."

"Mmm, well don't let me stop you from getting that jacket off."

He nipped at my lip. "Maybe I'm hoping you'll help me jacket off instead."

"Really? You went with that instead of 'I'm hoping you'll get me off instead'?"

His laugh vibrated against my lips. "Cut me some slack. I'm a little, uh, distracted."

He punctuated his statement by moving his hips forward, letting me feel how distracted he was. I made a soft noise as he pressed his bulge against me and he took that opportunity to slip his tongue into my mouth, flicking it against mine as he deepened our kiss.

That was it for jokes, at least for a while. I was distracted by his distraction, lost against his body as I imagined where we'd be in another heartbeat, and another, and on. He rubbed against me, little movements that made my body tingle, and when his hands slipped beneath my shirt again, I didn't shriek, even though they weren't much warmer than they had been the first time.

They warmed up quickly as he traced little patterns along my waist, bringing his hands up to my breasts. When he realized I didn't have a bra on under the baggy sweater he'd caught me wearing, he groaned and gripped my breasts, squeezing lightly as his hips moved forward again.

"Want you," he murmured. "Kels, I want you so fucking much."

"Already?" I teased.

"The fuck you mean, already?" he grumbled. "I've wanted you for fucking *ever*." He let go of one of my breasts, withdrawing his hand from my shirt so he could move it to my neck, cradling my head as he kissed me harder. "You have no idea how much I've wanted this."

And as much as I'd worried, as much as I'd spent the whole night trying to figure out if I was doing the right thing by telling Jimmy I wanted to be with him, I knew it was true.

I knew it was true in the way his lips moved, in the way he clutched at me. And in the way he breathed, in the very taste of his mouth and the warmth of the air brushing against me.

He wanted me.

It was my turn to guide him. I eased him away from me, just slightly, just enough that I could plant a final, searing kiss on his mouth before taking his hand. There would be time for the bedroom later; for now, the living room was right there, cozy and warm and glittering with lights from my stupid, ugly little Christmas tree. I led him to the couch, intending to make him sit so I could straddle his lap and pick up where we'd left off before Alex and Em had interrupted us the night before, but Jimmy stopped me before I could.

He kissed me lightly, then set to work undressing me. Piece by piece and bit by bit, he unwrapped me, taking his time and admiring each part of me that I didn't feel called for admiration. It was hard to understand why I felt that way as he looked at me, his eyes feasting fervently as they glided across my body. It was harder still when he touched me, using his fingers to map out every inch of me that he could, the piercings in my nipples and belly button his waypoints as he explored my torso.

I loved the way his hands felt, the slight roughness of his fingertips and the controlled yet eager way he worshipped my body. My body responded to him, electricity dancing across my skin as my nipples hardened and wetness started to pool in my panties. His hands kept learning every inch of me as he kissed me again, lips lingering enticingly before he pulled away and dropped to his knees.

It was unexpected and I watched, entranced, as he peeled my pajama pants down my hips. He didn't look up at me, just took in each new patch of skin he revealed, until I was left in my panties. That was when he glanced up, letting me see the stupid little smirk on his face before he pushed it against my mound.

"Oh," I breathed as he teased me through my panties, his tongue moving against the spot I knew had to be damp. The corners of his eyes crinkled and I knew he was smiling even as he kissed my pussy deeply.

My panties were clinging to my lips and he traced his tongue along them, confidently in control and not letting so much as a hint of his mouth touch my bare skin. I whimpered, toying with my lip ring as need washed over me, too nervous to grab his head and push him against me like I wanted to, but barely able to keep my knees from shaking as he played his little game.

Just when I thought I couldn't take another moment of it, though, Jimmy's hand began moving up between my legs. I swallowed hard, watching as his fingers walked closer and closer to my dripping pussy. First my knee, then up to my inner thigh, and then I was trembling as his hand moved higher, and higher, and when I was *certain* he was going to touch my pussy, he didn't.

Instead, he carefully pulled the crotch of my panties away from my lips, moving it to the side and holding my gaze as he pushed his mouth back between my legs. I braced myself for another round of his teasing, only to cry out as he plunged his tongue into my folds and started licking me *right*.

So fucking right.

I had no choice but to brace myself against his head. I just didn't. Not with the way he was eating my pussy like he was starving. Not when I was captivated by his gaze, dark eyes intense and boring into mine as his tongue lapped at me, greedy in its need to taste me and indulgent in its need to savor me.

When he pulled away, I couldn't stop myself from groaning in disappointment. He laughed, pressing a kiss against my thigh.

"I want these off," he explained, tugging my panties down. "And I figured there's this perfectly good couch right here that you could chill on so you don't fall when I make you come on my face."

The fucking *sass* of him.

But he had a point.

It didn't take long before I was coming on his face. I had no idea where Jimmy learned to eat pussy like that, but *fuck*, was he good at it. His tongue swirled around my clit before lapping at it, then dipped into my entrance before he started sucking on my clit. I could barely keep track of what he was doing, losing myself once he reached up so he could hold my breast and play with my nipple while he licked me.

That was probably what did me in, honestly, because it was only a few moments later that I was gasping his name.

"Don't stop, Jimmy," I whimpered. "Right—ungh—*fuck*."

And I swear, seconds before my thighs tightened around his ears and I clutched at his head for dear life, I felt the little jackass smirk again.

Not that it mattered. He could smirk all he wanted if he was going to keep eating my pussy like that.

"Doing all right?" he asked, sitting back and grinning with pride after my orgasm finished ripping through me.

"Mmm," I groaned, closing my eyes as I tried to recover. "Give me a sec."

"Whatever you need."

I flicked one eyebrow up, then opened my eyes. "Undress."

He laughed, startled. "Huh?"

"I need you to strip." I waved a hand at him. "You are wearing an unfair amount of clothing. *And* you've seen me almost-naked way more times than I've seen you almost-naked." I gestured at him again. "Pants off. Now."

I don't know if I quite *leered* over Jimmy, but I definitely indulged in the sight of him. Lights from the Christmas tree danced along every gorgeous inch of skin as he undressed for me. He wasn't so much thin as he was lithe, which was similar, but he deserved a much prettier word than "thin" considering how attractive he was. His stomach was flat but not overly muscled and his shoulders were pulled back confidently as he turned towards me.

And his cock was, of course, hard as a rock and fucking *delectable*. But as much as I wanted to taste him again, I wanted something else more.

"You should come over here," I said when his eyes met mine again.

"Yeah?" he asked.

"Mm-hmm. I want you," I replied. "Like, right now."

"I want you like, constantly." His throat flexed as he swallowed hard. "I, uh... I know you said you can't, um..."

"You want to know if you have to wear a condom?" I asked.

"I have one," he said. "And I swear I'm... you know. I don't have anything. But I wasn't sure if you'd want me to wear it."

"You were pretty confident you'd be getting in my pants, hey?" I asked. He licked his lips. "A guy can hope."

I laughed. "I don't have anything either. But it's your choice. If you're more comfortable wearing it, wear it."

"You gonna judge me if I don't?"

"Not even a little bit. I trust you."

He didn't quite groan, but I definitely heard a soft noise escape his lips as he joined me on the couch.

I finally got to straddle his lap like I'd planned to before he'd blown my fucking mind with his tongue, though I didn't sink down on his cock right away. I needed to touch him first, to kiss him and feel the warmth of his chest beneath my palms, to take my turn letting my hands talk. And he let me, far more patient than he should have been as I explored him tenderly, running my hands down his arms and along his stomach and through his hair before carefully positioning myself over him and sinking down.

His mouth dropped open as I took him inside me. I don't know if mine did or not; I was so focused on the feeling of his cock entering me, my walls stretching around his thick, hot shaft, that I could barely think. He hit all the spots I needed him to, satisfying that hollow craving I'd been desperate to fill, though it took a second attempt before I could get all of his cock in my pussy.

I sighed once I had, pausing with him buried deep inside me. His hands were on my hips but moved around my waist, pulling me forward so he could kiss me. We stayed in that heartbeat as long as we could, our bodies entwined and our lips joined, living in a moment that was just as it was meant to be.

It was just perfect.

When I couldn't take it anymore, I started moving, lifting myself before sheathing him inside of me again. Jimmy moaned, a lovely, thrilling, gorgeous sound that I *felt* surge through me, and I had no choice but to roll my hips faster, eager to hear it again. His hands moved from my waist to my lower back, then down to my ass. He grabbed a handful, making that beautiful noise again as he urged my body forward faster and harder.

Bliss seared through me, his cock possessing my body in a way I couldn't say I'd ever experienced before. It was insistent, almost demanding my pleasure, and I had to steady myself on Jimmy's shoulders as I rode him. My fingertips dug into his back as I realized I was going to come *again*.

I whispered it to him and he half-laughed, half-moaned. Sweet words left his lips, little urgings, things I felt more than I heard as I worked myself to another orgasm. I was close, so fucking close, when the words became more urgent and his hands tightened on my ass, the tone becoming more desperate and needy.

"Gonna come," he groaned, almost anguished. "Can't... *fuck*, I can't—"

"It's okay," I whispered, my lips brushing against his ear. "Come inside me, Jimmy."

He groaned again, then gasped, then made a noise that was astoundingly hot and tilted his head back. Moments later, his cock throbbed and I felt it as he spilled himself inside my pussy.

His face twisted in an eruption of torment mixed with ecstasy as I kept impaling myself on his cock. It was amazing, the sight of him, and the way his body surged. The sound of him, the feel of him, the way he clung to me as if he thought he would fall off the edge of the world if he let go... it was what I needed. I clutched at him as my second orgasm hit me like a tidal wave, washing over the both of us as I held him against me, quivering on top of his body as I finished.

Indiscriminate time passed as we sat on that couch. Slowly, the world reappeared around me, colorful Christmas lights caressing Jimmy's flushed cheeks. His eyes were closed, eyelashes brushing against his cheeks as he breathed steadily. At some point he'd let go of my ass, his arms ending up back around my waist so he could hold me close.

A heartbeat passed, then two, then more, and when Jimmy's eyes finally opened, he smiled at me through the heaviness.

"Can I stay the night?" he asked drowsily.

"You fucking better."

Both of us laughed, a tired sort of laugh, and all I could think when he kissed me again was how thankful I was he'd chosen me.

Twenty-One

Mom Guilt is real.

It manifests in different ways for different moms. I guess dads might have it too, but I wouldn't know; Baylee's dad was incapable of admitting guilt in any way, shape, or form, so I didn't have firsthand experience with what Dad Guilt might be.

But Mom Guilt, well.

Mom Guilt is the eighteen phone calls you make the very first time you leave your child with a babysitter, followed by the eighteen minutes of crying when you get home from wherever you were because you feel so bad for leaving your baby for The Very First Time.

Mom Guilt is crying on the toilet because you locked the bathroom door so you could get Two Fucking Minutes Of Peace, but now your child is sobbing in the hallway as the saddest little knocking sounds stab you right through the heart because they miss you.

It's hating yourself a little and then a little more when you indulge and do stupid things like get piercings because you trusted your ex-husband to actually pay the child support he said he would, and when he doesn't and you're down to your last pennies, you can't help but regret eating that slice of bread for breakfast because after dinner, your daughter is still hungry and you have nothing else to give her.

It's making those choices you have to make that hurt your child, not because you want to, but because sometimes what's best for them isn't what they want. It's telling your child no, you cannot stick a fork in the power outlet because it will fry your stupid little brain, only for them to not understand Why Mommy Is Being So Mean. Because they just... they don't fucking understand how electricity works yet, and when you remember that, you feel even shittier because it's easy to forget how scary and new the world is when you've only been on it for a hot minute.

It's counting down the days until they're eighteen and you can celebrate, sort of, because you got them to adulthood and technically they are Not Your Problem Anymore. It's knowing how *awful* that sounds, even though you know every parent in the world thinks the same thing at some point.

And it's knowing, without a doubt, that it doesn't matter if they're eighteen months or eighteen years old, that they'll never not be your problem anymore, and you couldn't be happier about that... but God *damn* if you don't want to sell them to the zoo sometimes.

Above all, Mom Guilt is unreasonable.

For example, when I woke up in Jimmy's arms the next morning, I really had nothing to feel guilty about. And I suppose I didn't feel guilty right when I woke up. Instead, I basked in the feel of his arm around me and listened to the steady thrum of his heart, trying to think of the last time I'd woken up in anyone's arms. Daniel had never been much for physical affection and the adult sleepovers I'd had post-divorce were less "sleepovers" and more "Okay, you're done? Cool, I gotta get home to my kid, see ya."

So, as far as the whole cliche of literally waking up with someone's arms around me went, there was a pretty good chance it was the first time it had ever happened. And as it turned out, I liked it.

I liked it a *lot*.

We had apparently been so exhausted that we hadn't moved an inch after I nestled next to him the night before, my head on his chest and his arm around my shoulders. It had felt natural, easy, like a routine we'd done countless times before and would do countless times more, even though it was the very first time. And I was content to stay there, dozing lazily with the occasional gentle breath brushing my forehead, but the universe had other plans.

At least, my universe did.

Jimmy startled when my phone started ringing, jostling me out of the half-asleep state I'd fallen back into. I snorted back a laugh at the confusion on his face, then flopped ungracefully onto my back so I could roll over and grab my phone from the nightstand. The screen was blindingly bright and I winced, squeezing my eyes shut as I answered.

"Morning, sweetie," I said.

"Hi, Mom," came the subdued response. "Sorry I didn't call right when I woke up."

My eyes flew open.

"What's wrong, Bay?"

"Nothing," she said.

I waited.

"I just miss you," she continued.

My heart ached. "I miss you, too. Is everything okay?"

"Uh-huh."

And then silence.

My daughter did not *do* silence.

Tension ran through me, so obvious that Jimmy seemed to notice and rolled onto his side, his forehead creased as he studied me. I sucked lightly on the piercing in my lip.

"What fun plans does Dad have for you today?"

She sighed. "I dunno. Probably boring stuff. He said I gotta go to the mall and get a dress for church with Grandma. I told him I don't like church and I hate wearing dresses and then Grandma said Santa wasn't gonna bring me any presents if I didn't go."

I swallowed back what I wanted to say, which was that her grandmother was a detestable hag who definitely didn't have a stick up her ass because that would've implied she was capable of unclenching her tight excuse for a butthole, and tried to sound comforting instead of disgusted.

"Well, don't tell your grandma I said this, but that's not true at all," I said, my voice almost instinctively quiet, like the sheer mention of the hag was enough to make me wary.

Her tone brightened cautiously. "So I don't hafta go to church?"

Ah, fuck.

"I'm not saying you don't have to go to church," I said carefully. "If you really, really don't want to go, you can try talking to your dad. But Santa will bring you presents either way. If he doesn't bring them there, I'll make sure he leaves them here for when you come home."

"Oh," she said miserably. "Well, I guess that's okay. But if I have to wear a dress, I'm not going to be very happy, Mom."

Her attitude was almost funny.

Almost.

We talked a bit more and I got the gist of what had her so upset: Daniel's mom had brought breakfast over and Daniel told her it would be rude to call me while Grandma was there. So she'd already been annoyed, and when Daniel told her she had to wear a dress—which she didn't actually hate, but she was going through a phase where she was trying to develop her own style, so being told what she could and couldn't wear was the real issue there—she'd gotten even more upset.

And then of course, Daniel's mom implied that she was going to end up on the naughty list for doing *one* thing after Baylee had spent a whole year being as good as she could possibly be, and Santa had told her the day before that she was on the nice list, and she still didn't understand why not wanting to go to church was something that was bad, and now she was panicking that the Christmas wish she wouldn't tell me about wouldn't come true.

I promised her she was still on the nice list and that I was certain Santa was still going to try to make her Christmas wish come true, but that maybe she should tell me what the wish was so I could double-check with Santa about it. She still refused, of course, but by the time I heard Daniel in the background telling her it was time to go with Grandma to the mall, she did sound a bit happier.

"Have fun at the mall, sweetie," I said.

"Maybe," she said.

"At least try."

"Well, *duh*," she said, giggling.

"Don't say 'duh,'" I heard Daniel scold in the background. "It's rude."

Baylee's giggles stopped and she sighed. "Okay. I gotta go, Mom. Love you."

"Love you. Talk to you at dinner."

We hung up. Frustrated, I sat back against the headboard, fidgeting with my phone as the Mom Guilt took over.

"You're upset," Jimmy said, propping himself up on his elbow. "Talk to me."

And how was I supposed to explain it to him? That my skin felt like it was crawling, that my stomach was roiling, that while I was lying in bed thinking how good it felt to wake up next to him and how much I'd enjoyed last night, my daughter was being made to feel like she was a bad kid because she didn't want to wear a dress and go to church.

As much as I tried to explain it, he didn't seem to get it.

"I should be doing something to help her," I told him.

"What could you do?" he asked bluntly. "Seriously. Like yeah, it's a bad situation. Yeah, your ex is a douchebag of the highest level. But you said it yourself, there's nothing you *can* do, not until he brings her back. You can't feel shitty for enjoying yourself."

"I can and I will," I said stubbornly. "Just try and stop me."

He raised an eyebrow. "Is that an invitation?"

My mouth dropped open. "An invitation for *what*?"

The shadow of a smirk was on his lips, as much as he tried to fight it back. "To stop you from feeling shitty."

I stared at him, speechless. I mean, yeah. It kind of was what I'd said, wasn't it? And what he was insinuating... I mean, it was also entirely inappropriate, but since when was I someone who cared about what was appropriate?

Very deliberately, I put my phone back on the nightstand, then looked at Jimmy pointedly.

"Let's see you try, Jimbo. Make me smile."

He didn't waste a second, getting to his knees and moving in so close he was practically pinning me against the headboard. Instantly, his lips were on mine, a searing, scorching kiss that completely took my breath away. A confident hand moved to my knee, nudging my legs apart so he could tap his fingers along my inner thigh.

"Is it working yet?" he murmured against my mouth.

"Mmm," I replied. "Not quite yet."

"Too bad," he said casually, grabbing my wrist and guiding my hand to his cock. "'Cause it's working for me."

I almost smiled when I wrapped my fingers around his throbbing shaft.

"That was fast," I said as he let go of my wrist so he could grab my breast again.

"Fast?" he scoffed, nipping my lip. "I had to sit there staring at your naked ass while you chatted away on the phone. You know how fucking hard that was?"

"I have some idea," I said, stroking him purposefully. "But no one said you had to stare at me."

"Like I'd give up the chance to see you naked." He bit my lip again, harder that time. "You know how friggin' hot you are? How friggin' addicted I am to your body?"

That didn't get a smile, but a rush of tingling warmth danced across my skin, bringing redness to my face and wetness between my legs.

His fingers kept doing that maddening thing, tapping along the sensitive flesh on my thigh, drifting closer and closer to my pussy but never quite making it all the way there. I kept rubbing his cock, the smooth heat of his shaft almost as maddening as the feel of his fingers, until I couldn't take it any longer and had to squirm in place, desperate for *some* kind of friction.

The slight movement didn't go unnoticed. For a moment, I thought Jimmy was going to give in and start fingering me. Those tantalizing fingers of his moved up, and up, and just when my breathing quickened and I was nearly quivering with anticipation, he traced his fingers along my pussy lips... and nothing more.

I whimpered against his mouth and felt the soft puff of air as he laughed.

"Working yet?" he asked.

"No," I muttered, fooling absolutely no one.

He slid his tongue into my mouth as the hand on my breast focused on my nipple. I inhaled sharply as he rolled the hard little nub between his fingers, mindful of my piercing, then ran his thumb along it quickly. That earned him another squirm, so sudden that I almost managed to push his hand against my clit, but he was too fast.

"Jimmy," I pleaded.

"Kelsie," he mocked.

"You're torturing me."

"Hmm." He ran his thumb across my nipple again. "We can't have that now, can we?"

"Not at—oh!"

I wasn't expecting him to grab me, moving me away from the headboard in one quick motion. Before I even realized what was happening, he had me on my back, and that was it. In that sudden moment of shock, I laughed.

Jimmy grinned triumphantly, moving between my legs. "How about now?"

I fought back a smile. "I dunno..."

"No?" he asked innocently.

I should have said yes. Instead, I *shrieked* as he tickled me, writhing beneath him in a completely futile attempt to escape.

"Now!" I gasped between what I refused to acknowledge as laughs. "It's working now!"

He didn't stop. "What was that? Sorry, you're going to have to repeat yourself, I can't hear you over all the laughter."

I managed to free one of my arms and clutched at his forearm, shoving it away. He retaliated by grabbing my free arm and pinning it to the bed. I tried to do the same thing with my other arm but barely managed to touch him before he was in control of that one, too. He moved it above my head, adjusting so he could use one hand to hold both of my wrists. I tensed, half-expecting him to start tickling me again, but he just touched the side of my face.

"You good?" he asked.

Confused, I nodded. Carefully, he pressed his lips to mine.

"Just making sure," he whispered.

There were no words for the way that made me feel. How could there be? How could a word ever explain the way my heart soared and fell at the same time? How could anything describe the feeling I had from something so simple as him taking that moment, pulling back so he could check in to make sure I was okay?

All I could do was smile.

He felt it and responded with one of his own. The hand on my face moved down my body, no longer teasing or tantalizing or tickling but simply traveling to its destination. He shifted, grabbing his cock so he could guide it inside me as he kissed me again.

It had started fun and silly and wild, but things had morphed, changing into something much, much more. It was only when he sank inside me completely that he let go of my arms, and I moved them only so I could wrap them around his body and hold him close as he began moving inside of me.

Nothing existed in the world except us, except lips and limbs, gasps and sighs, gentle movements as he entered me again and again. Hair was brushed away from my forehead and kisses found my lips, my cheeks, my forehead. He worshipped me as he filled me, completing me in a way that I didn't think was possible and was terrified to already start acknowledging. How something like that could happen to me, like this, so soon... there weren't words.

It amazed me.

He amazed me.

Jimmy's lips didn't leave mine as I came, taking my cries of explosive bliss for himself as he pushed inside me harder and harder. I hugged him to me, hands splayed on his back, his body giving so much to me and taking everything I wanted to give. His own orgasm wasn't far behind and as I felt him finish, his breath hot against my skin and his body stilling for a heartbeat before he thrust those final few hard, deep times, I smiled again.

He collapsed next to me on the bed, bringing me back into his arms as we both caught our breaths and let our bodies drop from the high we were riding. For a while, we didn't speak, just lay there, Jimmy's fingers tracing light patterns along my arm.

"So this is gonna be a thing, right?" he asked.

"What?"

"You and me."

Such simple words, yet they meant so, so much.

Especially because something was missing.

"'You and me' aren't it, though," I said. "I have a kid, Jimbo."

"Oh yeah, little what's-her-face. Brittany? Bentley?"

I rolled my eyes. "I'm being serious."

"You don't need to be," he said. "It's not like it's some big revelation, Kels. What do you want me to say, I'm cool with your kid? 'Cause I thought that was implied but if it's that big a deal, I'll say it for the record. I'm cool with your kid."

"Is she going to be cool with you, though?"

He paused. "I... what?"

I shifted, my face burning. "I don't know how to do this part of it. I've never, like, introduced someone to her. I don't know what she'll think or how she'll take it or if... I mean, yeah, obviously I want this whole you-and-me thing to work but I don't want to get her hopes up in case things... you know. But not telling her would mean we'd have to pretend like there's nothing happening when we're around her and Leia which is... it doesn't feel right."

Jimmy hugged me a bit closer. "We don't have to figure it out right now, you know."

"I know. Daniel's not bringing her back until the day after Christmas."

I couldn't see his face, but I almost felt him wince. "Sorry. I meant—"

"—that we can think about it." I kissed his chest lightly. "I know."

We fell silent and I was half-dozing against his chest when he spoke again.

"You aren't selfish, you know," he said out of nowhere.

I chuckled. "Uh, okay. Where'd that come from?"

"Last night." He pulled me in closer, kissing the top of my head. "You said it when you were trying to talk me into not wanting you. And I was thinking about it and that's like, a big thing for you. You say it a lot. And you're not."

I shifted uncomfortably. "I mean, I am."

"Not." He trailed his fingers down my arm. "You're not gonna believe me right this second, I know. But you're not. You do a ton of stuff for other people. Thinking of yourself once in a damn while doesn't make you selfish."

"Jimmy, I—"

"It doesn't. I mean, think of it. Think of *this*. Your argument was basically that giving me what I wanted—a.k.a. you—was selfish... of *you*."

He was right. I didn't believe him right that second. But I appreciated the sentiment all the same.

"Anyway," he continued. "I'm the selfish one."

I rolled my eyes. "How d'you figure?"

He grabbed my hand and guided it down his body. I made a noise that was somewhere between bewildered laughter and impressed astonishment as I felt his erection beneath my palm.

"You're ready again?" I asked. "Jesus. How do you ever get anything else done?"

My head jostled as he laughed. "The benefits of me being twenty-one, babe."

I jolted upright as I looked at him with alarm. "What was that?"

"What was what?" he asked, confused.

"Babe?" I repeated. "*Babe*?!"

He fought back another laugh. "Well, what else am I gonna call you?"

"I don't fucking know," I said. "But you don't feel like it's a little weird for you to be calling *me* 'babe'?"

He shrugged. "I mean, I'm not gonna call you 'mama' if that's what you're—"

"Not a chance. Not a *fucking* chance, Jimmy."

"Well, I gotta call you something, babe. You get to call me Jimbo and I don't complain."

"You can call me Kelsie. Maybe even Ms. Bauer if I think you need to be particularly formal."

He flicked an eyebrow up. "Hmm. Ms. Bauer. That's kinda kinky. I like that."

He said it like he was joking, but if the way his cock twitched beneath my palm was any indication, there was a lot more truth to it than either of us was willing to admit.

And honestly, given the way he fucked me after that whole conversation, I don't think either of us minded.

Twenty-Two

THAT WEEKEND DIDN'T TURN out the way anyone expected.

One might blame Jimmy on account of the whole "getting thoroughly and completely fucked Friday night and Saturday morning and Saturday morning and Saturday morning and Saturday night after he finished work and some indiscernible number of times as Saturday turned to Sunday and Sunday morning et cetera et cetera" thing, but one would be very, very wrong.

Or one might blame Em, since she was the one who had shown up unannounced to extend an olive branch so we could make amends, and in doing so, instigated the whole getting thoroughly and completely fucked by Jimmy on Friday night and Saturday morning and Saturday morning and... well, one gets the picture.

One might even go so far as to say it was Daniel's fault, depending on which point in time one was basing their expectations on, since up until Thursday afternoon, one may have expected the weekend to include plenty of cheesy Christmas movies and candy canes and walks around Pueblo to see the Christmas lights.

However, one would be wrong in all instances.

It was Mike.

It was all Big fucking Mike's fault that weekend flipped so suddenly and so jarringly that I nearly ended up with a concussion from the emotional whiplash I'd experienced.

"I owe Alex," Jimmy said, doing nothing to untangle himself from my arms as the clock ticked closer and closer to the time he had to be at work. "And he promised Leia they were gonna do something together today."

"I understand," I said, doing nothing to move away from him. "You don't have to explain yourself to me."

"I know." He groaned, finally shifting so he could get out of bed and get dressed. "But I figure it doesn't hurt so that when I ask if I can come back tonight, you're more likely to say yes."

"Joke's on you. I would've said yes anyway."

"Good." He pulled me in for one more searing kiss that lingered, and lingered, and lingered until he made a soft noise of regret and pulled away. "So I'll see you tonight?"

"You fucking better."

One more kiss, then another, then he really did pull himself out of bed and got dressed. I watched lazily, only getting out of bed and wrapping myself in my bathrobe when he was pulling his shirt on so I could follow him down the stairs and kiss him one more time before he left.

And one more time after that.

And then he really did leave for work, though it was at exactly the time he was supposed to be arriving at work.

I pretended it was the fact that he was late for work that clued Alex—and by association, Em—into the fact that Jimmy stayed the night, which she disproved the moment I picked up the phone when she called that afternoon.

"So you made that decision pretty quick, hey?" she asked instead of saying hello.

"What decision?"

"To fuck my brother." She paused, then gagged. "I can't believe I said that out loud."

"He told you?"

I could almost hear her roll her eyes. "Right, because I've had so much time to talk to him since he spent the night at your place and then went to work."

"Oh. He told Alex."

"I'm sure at this point he's told Alex so much that he's regretting hiring him, but no. He left work early last night so we kind of suspected, but when he showed up today—"

"*Oh.* Because he was late."

"It was more the huge hickey on his neck."

My face went red. "Oh."

There was a long, tense silence. Just when it started going on long enough for me to start panicking that Em hadn't actually meant it when she said she'd be okay with me getting together with Jimmy and wondering how in the fuck I was supposed to choose between the two of them, she started laughing.

"So you and him are a thing?" she asked.

"I think so," I said.

She stopped laughing. "You don't know?"

"Well, I mean, we did say that we were a thing now, so..."

"So... yes."

"I'm still kind of processing it all. A lot happened really fast."

"Hopefully he wasn't too fast, I mean—oh my God, I can't do this."

I burst out laughing. "Do what?"

"Joke about you and my brother. Ground rule time, no more telling me the dirty details of what you're doing with him."

"I didn't say shit. You're the one who—"

"Yeah, yeah, you're the one fucking my brother so I'm going to blame you for it."

I rolled my eyes, though I couldn't stop myself from grinning. "Fine. I'll accept it."

"Good. Wanna go to the mall?"

"Now?"

"Yeah."

"Today?"

"Uh... yeah."

"Are you insane, Em? It's the Saturday before Christmas."

"Yeah, and Alex and Leia want to have a—she hasn't called him Dad but I'm trying to mentally prepare myself for it maybe happening one day so bear with me—they wanted to have a dad-daughter date." She paused, sniffled, and when she spoke again there was a thickness to her voice. "Which is awesome, because it means I have no kid to deal with this afternoon and we can, you know. Hang out and pretend like everything's normal."

That sounded pretty good to me, so I took the shower I'd been lazily putting off and met Em at the mall.

I can't pretend it wasn't awkward at first. It was. Like, it was weird enough that we'd been fighting because up until then, I couldn't think of a time that Em and I had fought before. But to add in the Jimmy factor... well. We had only just made up and now our dynamic was already being shaken up again.

But she forgave me and I forgave her, so it was going to be okay. It took a little time, but that awkwardness left, and by the time both of us had enough of the throngs of people desperately shoving their way through a busy mall, forging and scouring through picked-over bins of materialistic junk that Em and I pretended we were too good for while conveniently ignoring the fact that we had already purchased most of our materialistic junk, things were almost back to normal.

"Wanna come over and drink beer while we watch a shitty Hallmark movie?" Em asked as we left the mall.

"Sure, but probably just one," I said. "I'm driving."

"Or you could leave your car at my place and Jimmy can drive you home after work," she said. "Since I'm assuming you two are going to fuck like rabbits whenever he's available for the next little while."

"I'd like to point out that I'm not the one who set and subsequently broke the ground rules," I replied. "But yeah, he's coming over again tonight, so—"

"And now you've broken the ground rule." She elbowed me, then looped her arm through mine as we walked towards our cars. "I missed you."

"I missed you, too."

When we got to Em and Alex's place, we ended up forgoing the beer for a much more festive peppermint schnapps spiked hot chocolate while we watched some movie where a strong, independent business woman moved from the city to some town in the middle of butt fuck nowhere to take over a failing flower shop for some reason that seemed to include impressing the local hermit-slash-woodsman who was secretly a prince.

"Alex is okay with alcohol in the house?" I asked as she refilled my mug and added a generous splash from the schnapps bottle.

"So far," Em said. "I didn't know if it made me an asshole to not want to give up alcohol but he said he could handle it and that it wasn't fair to me. So we figured we'd try it out for a while and see. I keep it out of sight and locked up, not that he needs that. I mean he's been sober for decades. But just in case." She shrugged and sipped her hot chocolate. "I trust him and I trust he'll tell me if it's an issue. Plus he's got Mike, too."

Fuckin' Mike.

"What?" Em asked as she saw me tense.

"Nothing."

"Kelsie," she said, a warning tone in her voice. "Don't keep shit from me. That's how we—"

"Fuck. I know." I sighed. "Just, do you happen to know if Mike got the check I sent him? I gave it to Jimmy on Thursday but I forgot to ask if he'd given it to him."

"For the Taylor Swift tickets?"

I nodded and she shrugged.

"I'll get Alex to check with him if you're too busy sucking Jimmy's—"

"Jesus *Christ*, Em!"

She cackled and threw a few pieces of popcorn at me. I managed to catch a couple of them, but a few bounced off my chin and dropped down the front of my shirt.

"Can I ask you something serious?" I asked as I fished ungracefully for the scattered popcorn in my cleavage.

"Can it wait until you're done feeling yourself up?"

I shrugged, grabbed whatever pieces I could find, and popped them in my mouth. "Now?"

She sighed dramatically. "I suppose. What's up?"

And as much as I knew what I wanted to say, the words didn't come. I pressed my tongue against my lip piercing, frowning as I tried to make sense of the thoughts I'd already put together.

"Kels?" she asked after a moment.

"Yeah," I said. "I just... okay. I don't know if it's too early to be thinking about this but... how do I, you know... like, when you and Alex got together and Leia..."

"Are you trying to figure out how you're gonna tell Baylee about Jimmy?" she guessed with perfect accuracy.

I nodded, tapping my fingers distractedly on my mug of hot chocolate.

"I think you just tell her," she said after a moment. "I mean, I know that's easier said than done. Alex and I stressed about it for ages. Well, I did, anyway. But like, I read articles and shit, I made pros and cons lists, I tried to think of every possible question she might have, and when we finally sat down and told her about it—" She stopped, laughing as she shook her head. "She just told me I had better buy more macaroni and hot dogs because she'd got it into her head that it was Alex's favorite food."

I nodded. "Yeah, but..."

"But Baylee isn't Leia," she finished. "And then there's Daniel."

"Exactly!" I almost spilled my hot chocolate. "Like, I can't tell Baylee not to tell Daniel about Jimmy, but if he finds out I'm seeing someone... I don't even want to *know* what shit he'll try to pull."

"Right," she said. "Shit. I meant that Baylee has a dad so she might... but yeah, that's worse."

"But I can't keep it a secret," I said. "I mean, it's not fair, but it's also not realistic."

She looked at me warily. "Because...?"

"Get your head out of the gutter. I mean that we see each other regularly because of the girls. And Baylee might not be *the* most observant kid, but she's not stupid."

"Ah. Right."

"And because I'm going to have a hard time keeping my hands off him since he's pretty freakin' hot."

Em groaned and threw more popcorn at me as I took my turn to cackle wildly.

"Ignoring that part of it, you've got a point," she said. "Leia will know something's up, too."

"But it's way too early to... to say anything," I said. "Right?"

She shrugged. "Maybe. But I mean, do you think Baylee's going to be upset or excited about it?"

I shook my head. "I have no idea. I know she likes Jimmy, so I doubt she's going to be upset, but I don't know. And if she's excited, that's great... unless something, um, doesn't work out."

She sipped her hot chocolate, studying me over the rim of the mug. "Are you saying that because you're not sure if you want to be with him or—"

"No," I said firmly. "I do. A lot. But if he doesn't—"

"He does." She put the mug down on the coffee table. "Look, if you think Baylee's unobservant, you should see Alex sometimes. He didn't notice the hickey until after he figured it out. He said that Jimmy's practically glowing, Kels. Like his feet aren't even touching the ground, he's so fucking happy."

"Huh. I didn't think I was that good in the sack," I muttered.

"You know damn well it's about way more than how good of a fuck you are," she said. "So unless you're planning on keeping this from the girls for ages while you try to figure out something that everyone else already knows, that's a non-issue."

I toyed with my lip ring and didn't say anything.

"You have enough other shit to stress about," she said. "You don't need to add this to it. If you want my opinion, tell the girls. Maybe after Christmas since... I mean, Leia shouldn't find out before Baylee does. Whether you do or you don't, it's going to be the right decision and it's going to be the wrong decision. You never know what's going to fuck a kid up, but at the end of it all, Baylee's always going to know you tried to do what was best for her."

And she had a point. A really good point. So when Jimmy picked me up later that night after work, though thankfully before Alex and Leia had returned, I told him what I'd decided.

Well, not while we were driving. While we were driving, I made it clear I'd probably had one too many spiked peppermint hot chocolates and told him what I was going to do to his cock when we got back to my place.

And then when we got back to my place, I did all those things I told him I was going to do to his cock, which involved trying to suck every last drop of cum out of him as he sat on the couch in the living room, the Christmas lights twinkling in my eyes as he ran his fingers through my hair.

And once that was done, Jimmy had to hold me for a while as he recovered, murmuring again and again how amazing my mouth was and completely bolstering my confidence when it came to cock-sucking.

It wasn't until after Baylee called to say goodnight—thankfully sounding much more cheerful than she had when she called at dinner to tell me her favorite part of the day, which was slightly more cheerful than she had been when she called in the morning, though she did almost cry when she said Daniel told her she wouldn't be able to call me until after church the next day—that I mentioned it.

"I gotta ask," Jimmy said as I hung up the phone, laughter in his voice. "Ask what?"

"The singing. D'you—"

"Every single night," I said. "And I'll probably cry when she finally tells me she doesn't want to sing her goodnights anymore."

"Ah."

"And yes, I realize I suck at singing."

"Your words, not mine."

I rolled my eyes, then took a deep breath. "So. Speaking of Baylee. What do you think about coming over the day after Christmas and spending it with me and her? That's when she'll be, um, opening her Christmas presents from me and Santa."

He studied me, a half-smile on his face. "Isn't she gonna wonder why I'm there?"

"Not after I tell her that we're... you know."

"Fucking?"

I smacked his arm. "I am *not* telling her we're *fucking*!"

He laughed and pulled me into his arms, kissing my cheek, then my jaw, then my neck. "You're gonna tell her you're my girlfriend?"

Girlfriend.

It was such a stupid word but it made my heart flutter all the same.

"Yeah," I whispered. "I'm your girlfriend."

His arms tightened and his lips travelled to my collarbone, teeth grazing my skin lightly before he slipped a hand beneath my shirt.

"And I'm your boyfriend," he murmured.

"You are. Will you be there?"

"I fucking better."

My heart fluttered again and I pressed a kiss against the side of his head. "Good."

I felt him smile as he pushed my shirt up, fingers teasing along the edge of my bra before he delved beneath it.

Then, I felt his expression change to one of confusion.

"What the..."

I looked down as he pulled his hand out of my bra, accompanied by some exceptionally crumbled popcorn, and started laughing so hard I couldn't tell him why I had popcorn in my bra.

The laughter might have put his exploration on pause, but it definitely didn't stop him from continuing his expedition once I'd calmed down. He undressed me both carefully and carelessly, letting his clothes and mine fall arbitrarily around the living room until we were both naked, making love on the carpet next to the Christmas tree.

And that's what it was: making love. It wasn't fucking or sex or hooking up or getting off. There was no pretending it was anything less than what it was. I couldn't say it, not out loud, not so soon.

But I felt it.

And I was sure he felt it, too.

At some point, we made it back up to my bedroom. I wasn't sure when; time both mattered and didn't, not when Baylee wasn't home and Jimmy was occupying all my senses. We made love again, and a time or two after that, and I slept safe in his arms, his body curled up behind mine and holding me close.

And it was good. It was so, so good.

Twenty-Three

Since Baylee wasn't calling first thing the following morning, Jimmy woke up before I did. And that was wonderful because it meant I got to wake up with something hot and thick and hard resting on my ass and fingertips gently tracing patterns along my waist.

I didn't say anything as I blinked the sleep from my eyes, just luxuriated in the feel of him until I was ready to press myself back so his cock was nestled comfortably between my ass cheeks.

He groaned when I did, the pattern he was making near my ribs stuttering as he pushed himself forward. That hand began to trace across my ribs and up to my breasts, groping me with a sleepy satisfaction that was almost wholesome in its appreciation. I murmured my approval as he fondled me, playing with my nipples and dragging his fingers along my cleavage.

"Can I?" he eventually breathed against my neck, pushing his hips forward and grinding against me harder.

"How do you want me?" I replied.

He nuzzled against me, his smile obvious. "Just like this."

I almost protested; I almost asked him if he'd somehow forgotten I had a dump truck ass even though his cock was literally nestled against it, and that meant that spooning wasn't a position that would be possible. Thankfully, I didn't say anything, because apparently I'd forgotten that Jimmy had an exceptionally decent sized cock.

It still took some work for him to get his head inside my pussy. When he did, my mouth fell open. I *felt* tight, like I was stretching even more than usual to accommodate his thickness, almost to the point that I couldn't handle it. I whimpered as he pushed forward, his cock demanding space inside of me in a way I was all too happy to allow, and just when it seemed like I couldn't take any more of him, I felt his pelvis press firmly against my ass.

He held himself there, slipping his hand down my body and between my legs, his fingers clumsy as he shoved them against my pussy. It took him a moment, but he found my clit, making my body twitch. He made a pleased noise, then began to move.

And oh God, was it good.

His cock must have been soaked with my juices by the time we both finished; I swear I was gushing against him as I came, my body reacting in a way that was familiar in the most unfamiliar way. And when he finished, I couldn't help but think I would never get tired of the noises he made when came, or the way his arms shook even as they tightened around me. I wouldn't ever stop loving the feeling of him drenching my pussy, the way his cock throbbed as he flooded me with wave after wave of cum.

It was *so* good.

I was kind of hoping for a repeat of the previous day, a mix of dozing and fucking and soft conversation surrounded by sheets and blankets, and we seemed well on our way there when there was a knock on the door.

"Who's that?" I asked, frowning.

"I dunno," Jimmy said. "It's not me."

I laughed, then reluctantly peeled myself away from him. I took a moment to stretch before grabbing a pair of jeans and pulling on a hoodie as Jimmy sluggishly pushed the covers back.

"You can stay here," I said, leaning over and kissing him as whoever it was knocked on the door again, louder this time. "I'll be right back."

Thank God he didn't listen to me.

"Kels, your phone is ringing," he called as I reached the bottom of the stairs.

"Let it ring," I replied. A third round of knocking started, more urgently this time. I glared at the door, bewildered and annoyed and puzzled all at once. "What the fuck?"

What the fuck didn't even begin to cover it.

The moment I opened the door, a whirlwind of energy burst forward.

"Mom!" she shrieked, nearly tackling me to the floor as she threw her arms around me.

"Baylee," I said dumbly, looking down and belatedly hugging her back. "Hey, sweetie."

"There," Daniel said, folding his arms moodily as he stood shivering on the doorstep. "She's home."

I stared at him, eyes wide, thoughts racing through a blank mind as I tried to process what was happening.

"I missed you," Baylee whined, pressing her head against my stomach.

"I missed you more," I said. "Why don't you go—"

And then I stopped.

Because Jimmy was upstairs.

And so was Baylee's bedroom.

But I couldn't very well ask Daniel what the actual *fuck* was going on while Baylee was standing there because unlike Daniel, I had no desire to use my daughter's presence as a weapon or a tool or to make a point.

I paused long enough that Daniel took note. An eyebrow flicked up as he looked at me and my heart started to pound, so hard that my legs began to feel like rubber.

And then Jimmy saved me.

"Okay Kels, I got the last of those present—uhh, pres... presentations, uh, presentation folders put away," he said, thundering down the stairs and faking shock as he saw Baylee standing there.

Or maybe it wasn't fake.

Yeah, he might've been playing along, but it probably wasn't entirely fake.

"Jimmy?" Baylee said, letting go of me. "What're you doing here?"

"I was, uh, helping your mom with... with this thing she has to do for work," he said.

Baylee frowned suspiciously. "On Sunday?"

"Uh-huh."

"That's weird."

Jimmy chuckled. "Yeah, that's what I said, too."

"Right," I said. "Bay, go put your things away in your room."

"Okay," she said obliviously, and she grabbed her bags—including a couple I'd never seen before stuffed full of new toys and presents and clothes—and practically skipped up the stairs.

I waited until I heard her footsteps in the hallway before I turned to Daniel.

"You've moved your spare key," he said conversationally. "I was starting to worry we'd freeze to death waiting for you."

"What the fuck?"

"Language, my dear."

My face went red. "What do you want?"

"Nothing," he said stiffly. "She wanted to come home."

"I'm supposed to believe that after you showed up and fucking—"

"Do you always swear so much?"

"—took her with no fucking notice?" I said, ignoring him.

"Perhaps I had a change of heart," he said.

"Tell me the truth," I said, gritting my teeth.

"Perhaps you should have your..." He motioned at Jimmy, who was still standing somewhat behind me. "... whoever that is, go to the other room."

"Nah," Jimmy said coldly. "I'll wait here, if you don't mind."

Another eyebrow flick from Daniel.

"Jimmy can wait there," I said.

"Jimmy," Daniel repeated, then a look of recognition crossed his face. "Are you Jimmy Reilly?"

"I am," Jimmy replied cautiously.

"Hmm." Daniel took a breath, his mouth twisting as though he'd smelled something bad. "Well, Mr. Reilly, perhaps you can inform Mr. Acton that Baylee is home safe and sound."

I stared at Daniel, trying not to let my confusion show and failing miserably. "What does Mike have to do with this?"

During my marriage to Daniel, I got used to being made to feel stupid. He had it down to a simple look, his cold eyes full of a condescending impatience that used to make my skin crawl and my spirit shrink smaller and smaller. It was terrifying what that man could do with a look, how he could reduce me to feeling like I was simply a husk of a human going through the motions of life with no more sense of self than a cockroach.

He controlled me with looks like that, consumed me, used them as warning sirens to the storm that could come should I choose not to heed him. Looks like that would make me freeze, shake, tremble from across a room.

Looks like that had terrified me for years.

Right then, standing on my doorstep in the frozen air of a Sunday morning, Daniel tried to give me one of those terrifying looks. I saw the hint of psychopathy, the twinkle of a man who knew how to cause pain and enjoyed it, who wanted to throw some biting remark at me...

And who couldn't.

"You seem to have friends in high places that you don't even know about," he said instead, disdain barely disguised beneath the acute politeness of his tone. "That's very interesting, my dear."

"Don't call me your dear," I said.

He smirked. "My dear—"

"Did you not hear her?" Jimmy said from behind me. "Or are you that fucking stupid?"

It was a risky statement. It could have gone incredibly badly. I don't think Jimmy thought through how badly mouthing off like that could have gone, though I couldn't blame him. He'd never had to stand in front of Daniel, shaking like a leaf and staring him in the eyes while trying to keep track of where his fists were in case I had to duck.

But it didn't go badly.

Not for me, at least.

Daniel, on the other hand, had a strange look on his face. It took me a moment to recognize it as nerves.

"As I said." He stopped, clearing his throat. "Please inform Mike that Baylee is home. Should she wish to spend time with her family again, I will ensure we discuss it with plenty of notice."

"Would you like to tell me why you've had this change of heart?" I dared to ask.

"No," he replied. "I would like to say goodbye to my daughter."

There was no use pressing for more information. Daniel wouldn't tell me any more than he had to simply because something had caused him to give up an iota of control and he was going to grasp at any and all other things that he could control. Whatever Mike had done, it had shaken him, so badly that he'd skipped *church* and brought Baylee home when he'd gone to all that trouble to get her for so long.

It had shaken him more than anything had shaken him before.

And that was saying something, because the man who knelt down to hug my daughter and tell her that he loved her was not the kind of man who let much shake him. Not visits from police officers responding to reports of a domestic incident. Not being served divorce papers. Not the fact that he'd lost control of his temper and put me in the hospital. I mean, he was the kind of man who manipulated a girl for years and years, with no reservations and no repercussions and, most significantly, no regrets.

It took a lot to shake a man like that.

As he left, I didn't know if I was impressed or terrified that Big Mike was such a scary motherfucker that the scariest motherfucker I knew was afraid of him.

And I didn't know if I brave for all those times I'd backtalked to him, or just incredibly stupid.

I didn't know what he'd done, what he'd said, how he'd managed to track down my ex-husband and my daughter. I didn't know what connections he had. Jimmy didn't seem to either, not that I could ask him right that second, but when I texted him later that day, he swore up and down that he had no idea.

Alex might have known. He probably did. Em probably did, too. I mean, she probably instigated it; I didn't know how else Mike would have even known what happened or who Daniel was.

And I could have asked her. I could have called her and said Baylee wanted to play with Leia and then grilled Em for details. I could have pushed and pressed and insisted that she tell me what she'd done. I could have demanded that Mike tell me how he found Daniel, how he'd managed to do what I never could and stir up some semblance of emotion from the icy depths of Daniel's would-be soul.

And maybe I should have. I mean, knowledge like that could be invaluable. It could have changed everything. Whatever Mike knew or did, I could have used that to cut Daniel out of my life once and for all.

Or maybe not. Maybe Mike dealt in veiled threats and backroom deals. Maybe he'd manipulated the manipulator, somehow finding something that Daniel was afraid of and would take seriously. And maybe I could leverage that, find a way to make Daniel agree to get the fuck out of my life forever.

Because I was tired of having monsters in my life. And he was a monster, the worst of them all. I might have had all sorts of little monsters in me, but they were only there because Daniel had laid them there like little parasitic larvae. He was the father of my monsters.

But he was also the father of my daughter.

And if there was one thing I could remember about the girl I'd been before Daniel ruined me, it was that I'd hated being told what to do. I'd hated being told what to wear, who to talk to, how to act, and what to think. Daniel had done what my parents couldn't, which was to break me, subdue me, turn me into a docile little woman who would nod when she was told to and come up with excuses for her blackened eyes when necessary. And God help me, I would never let anyone fuck with Baylee's mind the way Daniel had fucked with mine.

Daniel got to me because my parents tried to force me to be the daughter they wanted instead of the daughter they had. Growing up with them was a battle and the scars from that had left me vulnerable.

Baylee would never end up with scars like that because there were no conditions for my love. She had it, wholly and completely, forever.

In my daughter, I saw the girl I might have been. And even if that wasn't the girl she wanted to be, that was okay; she could be anything she wanted. But I saw bits of myself in her that I recognized vaguely, like they were childhood friends who I hadn't seen in decades. And one of those bits was her inherent need to pave her own way, to make her own choices, to go against what people said simply because complacency wasn't in her blood.

I couldn't be the bad guy, not when it came to Daniel. Taking away her ability to choose to have him in her life would only push her towards him. I knew that as much as I knew I'd love my daughter with everything in me, no matter what choices she made.

There was no question that he loved her too, or at least, the way that he felt about her was the closest to love he was capable of. He hurt me, but he wouldn't hurt her, and that was what mattered most.

She would understand, one day. I dreaded the thought of the day she realized what kind of man her father was. I dreaded dealing with the broken heart caused by the one man in her life who was supposed to never let her down. But it was a discovery she had to make on her own, and when she did, I would still be there, loving her unconditionally.

And maybe that would be enough to patch her heart back together.

Still, maybe I should have asked Em and Mike what they had done. Maybe I should have known what kind of people I had in my corner. Maybe I wanted to know so that I could have that moment of vindication after all those years of putting up with him, so I could get vengeance for all the horrible things he'd put me through, so I could punish him the way he'd punished me.

But I'd already dedicated enough of my life to Daniel. So instead, I chose ignorance.

I chose hugging Baylee so tightly and for so long that she took a huge, gasping, dramatic gulp of air when she finally managed to squirm away.

I chose telling her to go upstairs and bring all of her new clothes down to the washing machine so I could sneak a kiss with Jimmy and whisper to him that we'd talk later and figure out a new plan for telling Baylee about us, oh and also, could he give me a ride back to Em's to get my car and pretend like he'd brought me home out of the kindness of his heart so she didn't suspect anything?

I chose to be the bigger person, to let the universe punish Daniel, to focus my energy on the things I could control—the things I *wanted* to control—the things that would bring me joy and happiness and all things *good* instead of giving one more second of my time to thinking about *him*.

I chose to be selfish, and I didn't feel guilty about it at all.

Twenty-Four

JIMMY AND I DECIDED to wait until after Christmas to tell Baylee about us, like we'd originally planned, and then promptly fucked that up.

The intent was to give her time to return to some semblance of normalcy. At first I wasn't sure if she'd need that time. I thought maybe she'd be regular old Baylee with her bountiful grins and bold statements and wild dreams, innocently oblivious to the chaos that had swirled around her life for the past few days. She was eight, after all, and maybe she would take everything that had happened at face value.

And she seemed to be okay, at least, for most of the day on Sunday. She seemed so okay that I almost wondered if I should bring it up casually, ask her how she'd feel if Mom started spending more time with someone she cared about very much.

It wasn't until bedtime that it became obvious that Baylee wasn't quite back to her normal self.

"I la-la-la-love you, my little firefly," I sang as I tucked the blankets around her and made sure the stuffie she pretended she was too old for was within reach so she could grab it after I left the room like she always did.

"And I la-la-la-*love* you, Mommy," she sang back.

She hadn't called me Mommy in a very long time. The word alone was still enough to trigger that tingling maternal instinct that something was wrong. Swallowing back my worry in the hopes that she wouldn't see it, I brushed her hair off her forehead so I could lean forward and kiss it.

"What's wrong, Bay?" I whisper-sang.

She was quiet for a moment, then opened her mouth. Then, frowning, she closed it before starting again.

"Can we break the no-talking rule tonight?" she asked.

I brushed her hair back again, trying to calm my own nerves. "Just for tonight."

Her mouth twitched and she nodded, but didn't say anything.

"Are you going to tell me why?" I finally asked.

"Uh-huh."

I waited for another moment as she seemed to think, then looked up at me.

"I didn't tell Dad I wanted to come home," she said. "I'm happy he did 'cause I wanted to but I didn't tell him that 'cause I thought Santa might think it was naughty 'cause he'd think I was being ungracious."

"Ungracious?"

"Grandma said little girls who don't wear dresses and go to church and listen to their dads are ungracious," she said. "And ungracious girls don't go on the nice list."

The fucking rotten old bitch. Two and a half *days* was all it had taken to make my little girl question herself.

"Your grandma is wrong," I said. "Very wrong. You're not 'ungracious' and those things aren't what make a little girl gracious or nice or anything."

"But what if it makes Santa put me on the naughty list?"

I glanced from left to right, then leaned in. "Tell you what. If you *really* want to know, I'll tell you how Santa decides who's on the nice list."

Baylee's eyes brightened and she nodded.

"You get on the nice list by doing good things for people and being nice to animals and always trying your very best," I whispered conspiratorially. "Santa knows when people try to do the right thing and even if we make mistakes, he understands. As long as you try to be a good person, Santa will put you on the nice list."

"Really?"

"Really."

She looked relieved for a moment before her face clouded over again. "Okay, but how did Dad know I wanted to come home?"

"That I don't know, sweetie."

She twisted her mouth. "Well, I'm glad he did. I dunno why he was so *grumpy* all the time. Normally when I have Dad Day we do fun things but now he wants to tell me what to do all the time and I don't want to listen to him. I think I'd rather be ungracious."

I slid my arm around her shoulders so I could hug her.

"Be ungracious," I said. "It's better than being disingenuous."

"What's disig... disjigin..."

"Disingenuous." I kissed the top of her head. "It means fake. If your choice is to be fake but polite or be yourself and be rude, be yourself."

"Be myself," she repeated, then untangled her arms from the blankets so she could hug me back. "I'm glad I get to spend Christmas with you, Mommy. Dad and Grandma are pretty dis-igneous."

"Disingenuous."

"What-ev-ev-ev-ev-ever," she sang, and I knew that she was going to be okay.

Still, I figured it couldn't hurt to let things settle for a few days before telling her about me and Jimmy. Once I was sure she was asleep, I called him.

"It means things for us—like, you-and-me us—have to be quiet for a bit," I said after I finished telling him. "I'm sorry."

"Don't be," he replied.

"It means we can't really... you know."

"Fuck?"

"I was going to say act any differently than we usually do, but it's good to know where your priorities are," I teased.

"My priorities are what's best for Baylee," he said. "You know what she needs better than anyone."

I couldn't hold back a smile as I looked down at my hands. "I don't want to feel like I'm making you wait for me."

"Make me wait," he said. "I don't care if it's a few days or weeks or months, whatever. Waiting for you is worth it."

He wasn't there, so he couldn't see me roll my eyes, but I did it anyway to cover up the way my heart fluttered. "That was cheesy as fuck."

"I can't help it if the truth is cheesy as fuck," he said.

"Smooth."

"You think so?"

"Mm-hmm."

"How smooth?"

I glanced towards the stairs, then lowered my voice. "Smooth enough to get your cock in my mouth, if you were here."

He let out a low, steady exhale. "Fuck. What'd I say about a few days?"

"Maybe Em will take one for the team and watch the girls for a while. Pretty sure she owes me at least one from when she and Alex first got together."

"God, I fucking hope so."

She didn't, though. Not because she didn't want to or anything, but because it was a few days before Christmas and so many other things came up that I almost didn't have time to refresh my hair color like I'd wanted to—almost. Even though they didn't live across the street anymore, Baylee and Leia weren't used to going for so long without seeing each other; between school and Girl Scouts and everything in between, they were together more often than not.

It worked out okay, though. The studio apparently wasn't very busy that week, so neither Jimmy nor Alex had to go into work very often. So it only made sense for them to tag along when the girls wanted to go ice skating and then see the Christmas light display at the zoo on Christmas-Eve-Eve. And even though Jimmy and I still had to keep our hands to ourselves and pretend like nothing had changed, it was nice to be able to *see* him rather than having whispered phone calls and text message conversations that I kept having to archive so Baylee wouldn't see them when she insisted on playing with my new phone.

Even though it was *really* hard to keep my hands to myself.

"You have got to stop walking in front of me like that," he dared to whisper while we were at the zoo and the girls had bolted ahead to get in line for hot chocolate, Alex following as he dug his wallet out.

"Like what?" I murmured back.

"Like with that fine ass of yours. It's driving me crazy."

"Don't look at it, then."

"What else am I supposed to look at?"

I snorted. "The Christmas lights? The animals?"

"There's Christmas lights here?" he asked innocently. "I hadn't even noticed."

I tried not to smile, but it was completely futile. "Stop staring at my ass."

"I can't help it. You keep walking in front of me and those jeans look so damn good..." He trailed off, then surreptitiously slipped his hand between us and down to my ass.

"You're torturing me," I breathed.

"I'm torturing myself," he replied, squeezing just firmly enough to make me stand a little straighter in the hopes no one had noticed the way

I'd jumped. "I thought grabbing your ass would help a little but all it's making me want to do is—"

"You two are taking some big risks right now," Em said as she walked up beside us.

Which was true, as much as neither of us wanted to hear it, and Jimmy reluctantly took his hand back.

"Sorry," Em said, sounding a lot more amused than she did apologetic. "What time are you and Baylee coming over tomorrow?"

"Tomorrow?"

"Christmas Eve? To stay the night? So we can spend Christmas Day together and the girls can open their—" She went silent, mouthing the words 'Taylor Swift tickets' "—at the same time? You said, and I quote: 'I'll be there no matter what.'"

"I didn't know if that was still on the table," I said.

She rolled her eyes. "Duh, Kelsie. *Duh*."

"You're taking after the girls now?"

"Who do you think they got it from? Anyway, you might as well come over for dinner."

"What about me?" Jimmy asked.

"You can come for dinner if you want. I'm assuming you're going home after, though, since you don't want the girls to know—" She went silent again, mouthing something that looked a lot like 'that the two of you are fucking.' "Or you could sleep on the couch, I guess."

"I'll probably just go home," Jimmy said, though he sounded a bit sad.

"Sorry," I said. "Next year you can have the guest room."

"I can have it?" he repeated. "Where are you going to sleep?"

"Probably also in the guest room."

Before he could respond with anything but a smile and Em could do much more than roll her eyes again, the girls raced back with steaming Styrofoam cups of hot chocolate, smiles bright with sugar-glazed excitement as we resumed our walk through the zoo.

What Jimmy and I *should* have done was have him come over to my place after Baylee was in bed that night so he could secretly pick up the gifts that "Santa" was going to drop off for her the next evening. That way, we could have quietly fucked each other's brains out and gotten it out of our systems.

But we didn't.

Instead, that night when I couldn't sleep because I couldn't stop thinking about his cock, I got out of bed and dyed my hair—not blue, but a shockingly festive candy apple red—then snuck the gifts into the car and covered them with a blanket so Baylee couldn't see them when we drove over to Alex and Em's. My intent was to sneak them into the house after the girls went to bed on Christmas Eve. But of course, between the excitement and the Christmas cookies and raucous singing of carols, they didn't go to bed until quite late.

And then, of course, we had to wait while they giggled and chatted and tried to listen for Santa's reindeer on the roof.

And by the time they fell asleep, Em and Alex had already put Leia's presents out because it was much quieter for them to sneak the gifts out of their hiding place than it was for me to go outside and trek back into the house, so I said they should go off to bed and that Jimmy could help me carry the gifts in.

And I wasn't fooling anyone with that excuse, but even though Em and Alex one hundred percent knew what I was doing, they very kindly played along and said their goodnights so they could go off and fuck each other's brains out.

Which left me, Jimmy, and the dreamy anticipation of Christmas morning as the only things stirring, unless Alex and Em had a mice problem we didn't know about.

Jimmy wanted to put the presents out, so I leaned against the wall in the living room, illuminated only by the warm, twinkling lights decorating the tree. They flickered as he tucked one last gift carefully in its place. He stood up, regarded the display of gifts nestled beneath boughs of pine, then bent forward to adjust one of the colorful packages the slightest bit.

"There," he said softly.

"Excuse me, Santa, have you seen my boyfriend?" I teased. "I thought I left him in here but—oh, Jimmy! I didn't recognize you. My mistake."

He turned and tried to scowl at me, with little success. "You saying I look like a chubby old guy with a beard?"

"You look nothing like Mike."

Any semblance of his scowl disappeared as he tried not to laugh. "Sorry to burst your bubble, but I ain't Santa, Ms. Bauer."

"Too bad," I sighed. "I was hoping I could sit on your lap."

"Well shit, maybe I spoke too soon." He glanced down the hallway that led to Leia's room, then without another word, pulled me into his arms and kissed me.

And I kissed him back, melting in his arms as that one kiss turned to two, and then three, and then—

"Maybe we should go down to the guest room," I breathed against his mouth.

"So Baylee doesn't come out and see Mommy kissing Santa Claus?"

I smirked. "You're such a smart ass."

"Watch yourself. Don't want to end up on the naughty list."

"I would've thought you wanted your girlfriend on the naughty list."

"Hmm... now that you mention it..."

I nipped lightly at his lip. "C'mon. Come fuck me before you go."

He made the softest, sweetest, most enticing sound, then let me take his hand and guide him through the darkened house to the guest room in the basement.

We kept it down as much as possible, though in hindsight, there was no need for it. Alex and Em didn't live in a shitty little townhouse with paper-thin walls. On top of that, Alex was a musician. There was soundproofing built into the damn place.

But Jimmy and I were both a little distracted at that point, so we didn't think of that.

It had only been two days since we'd last been together, but no one would have ever guessed that based on the desperate way we were pawing at each other. Jimmy practically tore his shirt off as soon as the guest room door closed, dropping it to the floor as he reached for me again. Strong hands cradled either side of my face, guiding my lips up to his, capturing my breath and my heart as he urged me back towards the bed. I let him guide me happily, reaching down to unbutton his jeans as we did that strange, lurching kind of walk that would have been much more efficient if we would've stopped kissing for five seconds.

Except we had no desire to stop kissing for even five seconds, so "awkward lurch towards the bed until the mattress hit the back of my thighs and I ended up on my back with a half-dressed Jimmy on top of me" it was.

I spread my legs for him as he pinned me down, running my hands along his sides and back as he moved my hair away from my face. He didn't try to hide his eagerness, kissing me with earnest passion full of fire and need and exhilaration. I tried to keep up with his lips, but he wanted so much of me all at once that it was all I could do to sit there, letting him take everything I wanted so desperately for him to have.

It was a moment of whispers, heartbeat after heartbeat urging each other on. He nestled against me, the rigid bulge I hadn't quite managed to free before we ended up on the bed pressing needily against my still-covered pussy. That didn't stop him from grinding forward, seeking whatever friction he could and driving me mad with the promise of more. I pushed my hips up to meet him, seeking more as my panties started to dampen, and more as that hollow ache of need began deep in my stomach, and *more* as my pussy throbbed insistently, desperate to be filled with *him*.

With all of him.

And he knew that; I said as much, multiple times, pleading in his ear for him to fuck me, please just fucking fuck me, Jimmy. And I felt him smirk and smile and chuckle as he kissed my jaw and neck and collarbone, positioning me so my legs were hooked over his thighs while his hands indulged in the rest of me. Fingertips pushed beneath my sweater—an ugly Christmas one, of course, because when the fuck else could I wear something so wonderfully tacky—and inched along my skin, leaving a lingering torture that made me eager for more.

By the time he finally touched my breasts, I was a mess. My body jerked when he toyed with my nipple, then trembled as he pinched it softly, then began to quake as he flicked the pad of his thumb back and forth across the hard, sensitive little bud. My breath hitched and Jimmy hesitated; as soon as he did, I seized his forearm and looked up at him frantically.

"*Don't stop*," I gasped, and he immediately resumed, and seconds later, I was fucking *coming*.

His cock was still pressed against me, that much was true, but I was certain that it had nothing to do with the sudden pleasure overtaking my body. It was a familiar sensation in a way that was entirely brand new, peaks and valleys of intensity that threatened to overwhelm me before receding, only to crash back through me seconds later. I clutched Jimmy's arm, my eyes closed and my body quivering. It was only when I squeezed his arm harder and tugged it away because my nipple was painfully oversensitive that he stopped playing with it.

If someone had walked in at the moment I opened my eyes, they would have been hard pressed to figure out which one of us had just came solely by the looks on our faces. Jimmy looked mind-blown, his eyes wide and round and so hilariously awed that I couldn't stop myself from laughing, though it was an exhausted, stunned-sounding chuckle as I rested heavily against the pillow.

"Holy *shit*," he said. "Did you—"

"Yep."

"Just from—"

"Uh-huh."

"I thought that was, like, an urban legend."

"Apparently not."

"Apparently...?" He trailed off, then looked stunned as the realization hit him. "That was the first time you've—"

"Mm-hmm."

"Holy shit," he whispered again. "So *I* made you—"

"—have a crazy intense orgasm just from playing with my nipples, yes," I said. "Yes, you did."

"Holy shit," he said for the third, and then fourth, time: "*Holy* shit."

Had my mind not just been completely blown into a hazy, drifting sort of place, I might have made fun of his inability to say anything else. Instead, I reached up and pulled his face down to mine so I could kiss away his ability to talk while I recovered.

Those kisses turned to more, of course, and my hands wandered as I worked to remove the rest of Jimmy's clothes. It took a bit longer than I wanted because I kept being interrupted by Jimmy undressing me, but eventually we were both stripped naked, skin pressed to skin as we held each other and touched each other and enjoyed every inch of each other.

His cock brushed against me as he moved, hard and throbbing and dragging drops of pre-cum all over my stomach and thighs and pussy. And I was soaked, my pussy *drenched*, so much so that Jimmy almost moaned louder than I did when he reached down and swept his fingers along my folds before delving two fingers into my waiting entrance. His thumb lazily massaged my clit as his fingers moved inside me, filling me just enough to make me positively desperate for more of him.

"Kels," he whispered. "Can I, uh…"

"Fuck me? Yes."

He laughed. "Yeah, but like… in a certain way? If it's okay with you?"

"Stop fucking around and tell me what you want."

Between his hesitation and the redness of his face, I was expecting something weird. Like, maybe not weird-weird, but maybe one of those things that you don't bring up in the middle of hooking up since it might warrant a bit more of a conversation, like anal or revealing that you're super into electrostimulation or using Red Vines as bondage ropes or something. And had it been something like that, I would've been willing to forgive it. After all, Jimmy and I were both kind of new to this and I trusted him, even if his theoretical timing had been a little off.

But it wasn't anything like that.

"I want to fuck you from behind," he finally muttered.

"Like… like doggy style?"

He nodded and I pressed my lips together, trying not to laugh.

"I mean, yeah," I said. "You don't even have to consider it your Christmas present or anything."

He groaned, pressed his forehead to mine as a shiver ran through him, then kissed me one last time before moving away so I could turn over. I grabbed the pillow from the head of the bed and tucked it beneath me, got on my hands and knees, then looked over my shoulder at the man who had his eyes completely glued to my ass and thighs.

I didn't know what he was seeing, obviously, since my eyes were on the front of my head, but the look on his face told a story so clear that I could almost picture it. His eyes moved back and forth, taking in the roundness of my ass and the span of my thighs, which I knew were probably glistening given how glazed my pussy was. Then his fingers, again, spoke the rest of the story; he trailed them up the back of my thighs, mesmerized as he touched the scorching place between my legs.

Then he was moving, leaning forward and pressing a sudden—but not at *all* unwelcome—kiss against my ass before he positioned himself behind me. His hands traveled along my body again, touching my hips, my sides, and my lower back before lingering on my ass for a long, deliciously expectant moment.

When he was done caressing every inch of my ass, I felt him shift, then the heat of his hard cock was pressed against me. One hand was on my hip and the other was, I'm sure, wrapped around his cock so he could guide it into me, but I was so fucking *ready* for him that I doubted he needed it. His thick tip pushed inside of me, forcing my pussy to stretch around him. My juices allowed him to move smoothly, though he took it slow, letting me feel it as he filled me up inch by glorious inch until he was stuffed inside of me with his hips pressed against my ass.

"Jesus," he breathed when I moaned. Then, when he still hadn't started fucking me and I pushed back so his hips pressed against me harder: "Holy *fuck*."

He let me do that a few times, gliding forward before fucking myself back on his cock, before he moved both hands to my hips and thrust forward. I bit my lip, curling my fingers around the sheets beneath me as he did it again, and then a bit harder, as if he was testing to find out my limit. He was waiting, I think, for me to whimper or cry out or tell him to slow down or even stop.

But I had no intention of doing anything of the sort.

Slowly, his confidence grew, and those slow little thrusts came faster and harder until he was plunging himself into me. I could barely stifle my noises as he pounded me, my ass bouncing as his body slapped against mine. Biting my lip, I lowered myself, bowing my head and pressing my face against the mattress so I could moan a little louder without worrying that anyone would hear me.

Aside from Jimmy, of course, who heard me, then promptly made the fact that I was trying to muffle my cries irrelevant when he made a groaning sound of his own. Not that I cared because, honestly, the sound of him was just...

It was so hot.

I knew I was going to come again. I mean, there was no question about that. I was balancing on that line of desperate and overstimulated, my heart as full as my pussy was, my body greedy for the pleasure I knew he could give me. I braced myself against the mattress with one hand so I could slip the other down between my legs.

I fingered my clit for maybe ten seconds before Jimmy realized what I was doing and decided he was having none of that. Instead, he paused with his cock buried inside of me, leaned forward, and used one hand to shove mine out of the way so he could replace it with his. The other hand slipped around my body and up to my breast so he could pull me back up, strong arms supporting me as he began to ravish my pussy again.

There was no staying silent for me at that point.

His lips were on the back of my neck. He kissed me there, then moved his mouth to where my neck met my shoulder. Another kiss, then the slight pressure of his teeth as he bit down. And I have no idea why that was so hot, but apparently I was *super* into him biting me because without warning, I came again.

Hard.

Almost screaming hard.

Hard enough that Jimmy hurriedly moved his hand to my mouth, stifling my cries as he kept moving inside of me, and I was impressed that he managed to have the presence of mind to do that because even before I was done coming, he was shooting his load inside of me, flooding my pussy walls with spurt after spurt of cum.

My arms shook as I tried to hold myself up, my body heavy as those blissful spasms faded. Carefully, Jimmy lowered me to my stomach, still inside of me as I found my place on the bed. He kissed my shoulder again, then my neck, his breath hot even against my scorching skin. His hands moved to my back, caressing and massaging lightly before he reluctantly pulled out and collapsed on the bed beside me.

"Jimbo?" I murmured.

"Hmm?"

"That was fucking fantastic."

He snorted back a laugh, drawing me into his arms. "Tell me about it."

"Well, first you seemed terrified to ask if you could fuck me doggy style, then—"

"Ha, ha." He groaned, shifting again as I curled up against him.

"But seriously," I said. "Why were you so concerned?"

He didn't respond right away, which was strange. I frowned, glancing up at him as best I could considering he was holding me against his chest.

"Jimbo?" I asked.

His mouth twitched. "What's that rule about not talking about, like, previous partners in bed?"

I rolled my eyes and nudged him. "Rules are stupid. Tell me."

He sighed. "Does it sound like a humble brag if I say I've wanted to fuck someone like that for... like, way too long, obviously, but every time I tried it was... I felt bad?"

"Felt bad for what?"

"My, uh... I... Girls said it hurt," he finally said. "Because it's too..."

"Big?"

He coughed slightly. "Uh, yeah."

"Oh."

A beat went by, then vulnerability took over.

"Did I hurt you?" he asked. "'Cause if I did then, like, I don't want you to think you have to do it again."

"Not even a little bit." I pressed a kiss against his chest. "I appreciate your concern, but if you never fuck me like that again, I will be very, very bummed out."

He laughed, startled, but I felt him relax a bit as he nuzzled against me.

We stayed like that for too long, holding each other in the dimly lit guest room with the occasional murmured question and tender, honest answer. A while later, Jimmy untangled his arms from me, whispering some bullshit about how he should get dressed and go home.

I mean, it was accurate bullshit, but it was still bullshit.

"But I want you to stay," I said drowsily.

"I wanna stay," he replied, tugging his jeans on, then going to the bag I'd left on the dresser, digging out the pajamas I'd brought, and bringing them to me. "But this isn't how I want Baylee to find out."

I took my pajamas from him. "Yeah, but..."

He smirked as I trailed off. "But I'm right?"

I swallowed, then put my pajama top on.

"Stay and hold me for a bit, then," I asked. "Till I fall asleep. I sleep better when you're here."

And he almost questioned it, but he heard something in my voice that made him stop. Instead, he put his shirt on the dresser and climbed back into bed in just his jeans. I finished putting my pajamas on and curled up next to him as his arms settled against my body.

He was right. That much was true.

He was right, but that wasn't what had made me stop.

It was that he said 'I.'

I knew Jimmy cared about me and Baylee, even before "we" had become a thing. It was irrefutable, the way he looked out for both her and me. But that moment, hearing him say what he did—'This isn't how *I* want Baylee to find out'—said more than anything.

He was serious about this.

He wanted to make sure my daughter was okay.

He didn't want her to find out by walking in and discovering us together in a way that might upset her.

So that had touched my heart, which made it even harder for me to let Jimmy go home.

Which meant I pleaded with him to stay with me until I fell asleep even though I knew he was incredibly tired given the way he'd come inside me a short while earlier.

Meaning that it was entirely my fault that he also fell asleep and Baylee one hundred percent found out he and I were fucking by walking in and discovering us together.

Twenty-Five

I WOKE UP DISORIENTED, words in my mind that I had heard in my sleep, echoing and reverberating until I understood what they meant:

"Mom! *Mom*! Santa came while we were sleeping and—"

And.

And what?

And there were arms around me. I liked that there were arms around me.

There was a warm, sleepy body pressed against me. And I liked that, too.

Except that warm, sleepy body jolted upright, jostling my head uncomfortably.

"Shit," said Baylee, except she said it in a manly voice, which was weird because last time I had checked, my daughter did not have a manly voice.

And then I realized I was a drowsy moron and Jimmy was still beside me.

"Mom?"

I opened my eyes, my heart racing as I sat up to see my daughter standing at the foot of the bed, blonde hair flat on one side and tousled on the other, eyes as big as saucers as she stared. Beside me, Jimmy was frozen, though his heart was thudding so hard I could feel it.

At least he had his pants on. Thank God he'd insisted we get dressed.

"Bay," I said weakly. "I—Merry Christmas?"

"Merry Christmas," she repeated, still not blinking as she stared at the two of us.

I cleared my throat, trying to shake the sleep out of my voice. "I know you probably have questions right now and—"

"Is Jimmy your boyfriend?" she asked.

I looked at him helplessly. "I, um. I was going to tell you, sweetie, but yes, I—"

And then she *shrieked*, spun in a circle, and bolted from the room.

"Leia!" I heard her yell. "Leia, it *worked*!"

"What worked?" Jimmy asked.

Before I could tell him I had no idea what my daughter was talking about, a stampede of eight-year-old footsteps thundered down the stairs and burst back into the room. Jimmy inhaled sharply as Leia rounded the corner, trailing Baylee by mere inches.

"Uncle *Jimmy*!" she shouted.

"Oh, shit," floated an adult voice from somewhere above us.

Baylee crawled onto the bed and threw her arms around my neck, practically vibrating and speaking so fast I could barely keep up.

"Me and Leia both asked Santa if you and Jimmy could be boyfriend and girlfriend and he said he would see what he could do but that his magic powers didn't make people fall in love but Leia said that Santa could do anything so we used all our Christmas wishes and that's why I couldn't tell you 'cause if I had it wouldn't come true but I didn't say anything this whole time and it worked because now *it came true*!"

Somewhere in that string of gibberish, Em had raced down the stairs and joined us in the increasingly crowded guest room. Leia was doing a strange sort of jumping dance and grabbed her mom's forearm as soon as she entered.

"Mom, Uncle Jimmy and Kelsie are boyfriend and girlfriend now! Santa brought us Baylee's Christmas wish!"

I could have cried.

Scratch that.

I did cry.

I tried very hard not to cry, but it was a lot, you know? The intense fear that I'd scarred my daughter for life followed by the confusion as she celebrated something I hadn't even been aware of followed by the realization that my daughter and her best friend had given up their Christmas wishes—which yes, I know that Christmas wishes aren't real but *they* didn't—so that Jimmy and I could be together.

I don't know where my squalling turd of a daughter got her selflessness from, but it wasn't from me.

I did manage to hold the tears back for a bit. I didn't cry as I hugged my daughter, sharing a grateful look with Jimmy as we both let out relieved breaths. And I was particularly proud of the fact that I didn't cry when Baylee let go of me and jumped on Jimmy, barely giving him time to put his arms out to catch her before she hugged him.

And keeping my eyes dry when she failed to use her indoor voice to tell him she wanted him to make her mom happy and to take good care of her? That deserved a gold medal, especially when Jimmy solemnly promised her that he would.

I didn't cry when Em and Alex promised they'd never let me or Jimmy live this down. And I didn't cry when Jimmy looked at me nervously, apologized, and handed Baylee a long, thin package that contained a set of drumsticks with a picture of the drum kit he'd bought her wrapped around them.

Even though no one would have blamed me for wailing, I just laughed and kissed him, which made Baylee squeal and tap the drumsticks rapidly against the coffee table.

I still kept it together when Em *did* cry, right after Leia opened some weird recording equipment thing from Alex that he explained was for her and Baylee so they could play music together if they wanted to, just the two of them with a "band" backing them up, and when she asked about performing, he shook his head.

"It's just for you to have fun together," he said.

Leia looked at the gift, then carefully set it down beside her. She stood, ran up to Alex, and hugged him tightly.

"Thanks, Dad."

Em had to leave the room for a minute, and I didn't cry while she was gone and Alex slipped me an envelope that he explained was a gift from him—*just* him.

"You do so much for me and Em without ever asking for anything back," he said quietly as Jimmy showed the girls how to work the recording thingie. "Consider this a small token of my gratitude."

My mouth dropped as I opened the envelope. "Alex, this is too much."

"It's not even close to enough. You're so damn thoughtful about everything that I didn't even realize how much harder I was making things for you."

"I... I just want you and her to be happy," I said. "She's my best friend."

"You know damn well you're more than her friend." He smiled, glancing at the girls and Jimmy before looking back at me. "You're family."

It took some effort, but I managed to keep my eyes dry as I flipped through the brochure he'd included in the envelope detailing all the amenities and packages available at the luxury spa he was sending me and Em to for a weekend away, just the two of us. I maintained my cool as he handed me another envelope, awkwardly explaining that this one was from Mike, then watched nervously as I opened it to see a donation in my name to the women's shelter in the exact amount of the Taylor Swift tickets.

And that was really something since it... well.

It said a lot.

It said that Mike had never intended to make me pay for the tickets, but that he understood—that he *knew* giving me my check back would have been insulting and humiliating and frustrating for me. So he cashed it, that check I'd written using funds my ex-husband had tried to buy my daughter with, and then turned around and sent it back into the world to help the next woman who ended up with a man like Daniel. He let me have my pride in a way that let him keep his pride, and that... well.

I understood Mike a little better now.

I didn't cry when we got Baylee and Leia to sit next to each other so Jimmy could surreptitiously hit record on his phone as they both had huge paper-wrapped boxes placed in front of them. I almost cried laughing when the girls realized that there was a smaller paper-wrapped box in the big one, and another one, and six more before they finally got to a small, flat box right in the middle.

And it was a close fucking call when Baylee opened that small, flat box, saw the words "Taylor Swift concert," and burst into tears that overwhelmed her so much, it took nearly ten minutes before we could resume opening presents. It was even closer when I held her as she cried, listening to her whimper that she was so excited, she was just so excited, and sorry, she needed a minute because she never in a hundred million thousand trillion years thought she'd get to see a Taylor Swift concert and I realized that everything horrible, awful, horrendous thing that I'd had to go through to get those tickets was worth it.

I was fine right up until Baylee handed me a messily wrapped gift and said that she had made it herself while she was at her dad's and he said she had to have quiet time.

It was a picture frame, like one of those cheap wood ones you can get at any craft store, but it had two openings on it. She'd painted it and bedazzled it with every color of rhinestone in the universe, glued pompoms across one edge and ribbon across another, and there had clearly been an incident with glitter that had been hastily covered up with construction paper.

On one side, a picture she had to have gotten from Em: me and her at the concert after she'd finished playing tambourine with the Poplins and I'd lifted her into the air to tell her how proud I was of her.

On the other, a drawing with careful lettering done in marker:

Home Is Where My Mom Is

Love, Baylee

"Mom, it's supposed to show I love you," she said.

"I know, sweetie."

"And you're s'posed to be happy," she said. "You have a boyfriend now and we're going to see Taylor Swift together and it's *Christmas*! Why are you crying?"

I sniffled and looked up.

In that room was my boyfriend, a man who had chosen me and my daughter above any level of normalcy.

In that room was my family; aside from Baylee, not by blood, but the family I'd chosen and that had chosen me.

In that room was my daughter, my sweet, smart, selfless girl. I sniffled again, then hugged her tightly.

"'Cause I'm happy, Bay. I'm really fucking happy."

"You shouldn't swear," she giggled. "Dad says it's ungracious."

"Fuck that. It's a good day for swearing."

Acknowledgments

My books would not be possible without some very special people:

My proof-readers, editors, and beta readers are extraordinary people who I am incredibly grateful to. Special thank you to Jason Caldwell, Nora Fares, John, and Chasten.

To Paul M, Kevin Matheny, centralsquareguy, KW, AG, PM, N, ED, KJ, MidNyt, RP, Caleb Waters, and all my incredible supporters on Patreon and in my Cheryl's Terrors group - thank you. Your enthusiasm, support, and belief in me means more than I can ever say.

I am lucky enough to be surrounded by friends and family who have read, supported, and encouraged my writing. To all of you, thank you, and I stand by what I said: you're the one who has to look me in the eye if you read something you didn't want to think about me writing! But also, thank you for not making it weird. I am so grateful for the special people in my life.

And finally, to the man I love more every single day: I love you. You're my everything. Thank you for standing with me, encouraging me to follow my dreams, and being my happily ever after.

Also By Cheryl Terra

Find all of Cheryl's books by visiting **cherylterra.com/stories**
Each series is listed in chronological order

Standalone Stories

One Little Question
When It Rains
Another Last Call
Selfish Love
What Happens In Vegas
Sore Loser
The Happiest I've Ever Been

The Unicorn Confessions

The Unicorn Confessions
Unicorn For Sale
Death of a Unicorn

The Love Across Canada Universe

Theo + Aspen:
Get Over It
More Than Words

Sean + Rick:
The Devil Made Me

Noah + Lacey:
Runaway
Waking Up
Finding Home
Of Daffodils

Collaborations with Jason Caldwell

Unseen Love
No Strings Attached
As You Wish

Get Free Books

If you want to be the first to know about new books, upcoming projects, and exclusive freebies, visit **cherylterra.com/freebies** to sign up for Cheryl's mailing list.